THE DEPUTY'S SECOND CHANCE

BRENDA HARLEN

Harlequin

SPECIAL EDITION

Recycling programs for this product may not exist in your area.

ISBN-13: 978-1-335-18029-2

The Deputy's Second Chance

For questions and comments about the quality of this book, please contact us at CustomerService@Harlequin.com.

Harlequin Enterprises ULC
22 Adelaide St. West, 41st Floor
Toronto, Ontario M5H 4E3, Canada
www.Harlequin.com

HarperCollins Publishers
Macken House, 39/40 Mayor Street Upper,
Dublin 1, D01 C9W8, Ireland
www.HarperCollins.com

Printed in Lithuania

She exhaled a quiet sigh of relief, grateful for his unquestioning support.

"Anyway, all of that was just a lead up to saying that this was the best Valentine's Day I've had in a very long time," she said. "So thank you for that."

"You're welcome," Flynn responded, turning to smile at her at the same moment that Meg leaned forward to kiss his cheek.

Her lips landed awkwardly at the side of his mouth.

She quickly pulled back, because it was awkward.

It was also, unexpectedly, tingly.

Tingly?

She mentally rolled her eyes at the completely inane and totally inappropriate description.

Flynn was her friend.

One of her best friends, in fact, which meant that she absolutely should not be feeling any kind of tingles around him.

"I'm so sorry," she said.

Her cheeks were burning with embarrassment; her body was humming with awareness. But it was easier—and much smarter—to focus on the embarrassment rather than the awareness.

"No need to apologize," Flynn said.

And though the words were casual enough, there was an uncharacteristic huskiness in his tone.

Dear Reader,

Welcome back to Whispering Canyon! I'm excited to return to Wyoming—and to catch up on what's been happening with some of the town's local residents.

Flynn Chandler and Megan Wheeler were introduced as secondary characters in *The Rancher's Temptation*, but there was a hint of a spark whenever they were on the page together.

Of course, neither of the wounded hearts was willing to acknowledge it at the time. And even now, Flynn and Meg's friendship means too much to them to risk jeopardizing it—until an accidental kiss leads them to wonder if they were meant to be more than friends...

But as Flynn and Meg continue to deal with the traumas of their respective pasts, it's going to take the machinations of one sweet little girl—along with the help of some meddling grandparents—to make them see that the path to happily-ever-after only requires them to walk together.

I hope you enjoy *The Deputy's Second Chance* and will look for more stories coming from Whispering Canyon soon!

xo *Brenda*

Brenda Harlen is a former attorney who once had the privilege of appearing before the Supreme Court of Canada. The practice of law taught her a lot about the world and reinforced her determination to become a writer—because in fiction, she could promise a happy ending! Now she is an award-winning, RITA® Award–nominated, nationally bestselling author of more than sixty titles for Harlequin. You can keep up-to-date with Brenda on Facebook and X, or through her website, brendaharlen.com.

Books by Brenda Harlen

Harlequin Special Edition

The Cowboys of Whispering Canyon

The Rancher's Temptation

The Deputy's Second Chance

Match Made in Haven

Claiming the Cowboy's Heart
Double Duty for the Cowboy
One Night with the Cowboy
A Chance for the Rancher
The Marine's Road Home
Meet Me Under the Mistletoe
The Rancher's Promise
The Chef's Surprise Baby
Captivated by the Cowgirl
Countdown to Christmas
Her Not-So-Little Secret
The Rancher's Christmas Reunion
Snowed In with a Stranger
Her Favorite Mistake
A Rancher of His Own

Visit the Author Profile page at Harlequin.com for more titles.

This book is for the warriors,
because everyone is battling something.

Prologue

Twelve months earlier

It wasn't easy to find a place at the back when the chairs were arranged in a circle, Flynn Chandler lamented as he took his usual seat in the usual room of the community center. No doubt the configuration was intended to accommodate a feeling of unity and facilitate sharing, but he wasn't big on sharing. Certainly not with a bunch of strangers.

But he wasn't here by choice. He was here because his mom was worried about him, no matter how many times he assured her she didn't need to be. And so, when she told him that she'd found a support group she believed would help, he'd agreed to attend one session in the hope that doing so might alleviate some of her concerns.

She'd lobbied for one a week for twelve weeks—as if that was a magic number that might miraculously lift the weight of the guilt he carried and banish the nightmares that plagued his sleep. And here he was now, in week four, because if the sessions hadn't helped, they hadn't hurt, either.

He spotted her as soon as she walked in, watched her as she looked around the room, assessing the setup very much as he'd done on his first day. A few people hovered around the table inside the door, chatting as they nibbled on donuts from Sweet Cheeks Bakery and sipped strong coffee. Flynn had no interest in conversation, carbs or caffeine. And apparently neither did the newcomer, who skirted the group to take a seat out of the direct line of sight of the group facilitator—Alex, easily identifiable by his clipboard and relaxed posture.

Her chosen seat, on the opposite side of the circle, put her directly across from Flynn, allowing him to study her as she settled and wonder what it was about her that had snagged his attention. It wasn't just that she was stunningly beautiful, though she was undeniably that. With blond hair tied in a loose knot at the back of her neck, big brown eyes fringed with thick lashes, high cheekbones, a straight nose, slightly pointed chin and creamy complexion—flawless except for a faint scar on her left cheekbone.

(Later, he'd discover that her eyes weren't actually brown, as he'd first thought, but closer to the amber of his favorite small batch bourbon whiskey. And that, in addition to the small scar on her cheek, she had another—nearly two inches long—that ran along her hairline, near her temple. Eventually he'd also discover that her smile tipped just a little bit higher on one side, though it would be several more weeks before he got to see that smile—and how it could light up a room.)

Flynn felt confident that this was her first session. He would have noticed her if she'd made an appearance in the group before now, though the certainty of that thought made him a little uneasy, as he'd paid no particular attention to any of the other group members.

Not Cheryl, with the pink highlights in her hair and nervous smile. Not Hugh, with his wide fingernails bitten to the quick. Not Albert, whose right knee jostled incessantly when he was seated. Not even Marilou, who usually sat motionless with silent tears running down her cheeks.

Flynn noticed these simple details but passed no judgment. Everyone had stuff they were dealing with and different ways of dealing with it—and not any of it was his business.

So what was it about *this* woman that made him wonder about her story?

She didn't say anything during the meeting, but she jotted some notes in a little book she pulled out of her backpack. Or maybe she was making a grocery list. A distinct possibility, he acknowledged, as he couldn't see what she was writing.

She was paying attention, though, even leaning forward a little when Alex responded to Marilou's question—apparently she did talk—about some common triggers of night terrors.

But before the meeting was over, right after Alex made his usual announcement that there were ten minutes left, she quietly pushed her chair back so that she could exit behind the circle rather than through it and did so.

And as Flynn watched her slip through the door, he discovered that he was sorry to see her go.

Chapter One

Birth, life, death.

As a surgical nurse at Whispering Canyon Medical Center, Meg Wheeler was well aware of the circle of life and had spent countless hours helping patients maintain their position in the middle of that circle. Death was inevitable, of course. But sometimes medical intervention could allow a patient to postpone the unavoidable, whether that patient was very young or impossibly old or at any stage in between.

Today, she'd scrubbed in with Dr. Nathan Duchesne. The vascular surgeon had transferred to WCMC only a few months earlier, and he was undoubtedly one of the most skilled specialists she'd ever had the privilege to work with. But always in surgery—even during procedures considered routine—there were things that could go wrong. Today, the final procedure on his operating list had been bumped when a firefighter, caught beneath a ceiling collapse in a burning building, was brought in.

Despite the team's best efforts, they hadn't been able to save him. The loss had shaken everyone, including the surgeon who'd announced time of death of the young man who wasn't only a community hero but a husband and father.

"I need a drink." Nathan stripped off his gown and scrub cap and dumped them in the bin outside the now quiet OR.

"There's no doubt you've earned one," Meg said.

"Do you think so?" His dubious tone wasn't one she'd ever heard from the usually cocksure surgeon.

"You did everything you could," she assured him.

"It wasn't enough."

She tossed her gown and cap in the same bin. "You're only human."

He slid her a look. "I'm a surgeon."

"My apologies." She lifted a hand to tuck an errant strand of hair behind her ear.

His gaze lingered on her ringless fingers. "Are you sorry enough to let me buy you a drink?"

"I can't," she said, feigning regret. "I have to pick up my daughter from preschool."

The mention of her child was usually an effective deterrent to most men, so she was surprised when Dr. Duchesne said, in a hopeful tone, "Maybe another time?"

"Maybe," she agreed, aware that she should be flattered by his interest. Because Nathan Duchesne wasn't just a skilled surgeon but an attractive man, with dark hair, piercing blue eyes, a strong jaw and toned physique.

But past experience had immunized Meg to the impact of a handsome face or charming smile, so that all she felt was mild discomfort at having to turn down the invitation of a coworker.

Still, she might have been more inclined to accept if she didn't suspect he was looking to share more than a drink. And while it wasn't uncommon for those who witnessed death to seek a human connection that would help them feel alive, she couldn't be that person for him.

She didn't want to be that person.

She had all the connections she wanted in her life.

Her parents and sister, her maternal grandmother, her cousin and best friend, Tess. And, of course, her daughter, Emma. The person whose life mattered so much more to her than her own. The person she would do anything to protect—and had.

Since that night, she'd built a protective shell around herself that no one had managed to penetrate. Only one person had somehow chipped through the outermost layer to become a friend in the past year, even if she'd resisted letting him all the way in.

Because there were still some things she didn't want anyone to know about her.

In any event, she wasn't too concerned about brushing off Dr. Duchesne. There were plenty of other nurses at WCMC to help the surgeon forget that, despite his superior education and his exceptional skills, he was only human after all. And she knew of at least half a dozen who would willingly stand in line for the opportunity to do so.

Meg left the OR and headed straight to the locker room. She didn't expect a hot shower would wash away the weight of the loss, but as she toweled off, she at least felt somewhat refreshed. Though she'd put in seven hours, the intensity of the day made it feel as if her shift had been twice as long. And, refastening her watch around her wrist, she was surprised to note that she still had a couple of hours before she was due to pick up Emma.

She spotted him as soon as she pushed open the door.

Flynn Chandler.

Former Army Ranger and military contractor turned rancher and undoubtedly one of Whispering Canyon's most eligible bachelors—even if he made it clear to anyone who expressed interest that he had no interest in changing his single status anytime soon.

He was leaning against the wall, his legs slightly stretched out in front of him, his cowboy boots crossed at the ankles, and scrolling on his phone, as if he had all the time in the world and nowhere else that he needed to be.

The Chandlers were akin to royalty in Whispering Canyon and Raylan Senior and Eleanor—the reigning king and queen who'd celebrated their sixty-fifth wedding anniversary the previous summer—had raised three sons together: Clayton, Raylan Junior—known as RJ, and Wyatt. Each of those three sons had gone on to have three more, with Flynn being the second born to RJ and Miranda.

The Chandlers weren't just rich and successful, they were also ridiculously good-looking, and any woman would be forgiven for indulging in a long look if one of them passed her on the street. Meg would be lying if she said she hadn't done the same on more than one occasion, but that had been "BE"—Before Emma—when she'd been young and happy and carefree.

Still, she wasn't oblivious to the fact that Flynn was an attractive man. He stood a little more than six feet tall, she guessed, with broad shoulders, narrow hips and long legs. And while other women might take note of his strong jaw with the slight dimple in his chin, his glossy brown hair that tended to curl at the ends when he needed a trim, or his dark blue eyes, Meg's first impression had been of taut muscles and brooding intensity. Then those blue eyes had locked on hers, and the force of his gaze—and the fear that he might actually be able to see into her soul—made her stomach flip.

Somehow, in the time that had passed since their first meeting, they'd become friends. Perhaps because they'd both seen and done things that others didn't know about and wouldn't understand. Whatever the reason, he'd become a fixture in her life—and Emma's life, too—even before her cousin Tess had hooked up with his brother Holt, followed by their marriage a few months later. And while Meg was usually pleased to see Flynn, she wasn't accustomed to seeing him at the hospital, obviously waiting for her.

He glanced up when she stepped into the corridor, as if he sensed her presence even before she spoke.

"Flynn."

He pushed away from the wall to meet her in the middle of the wide hallway. His gaze was serious, his mouth unsmiling. In other words, his expression was as inscrutable as always.

She suspected it was his experiences in the army that had

caused him to withdraw into himself—or maybe he'd always been that way. Not that she'd ever ask, because she knew that kind of question would quickly put an end to any conversation they were having. Some topics were simply off-limits, even between friends, and as someone who had her own boundaries, she was careful to respect his.

"What are you doing here? Is everything okay?"

"Everything's fine," he hastened to assure her. "I just thought you'd want to know that Tess had the baby."

She did want to know, and that happy news lifted her mood as nothing else could.

"Details," she demanded, already walking beside him to the elevator that would take them to the maternity wing on the second floor.

"Blake Leonard Chandler was born at 2:48 p.m., weighing seven pounds fifteen ounces and measuring twenty inches."

"Leonard, huh?" She was surprised to hear the newborn's middle name, as anyone who knew of the long-ago affair between Raylan Chandler Senior and Tallulah Leonard would be—and everyone in Whispering Canyon knew about the affair. Though the assignation had occurred almost six decades earlier, it came up now and again as a source of conflict between the two families. "Whose idea was that?"

"Holt's, apparently."

"He really does love her," she mused.

"Did you doubt it?"

She shrugged. "I hardly consider myself an expert on the subject."

"You don't have to be an expert to look at Holt and Tess and know that they're meant to be together."

Now she lifted a brow. "You say that as if you believe in fate."

"I'm not sure what I believe in anymore," he admitted. "But I'm rooting for them."

The elevator doors opened and he gestured for her to precede him.

"Room 2026," he said.

She made her way down the hall, arriving just as the baby's paternal great-grandparents were leaving the room. After exchanging pleasantries with the elderly couple, Meg and Flynn ventured into the spacious private room where Tess was sitting in bed with the baby in her arms. Holt was on top of the covers beside her, his arm across his wife's shoulders, the expression on his face one of unbridled love and complete devotion.

"I heard a rumor about a baby," Meg said.

The new mom looked up, a smile spreading across her face. "Come and meet your honorary nephew," she invited.

Meg moved closer to the bed, her heart swelling inside her chest as she got her first glimpse of the newborn. He was pink and plump and perfect, his tiny hands curled into fists, his eyes closed, his lips pursed. Beneath the knitted blue cap on his head, a few wispy blond hairs were visible.

"Oh, Tess," she murmured. "Look what you've done. He's absolutely beautiful."

Holt cleared his throat.

She spared a quick glance and a small smile for her cousin's husband. "Alright. I guess you do get some credit for knocking her up."

"Thank you," he said, grinning proudly.

"Do you want to hold him?" the new mom asked.

Meg held out her arms and felt a pinch in the vicinity of her chest when her cousin transferred the baby.

Love? Longing?

Perhaps a little of both, she acknowledged, blinking back the tears that filled her eyes as she remembered the first time she'd held her own baby in her arms, how her heart had immediately filled with so much love and joy.

So many hopeful dreams that quickly shattered.

She pushed those dark memories firmly away, refusing to let them cast a shadow on Tess and Holt's happy day.

"I know Emma must have been this small once upon a time, but I honestly can't remember."

"She was smaller," Tess confirmed. "Only seven five and eighteen inches."

"And eighteen hours of labor," Meg recalled, unlikely to ever forget *that* detail of the day. "How long for you?"

"It's not a contest," her friend chided.

"How long?" Meg asked again.

"Thirteen hours…minus ten," Tess admitted, a hint of pink color touching her cheeks.

"Three hours?"

"Three hours of intense labor," the new mom clarified. "The doctor suspects that my labor actually started two days ago, when I started having twinges in my back."

"Twinges," Meg echoed, shaking her head. "If I didn't love you so much, I'd hate you."

"But you do love me," her BFF said smugly.

"More than you know. But not as much as I already love this little guy."

"We knew you'd fall in love at first sight, which is why we want you to be his godmother," Tess said.

"And Flynn to be his godfather," Holt said.

Meg sent a glance across the room at the baby's surprised uncle, who she suspected was as uncomfortable with the potential responsibility as she was, likely for similar reasons. Not that his expression gave anything away.

"I didn't fall in love at first sight," he noted, as if that might get him off the hook.

"Yeah, you did," Holt said confidently. "You just didn't say it out loud."

"I'm touched," Meg chimed in. "Sincerely. But…I'm not sure I'm the right choice."

"I lived with you and Emma," Tess reminded her. "And I can't think of anyone better."

"You lived with me and Emma," she confirmed. "Which is why you, more than anyone, should know how I messed up with my kid."

The new mom's expression grew fierce. "What I know is that you are an amazing mom who would do anything for her daughter. I also know that if something happened and I wasn't around to raise my son, you would love him as much as I do." She pinned her cousin with her gaze. "Am I wrong about that?"

Meg shook her head. "No."

"And that's why we chose you."

Which was somehow daunting and reassuring at the same time.

"Kinda hard for me to say *no* now, isn't it?" she mused lightly.

"If you really want to say *no*, we'll find someone else," Tess said. "But we won't find anyone better."

"Okay, fine," Meg relented. "I'll do it."

Her cousin sent her a look that was a combination of amusement and exasperation.

Meg sighed, her chest tight. "I'm happy to be asked and honored to accept," she clarified.

"Now that wasn't so hard, was it?" Tess said.

"You have no idea."

"Is that why you picked me?" Flynn asked, shifting the spotlight away from Meg. "Because you knew you wouldn't find anyone better?"

"Nah, you were our default choice," Holt said, obviously teasing. "Because I've only got two brothers and the other one has his hands full with two kids of his own."

"I'm happy to be asked and honored to accept," Flynn said, parroting Meg's words.

"Obviously we haven't set a date yet for the christening,"

Tess informed them. "We're thinking probably April, when the weather's a little more predictable. But we'll check with you first to make sure there aren't any schedule conflicts."

"Please do," Flynn said. "Because there isn't anyone else on the ranch who can move cattle from one pasture to another."

"I think she was more concerned about Meg's schedule," Holt told his brother.

"Speaking of schedules," Meg said. "I need to be going. But I'll come back after dinner with Emma, so she can meet her new cousin."

"We'll be here," Tess said.

She returned the baby to his mom, then hugged both Tess and Holt before making her way to the door.

Flynn caught up with her again at the elevator.

"Coffee?" he suggested, when the doors opened.

"Did you not hear me say I had to go?" she asked, punching the button for the main level.

"I heard you," he confirmed. "I also saw you fighting back tears in there and thought you might want to talk."

"Don't all women cry over babies?" she said lightly.

"I don't know about all, but I know better than to attempt to fit you into any generic mold."

She was still mulling over that when the elevator doors opened again and Flynn took her arm, steering her in the direction of the cafeteria.

"Maybe you hang around with women who like to be manhandled," she said through gritted teeth, digging in her heels. "But let me assure you, I don't fit that mold, either, and I won't tolerate it."

He immediately released her and lifted his hands in a gesture of surrender.

And while Meg glared at him, he just stood there, patiently waiting.

He was always so damn patient.

So completely unfazed.

Usually she was unflappable, too. An important attribute in her profession. But there were certain things that pushed her buttons, and he'd pushed hers.

Inadvertently, of course.

And just because her emotions were a little raw was no reason to target Flynn.

"I'm sorry," she said.

"No apology necessary," he told her.

But there was. Because in the past twelve months, Flynn had been there for her more than anyone else.

"It's been a challenging day, and you got caught in the line of fire."

"I do have some experience with that," he remarked dryly.

Which she knew, of course. The whole town had been buzzing with the news when Flynn Chandler was medevaced to Landstuhl Regional Medical Center in Germany from an undisclosed location in the Middle East with life-threatening injuries. Three weeks later, when his condition had been downgraded to serious, he'd been transported home. Sixteen months later, there was no obvious evidence of those injuries—except to someone who looked in his eyes.

"I wouldn't mind a cup of coffee before I have to pick up Emma," she said now, offering an olive branch.

He gestured for her to precede him, accepting.

They ordered their drinks and before he could pull out his wallet, she tapped her ID badge to charge the purchase to her staff account.

"Do you want to tell me what happened up there?" Flynn asked, when they were seated at a table by the window.

As she sipped her coffee, he wondered if she might attempt to hedge or deflect. But he knew her well enough now to know when she was holding back.

And maybe she knew that, too, because when she finally

responded, it was to say, "I guess holding Blake and remembering when Emma was born took me back to those early days when I was certain my life couldn't be more perfect. Before everything changed."

Flynn didn't need her to fill in any more details. He knew that her husband had lost his job soon after Emma was born and that, instead of looking for another job, he'd started drinking. And when he was drinking, he got mean. Meg had packed up her daughter and left soon after that, but he knew that the scars of that experience remained.

"Birth, life, death," she murmured, speaking almost to herself.

And maybe she was thinking of the failure of her marriage or the loss of her husband, but he got the impression her preoccupation was with something more recent.

"You lost a patient today," he ventured.

She wrapped her hands around her mug and nodded.

"I thought it was exhaustion that was responsible for the shadows under your eyes, but I see now it's grief."

"What woman doesn't want to hear about the shadows under her eyes?" she said lightly.

"You don't need anyone—least of all me—to tell you that you're beautiful."

But maybe she did, because she seemed taken aback by his statement.

And perhaps a little wary.

"A statement of fact, Megan," he assured her. "Not an expression of interest."

She offered him a small smile. "Well, that's a relief."

"What happened?" he asked, unwilling to acknowledge that her quick response had chafed, just a little.

"Sometimes the odds are just stacked against us," she said. "In this case, it was a crushing injury that caused massive internal trauma. Multiple broken ribs, punctured lung, lacerated liver, significant hemorrhaging. Dr. Duchesne managed to locate and repair three tears while the team was monitoring the patient's vitals, giving him oxygen and pumping blood and epinephrine into him. But in the end…his heart gave out and we couldn't bring him back."

"I'm sorry," Flynn said sincerely.

Because he'd held the hands of enough dying men to understand that, even when death was inevitable, it still sucked to bear helpless witness.

"He was only thirty-two years old. A husband and a father. A firefighter."

"The blaze at the abandoned canning factory?" he guessed.

She nodded.

"I heard about it on the radio—and saw the smoke—when I was driving to the hospital."

"Now, because of our failure, there's a young widow who's going to have to push through her grief every morning to raise their child on her own."

"It wasn't your failure," he said, confident it was true. Because he knew she gave one hundred percent every single day. "What you did gave him a chance, despite the odds being stacked against him."

"Maybe." She swallowed the last mouthful of her coffee. "Anyway, getting to meet Blake today at least turned my focus back to the happy part of the circle."

"And now you'll go home and hug your daughter and all will be right in the world—at least for a moment."

"Her hugs are the best medicine," she agreed.

"Pizza can be pretty good medicine, too," he pointed out. "I could pick one up and bring it over."

"A tempting offer," she allowed. "But I promised Emma spaghetti and meatballs tonight."

"You know, I like spaghetti and meatballs, too," he said, his tone deliberately casual.

"Subtle," she said dryly.

"Maybe too subtle," he mused.

She rolled her eyes. "Would you like to come over for dinner, Flynn?"

He could feel just the hint of a smile tugging at the corners of his mouth. "I thought you'd never ask."

Chapter Two

Flynn recalled Megan's earlier words as he caught Emma when she raced across the room to fling herself at him. *Best medicine ever, indeed.*

"We're havin' s'ghetti and meatballs for supper and Mama said you're gonna eat with us."

"That's why I'm here," he confirmed.

"Did you bring me somethin'?"

"Emma," her mom admonished.

"But he's got a box," the little girl pointed out.

"So he does," Meg acknowledged.

"Dessert," he said, offering her the bakery box. "For everyone."

"Cupcakes?" Emma asked hopefully.

He chuckled. The sound was a little rusty, even to his own ears. Of course, he hadn't had much reason to laugh in recent years, but somehow, just being in the presence of this little girl seemed to lift the heaviness that weighed on his heart. "I'll let you have the first peek inside the box after you eat your dinner," he promised.

"Which will be on the table in twelve minutes," Meg said.

"I didn't mean to cut it so close," Flynn apologized. "There was a surprisingly long line at the bakery."

"No worries," she assured him.

"Can I do anything?"

"You can grate cheese for the garlic bread, if you want cheese."

"I want cheese!" Emma announced.

"Then you can help, too," Flynn told her.

"*After* you wash your hands," Meg said pointedly.

So Flynn carried the little girl into the powder room and they washed their hands together before making their way to the kitchen, where Meg had set the grater and a block of cheese on the counter.

Twelve minutes later, they were seated around the table with steaming plates of pasta, a basket of garlic bread and a bowl of salad that Meg admitted had been dumped out of a bag from the grocery store. It was, without a doubt, the best meal Flynn had eaten in a long time—and that included weekly Sunday night dinners at his mom and dad's place, because those meals inevitably left him feeling as if he'd been grilled more thoroughly than whatever was on the menu.

Instead, Emma kept them entertained with stories from preschool and adventures with Gramma Sunny and Grampa Marshall—the maternal grandparents who picked her up from preschool on the days that Meg was working. She was honest and funny, and anyone who heard her animated chatter might assume the little girl had lived a charmed life the entirety of her almost five years.

But Flynn knew differently.

"Unca Flynn—you're not listening to me," Emma said accusingly, and he knew he was busted.

Prior to Tess and Holt's wedding, he'd simply been "Flynn" to Emma. But when Holt became Uncle Holt, Emma decided that he should be Uncle Flynn. And though he knew Meg hadn't been entirely comfortable with the honorific, she hadn't protested his upgraded title.

"You're right," he admitted. "I was a little distracted, wondering if it might be time for dessert."

Her eyes grew almost as wide as her smile. "Cupcakes?"

"Nice save," Meg said to him.

He responded with a shrug.

"First we clear the table, then we have dessert," Meg reminded her daughter.

Or perhaps the reminder was for him, too.

He pushed his chair away from the table and began stacking dishes. When the tidying up was done, he set the bakery box in front of the little girl and lifted the lid.

"Cupcakes with sprinkles!" Emma clapped her hands together. "My fav'rite."

"I thought Great-Gramma Lula's brownies were your favorite," Meg said.

Her daughter nodded. "But cupcakes with sprinkles are my fav'rite kind of *cupcakes*." She picked a pink decoration off her treat and popped it into her mouth. "Paisley's mom got cupcakes with icing inside and she said that if the icing was pink, Paisley was gonna get a sister, and if it was blue, she'd get a brother."

"What color was the icing?" Flynn asked, aware that Paisley was currently Emma's best friend at preschool.

"Pink!"

"So Paisley's going to have a sister."

Emma nodded as she licked the icing off the top of her cupcake. "But she has to wait 'til summer for her baby and Mama told me Auntie Tess had her baby today."

"That's true," he confirmed. "You have a new cousin named Blake."

"A boy cousin." Emma wrinkled her nose at that. "Maybe Auntie Tess din't know to ask for pink cupcakes."

"I don't think that's quite how it works," Flynn told her.

"How's it work?" she demanded.

He looked at Meg, who was observing the interaction with undisguised amusement.

"Yes, please tell us how it works," she said.

He lifted a brow. "Do you really want me explaining the birds and the bees to your daughter?"

"I don't care about birds and bees," Emma said. "I wanna know about babies."

"Well." He cleared his throat. "When a boy and a girl love each other, they make a baby and sometimes it's a boy and sometimes it's a girl baby."

"But how do they make the baby?" she asked around a mouthful of cake.

"They, uh, join parts together."

Her brow furrowed as she chewed and swallowed. "Like Lego?"

He nodded, deciding that comparison worked as well as any. "Yes. Like Lego."

"When I build Lego, I can pick a blue brick or a red brick or a yellow brick—so why can't the mommy and daddy pick if it's a boy or a girl?"

"This is way above my pay grade," he muttered. "And far outside my realm of expertise."

"I don't understand," Emma said, frustration in her voice.

"Maybe your mom can explain it better," he said. "Since she's the only person in this room who's actually had a baby."

"Or we could go see Auntie Tess's new baby," Meg suggested, effectively steering her daughter's focus in a different direction.

"Yes! I wanna see the baby."

"Then you better finish up your dessert before visiting hours are over."

Meg knew that spending time with Flynn was good for Emma. Preparing and eating meals together and cleaning up afterward provided the little girl with an example of what life would be like if she'd been born into a traditional family with a mom and dad who cared about and supported one another. At the same time, it made her a little uneasy to realize how easily Flynn seemed to fit into the empty space in their lives, causing her to worry that Emma might start to think he was part of their family.

Because he wasn't.

And yet, over the past few months, whenever she'd needed somebody, he'd been there.

Truth be told, he had an annoying habit of being there sometimes even before she realized that she needed somebody. Almost as if he knew her better than she knew herself.

Perhaps that wasn't surprising, though, considering that the catastrophic failure of her marriage had taught her to question everything and trust no one.

But she couldn't survive for long on her own, no matter how much she wished she could. Being a single mom with a full-time job was occasionally overwhelming and always exhausting, forcing her to acknowledge that she needed to let others in and accept the help they were offering. Tess, her cousin and lifelong best friend, had been the first. Tallulah Leonard, her grandmother, was next. And, when she finally managed to forgive her parents for saying "I told you so" when she told them that her marriage was over, she let them in, too. And a good thing, as they absolutely doted on their only grandchild and provided both before- and after-school care for Emma when required.

Meg was also close to her sister, but Nicole was currently living and working in Alaska, and so their communications were limited to FaceTime calls and text messages. She'd additionally made some friends at the hospital, and though Meg was happy to hear about their relationship dramas—even when they shared more than she wanted to know—she didn't reciprocate. Because she knew that secrets could be wielded as weapons and she wasn't ever going to be defenseless again.

No one who knew what Meg had been through would be surprised to realize that her support network was—with the sole exception of her father—entirely female. At least it had been until the day Flynn Chandler asked her to have coffee and she said *yes*.

Even now, she didn't know what it was about him that allowed him to break through her usually impenetrable defenses. Maybe it was that she recognized the same defenses in him. Or maybe she'd seen that he was as damaged as she was. Or maybe she'd just really needed a cup of coffee.

Whatever the reason, that cup of coffee had been the foundation of a tentative friendship that had grown stronger with each day that passed. And now, almost a year later, he was one of her best friends.

Upon his return from his last mission, the former Army Ranger turned private military contractor had kept to himself. In recent months, Meg had been pleased to witness Flynn's reintegration into society. And while she didn't doubt that one reason for his evolution could be attributed to the adage that time heals all wounds, she suspected another cause was the unexpected bond he'd forged with her child.

If it had been left up to Meg, she wouldn't have introduced the taciturn vet to her impressionable daughter. But their paths had crossed by chance and Emma, often shy around strangers—and particularly men—nevertheless interjected herself into their conversation. Flynn hadn't known how to respond to the little girl at first, but Emma had pushed through all of his barriers as if they weren't even there, talking to him as if they were old friends—and it wasn't long before they were friends. And Meg realized that, instead of trying to free him from the burden of the baggage he carried, she needed to accept him for who he was, baggage and all, exactly as Emma had done.

But even more significant to Meg than the changes she saw in Flynn was the healing transformation that her daughter had undergone during that same period. She'd originally attended the support group in an effort to find coping strategies that might help Emma overcome the night terrors that had plagued her. Considering everything the little girl had witnessed in the first few years of her life, Emma's counselor wasn't surprised that she didn't sleep through the night, though she didn't seem to have any conscious memory of specific events but rather a fear of "the bad man" she'd seen hurt her mom.

It had been more than four months since she'd last woken up screaming—126 days, in fact—and though Meg was cautiously optimistic, she was reluctant to let her guard down, aware that the night terrors could return at any time. But she wasn't going to worry about that today, because today was a day of celebration.

And Emma was in good spirits as they made their way to the hospital, chattering away about Auntie Tess and Uncle Holt and all the fun things she would do with the baby, no matter how many times her mom told her that it was going to be a long time before Blake was even able to sit up, never mind engage in playful activities.

"Remember," Meg said, holding firmly to her daughter's hand as they exited the elevator. "Inside voice and no running in the hospital."

"I 'member," Emma promised.

And she did—until she stepped through the doorway of Tess's room, at which point she raced across the floor and launched herself at "Auntie Tess! Auntie Tess!"

Thankfully, the newborn was swaddled and snuggled in his dad's arms, safely out of reach of the little girl's flailing exuberance.

After receiving a big hug and kiss from her aunt, Emma sat back on her heels and looked at the now slight swell of Tess's tummy visible beneath the covers. "Mama said the baby was borned today, but how did you get him out of your tummy?"

The new mom chuckled softly. "You never ask the easy questions, do you, Em?"

"Did Unca Holt take it out?" she pressed.

"Um." Tess looked at Meg for help.

"Mama said Unca Holt put the baby in there," Emma continued.

"That's true," Tess agreed cautiously.

"Did you take the baby out, Unca Holt?"

"I was there when he was born," Holt said. "But Blake did most of the work himself."

"Sure, he did," Tess muttered, not entirely under her breath.

"Blake and his mom," the new dad hastily amended.

But Emma's attention had shifted again. "Can we get a baby, Mama?" she asked. "Can Unca Holt put a baby in you?"

"No!" Meg and Tess exclaimed in unison.

Emma's little brow furrowed.

"And now we're at a whole new level of awkward," Holt noted dryly.

Meg, cheeks burning, tried to explain the process in a way her not-yet-five-year-old daughter would understand. "A man has to love a woman to put a baby in her belly."

"Oh." Emma considered this for a minute, then tilted her head to look up at her uncle. "Don't you love Mama?"

"Um," Holt said helplessly.

"Of course, he does," Tess chimed in to reassure the girl. "But it's a different kind of love that makes a baby."

Emma huffed out a frustrated breath. "This is all very confusing."

"It is," her mom agreed. "So let's just focus on being happy that Aunt Tess and Uncle Holt have a baby and you have a brand-new cousin."

"Okay." But despite her apparent agreement, the little girl's tone was dubious. Then she climbed over Tess and off the other side of the bed for a closer look at the infant in Holt's arms. "Does he do *anything*?"

"He will, when he gets a little bigger," Tess said. "But right now, he mostly just sleeps and eats."

"Does he eat s'ghetti and meatballs?" Emma asked.

"Not yet," the new mom said.

"We had s'ghetti and meatballs for supper."

"And garlic bread?" Tess guessed.

The little girl bobbed her head. "Garlic bread *with cheese*."

"Yummy," her aunt agreed.

"Did you bring me any?" Holt asked.

Now Emma shook her head from side to side.

He pretended to pout. "You didn't bring me any leftovers?"

"There weren't any leftovers," she told him.

"You ate it *all*?"

She responded with another shake of her head. "Unca Flynn ate it all."

Holt's eyebrows lifted at that, but it was his wife who jumped into the conversation to ask, "Uncle Flynn had dinner with you tonight?"

"Uh-huh."

"Does Uncle Flynn have dinner with you a lot?" Tess asked curiously.

The little girl shrugged.

"Seriously?" Meg said. "You're interrogating a four-year-old?"

"I'm almost five," Emma reminded her mom, splaying all the fingers on one hand.

"And I wasn't interrogating," Tess denied.

"It sounded like an interrogation to me."

"Maybe because you're feeling defensive."

"I'm not feeling defensive," she said, just a little defensively.

Her friend snorted.

"Anyway, it's a school day for Em tomorrow," Meg reminded them all. "So I'm going to take her home now and get her ready for bed."

"And that sounds like avoidance to me," Tess mused.

"It's a fact," Meg assured her.

At the same time, her little girl said, "But I'm not tired."

Of course, she was asleep before they got home, leaving Meg to reflect on Tess's comments—and wonder how much longer she might avoid thinking about her complicated feelings for Flynn Chandler.

Chapter Three

Colby Chandler had always intended to live and work—and eventually marry and raise a family—on West River Ranch, like his father and grandfather and several more generations before him had done. Then Billy Garvey, the former sheriff of Whispering Canyon, was implicated in the cover-up of the shooting of family patriarch Raylan Chandler the previous spring. When it was announced that a special election would be held to fill the vacancy created by Garvey's arrest, Colby put himself forward as a candidate.

He didn't expect to win. He didn't expect the town's residents to vote for someone who had no practical experience in law enforcement. But he did have a degree in criminal justice from the University of Wyoming and the considerable influence of his family name weighing in his favor.

Two other candidates had thrown their names in the hat—Hillary Langley, a deputy sheriff from Howlett's Pass, and Lawrence Young, a sociology professor at nearby Bannock College. Colby was surprised, and deeply humbled, when he carried the vote by a landslide. Three days later, he was sworn in as sheriff.

Five and a half months later, he was finally starting to feel as if he had a good understanding of the job he'd been elected to do. Though there was a steep learning curve, he'd managed to navigate it with only a few minor stumbles, thanks mostly to Ken Holland, a retired deputy that he'd managed to talk out of retirement, at least for the short term.

A short term that, Ken had reminded him the day before, was almost up.

The phone on his desk buzzed, and he picked up the receiver as he continued to scan the proposed budget Gina Bonetti, his administrative assistant, had left on his desk that morning.

"Colby," he said.

"Flynn Chandler's here to see you," Gina announced formally.

Though he'd sent a message asking his cousin to stop by the sheriff's office at his convenience, he hadn't been confident that he'd get a response—never mind an in-person appearance less than twenty minutes later.

Colby had grown up on West River Ranch with eight cousins, all of whom had been born within a six-year span. In addition to being close in age, they'd developed close relationships, in some cases more akin to brothers than cousins. But none had been closer than Flynn and Colby's brother Ellis, and when Flynn had decided to join the army immediately after graduating from high school, no one was surprised that Ellis opted to go with him.

They'd enlisted together, deployed together, went to Ranger training together, kicked the asses of bad guys together and, when their enlistment ended, went to work for DHQ together—essentially performing the same duties for the private military contractor that they'd done for Uncle Sam without being constrained by the government's rules of engagement. At least, that was how Ellis had explained it to him.

Not that Colby actually knew what his brother and cousin had done as Army Rangers, because most of their assignments were highly classified. But he knew it had been tough on his parents, not knowing where their son was deployed between his occasional emails, video chats and even less frequent sat phone calls.

Then RJ Chandler got a call from someone named "Leo" at

DHQ telling him that Flynn was being medevaced to the US from an undisclosed overseas location.

The notes he'd scribbled during that call—

"hostage extraction,"

"ambushed,"

"lucky to be alive,"

"internal injuries,"

"medically-induced coma"—hadn't painted a clear picture, but he'd immediately booked two seats on a flight to Baltimore, so that he and Miranda would be there when Flynn's flight landed.

Wyatt and Kristin had stayed close to their phones, waiting for a call, desperate for any information about their son's status. But several days passed with no word from Ellis and no communication from DHQ.

After a week, while Miranda remained at her son's bedside and optimistic about his recovery, RJ came home to resume his duties at West River Ranch, obviously less so. But at least they knew Flynn's location and prognosis, however grim, while Ellis seemed to be MIA.

It was Flynn who updated the family on Ellis's status, though by the time he was able to do so, that update was several weeks out of date. And even then, all he could say was that Ellis had been alive the last time he saw him, without saying where that had been ("classified").

Sixteen months later, not much had changed.

Though Flynn had fought to get them more information from DHQ, there was rarely anything new to report. Occasional whispers about sightings would renew the family's hopes for a while, but official search efforts were hampered by the clandestine nature of DHQ's task in a hostile (and still unnamed!) country that they apparently hadn't had permission to enter in the first place.

Colby knew that Flynn had asked his former bosses at DHQ to send him in as part of those efforts, but for reasons they didn't deign to share with him—or at least that he didn't share with anyone else—they refused.

As hard as it was for Colby and his brother Jackson and their parents and grandparents to not know what had happened to Ellis—or even whether he was alive or dead—he suspected it was even harder for Flynn, who felt not just grief but guilt, as if he bore the responsibility for not bringing Ellis home. No doubt that was why he'd made excuses to skip out of more family gatherings than he'd attended since his return, hoping to spare Wyatt and Kristin the trauma of seeing their middle son's best friend without Ellis. But if that was his intent, it was an exercise in futility, because no one in the family would forget, not for a single minute of a single day, that Ellis was still missing.

"Sheriff?" Gina prompted, drawing his attention back to the present.

"Yeah. Thanks. Send him in."

She disconnected the call and, a few seconds later, a sharp knock on the open door preceded his cousin's entry to his office.

Flynn bypassed any number of more traditional greetings to ask, "What's up?"

"I'm doing well, thanks," Colby said. "How are you?"

His visitor stuffed his hands into the front pockets of his jeans. "Forgive me for assuming that you didn't ask me here to exchange basic pleasantries."

"Doesn't mean they can't be exchanged," he admonished, pushing his chair away from his desk and making his way to the coffeemaker on the credenza.

"Apologies," Flynn said dryly.

"You made good time," he noted.

"I was already in town when I got your message, picking up a few things from Nuts & Bolts," he said, naming the local hardware store.

Colby lifted the pot from the warmer and filled two mugs.

"Still trying to fix up that falling-down hunting cabin you call home?"

"It's not falling down," Flynn denied. "It's…rustic."

He snorted as he offered one of the mugs to his cousin. "Congrats, by the way, on your new nephew."

"I'm not sure how my brother and his wife having a baby entitled me to any kind of acknowledgment, but thanks," he said, accepting the proffered drink.

"I stopped by the hospital this morning to meet the baby," Colby continued. "He's a lot cuter than I expected."

"Looks like his mom."

The sheriff grinned at that as he settled behind his desk again. "Exactly what I said."

Flynn sipped his coffee, waiting—with thinly veiled patience—for his cousin to get to the point of this meeting.

Thankfully, Colby didn't make him wait much longer.

"I need a favor," he began, setting his mug in the middle of the blotter on his desk.

"Anything," he said, because Colby was family and Flynn was determined to never let his family down again.

"I was hoping you'd say that." His cousin smiled as he opened a drawer, pulled out a leather badge holder—complete with shiny badge—and set it on top of the desk in front of Flynn.

"You quitting your new job already?"

"That one says '*Deputy* Sheriff,'" Colby pointed out.

"So it does," Flynn noted.

"It's for you."

"Don't you already have two deputies?"

"I *had* two deputies," Colby agreed, emphasizing the past tense. "But Sawyer Wells is heading to Quantico at the end of March—"

"The FBI Academy?" Flynn interjected, surprised.

The sheriff nodded.

"Good for him," he said, and meant it. Flynn had gone

through school with Sawyer and was pleased to hear that he was pursuing his career ambitions, though he knew the lawman's absence would be felt in Whispering Canyon.

"And Ken Holland reminded me yesterday that he only came out of retirement as a favor to me—or more likely a favor to my dad, as they were friends back in the day—so that I wouldn't flounder through my first days on the job."

"No one thought you were going to flounder."

His cousin snorted. "I was a cattle rancher with zero experience in law enforcement."

"The same thing is true about me," Flynn told him.

"But you've served in the military, an experience known to foster leadership and teamwork skills, both of which are essential for effective law enforcement."

"I'm not interested in law enforcement."

"What are you interested in?" Colby challenged.

Flynn had no response to the question, so he remained silent.

"Yeah, that's what I figured," his cousin said.

"I keep busy enough at the ranch," Flynn assured him. "So you can tell my mom that you made the offer and I turned it down."

Colby seemed taken aback by that. "You think your mom asked me to hire you?"

"I know she's worried that I want to go back to DHQ, so yeah, I could see her coming up with this plan to keep my boots in Whispering Canyon."

The sheriff's gaze sharpened. "*Do* you want to go back to DHQ?"

A good question, and not one with a clear answer, Flynn mused, subconsciously rubbing his knuckles against his shirt where it covered the six-inch scar that was a memento of his last mission with the company. "I have no plans to do so at the moment."

"Good," Colby said. "Because you've got skills that would be a benefit to this department."

"Feel free to give me a call if you need help vaccinating calves or driving a herd of cattle into the mountains."

"I was referring to the fact that you located and elicited statements from the two witnesses who saw Gramps's shooter fleeing the woods last summer."

"They were hardly flying under the radar," Flynn pointed out. "And if Garvey had done his job, I wouldn't have had to make a trip out to California."

"If Garvey had done his job, I wouldn't be sitting in this chair right now," Colby noted. "But I am, and because I am, I need to hire some new deputies."

"You talked Ken Holland out of retirement once, I'm sure you can do it again."

"Unfortunately, he's not the only one who needs convincing, and his wife recently reminded him that they bought a condo in a retirement village on a golf course in Arizona because they planned to actually retire and play golf down there."

"Never understood the point of that game," Flynn remarked.

"Me neither," his cousin agreed. "But the point of this conversation is that I need a new deputy, and I need one that I can trust to have my back."

"Then you should keep looking," he advised.

"I trust you," Colby assured him. "Every bit as much as I know my brother trusted you."

"And where is your brother now?" he challenged.

"I wish I knew. But I do know that what happened in Afghanistan isn't on you, Flynn."

"You're fishing, Sheriff," he admonished.

The truth was, they hadn't been in Afghanistan but Azerbaijan. Because while training with local troops in Armenia, their team leader received intel that a group of hostages—humanitarian volunteers—was being held captive just across the border in Azerbaijan. The location turned out to be right, but something else went very wrong as they were leading the aid workers to safety.

The last thing Flynn remembered was hearing Ellis swear—and then the world went black.

"And you're not biting," Colby acknowledged.

"I can't tell you where we were, but I can tell you it wasn't Afghanistan."

The sheriff inclined his head, a wordless acknowledgment.

"Take the badge, Flynn."

"I haven't held a weapon since that last assignment," he told his cousin.

"Are you worried that you won't pass the firearms qualifications test?"

He shrugged. "It's a lot more likely I'll flunk the psych evals."

"I've got faith in you."

"I really don't think I'm the right person for the job."

"You said 'anything,'" Colby reminded him.

"Because I never imagined you'd ask something like this," Flynn grumbled.

The sheriff just smiled. "Well, that's on you then, isn't it?"

Meg knocked three times before turning the knob. Though she'd talked to her grandmother—on numerous occasions—about locking the door, Tallulah insisted that she wasn't worried about unwelcome visitors. "The neighbors are so damn nosy, they'd have enough details for the cops to make a composite drawing before any intruder found his way out again."

"Gramma?"

"In the kitchen," Tallulah responded.

Meg made her way down the hall then paused in the doorway for a minute, watching Lula. Her grandmother's once-blond hair was now gray and styled in a blunt cut that fell just above her shoulders. Her face was heavily lined—"alcohol will do that to you"—but her green eyes were clear and bright.

She wore minimal makeup these days—just a touch of mascara on her lashes and a swipe of gloss on her lips—and maximum jewelry—chunky silver hoops in her ears, a collection of silver bangles on both wrists and an assortment of pretty rings on her fingers, though the ring finger on her left hand was conspicuously bare—a bold and deliberate assertion of her never-married status. She wore an oversized flannel shirt, with the sleeves rolled up past the elbows, and a pair of jeggings with fleece-lined Crocs on her feet.

Looking at her now, it was hard to believe she was the same woman who—almost sixty years ago—earned herself a reputation for seducing (or allowing herself to be seduced by—depending on the perspective of whoever was telling the story) Raylan Chandler, a married rancher and father of two young sons. By all accounts, the affair was regrettable and short-lived, but it nevertheless resulted in a child. Another son, of course, as the Chandler men didn't seem capable of begetting daughters.

"Those don't look like cupcakes," Meg noted, as her grandmother dropped spoonfuls of dough onto a cookie sheet.

"Your cupcakes are already boxed up and ready to go."

"Emma's cupcakes," she clarified.

"There's fourteen kids in her class and you asked for two dozen," Lula pointed out.

"Fourteen plus the teacher and EA and parent volunteers."

Tallulah sent her a look.

"And maybe a couple extra for me and Em," she admitted, opening the box to peer inside.

"Uh-huh."

She closed the lid again. "Thank you. I could have picked up something from Sweet Cheeks Bakery, but Em prefers your cupcakes."

"I'm always happy to make them for her," Tallulah said.

"So, who are the cookies for?"

"No one."

"In that case—" Meg snagged one from a cooling rack and bit into it.

Lula slid the next tray into the oven and set the timer. "Good?"

"So good," she agreed, her mouth full.

Her grandmother selected a cookie for herself.

"Rocky Road, right?"

Tallulah nodded.

"Don't you usually put walnuts in these?"

"Yeah, but I decided to try almonds this time because Gretchen Frank doesn't like walnuts."

"So the cookies are for Gretchen Frank?" Meg asked, recognizing the name of one of her grandmother's nearest neighbors.

"Not specifically," Tallulah said. "But she's been coming around for coffee on Friday mornings for the past few months."

"Ah." She nodded. "The almonds are intended to camouflage the flavor of the cyanide."

Her grandmother's lips twitched. "You think I'm trying to poison her?"

"I imagine you'd rather spend the rest of your life in prison than have a weekly coffee date with any of the nosy biddies from your neighborhood."

"That sounds like something I'd say," Lula acknowledged.

"And have said—on more than one occasion."

Now Tallulah lifted a shoulder. "Gretchen isn't so bad."

"How and when did you come to this realization?" Meg asked curiously.

"She was part of the casserole brigade that showed up when I was released from jail last year."

It amazed Meg that her grandmother could speak so matter-of-factly about the incident when just thinking about Lula being arrested for shooting Raylan Chandler—a crime that no one actually believed she'd committed—and hauled off in cuffs, made her shudder.

"What did she make?"

"Something called *schinkennudeln*."

"Ham and cheese pasta," Meg translated.

"You've had it?"

She nodded. "My roommate in nursing school used to make it when we were studying for exams. German comfort food, she called it."

Not unlike spaghetti and meatballs was one of Emma's comfort foods—and a favorite of Flynn's, too.

"It is that," Lula agreed. "And I returned the baking dish with some *lebkuchen* inside."

"That was thoughtful," Meg said.

"Gretchen wasn't impressed. She bluntly told me that she's not a fan of most German recipes."

"So how did she explain the *schinkennudeln*?"

"It's easy to make and the ingredients are fairly inexpensive, and she had no intention of wasting a lot of time preparing a meal for someone who'd barely exchanged a handful of words with her in the more than thirty years they'd lived beside one another, even if she was almost certain that I'd been wrongly accused of attempted murder."

"And that's just the type of outspoken—and ornery—demeanor that would appeal to you," Meg mused.

"I can appreciate someone who tells it like it is."

"And how did you get from *lebkuchen* to Rocky Road cookies?" she wondered aloud.

"A few days later, I took over a lemon pie and suggested it was more suited to her disposition. She took the pie and invited me in for coffee."

"And that, to paraphrase Humphrey Bogart in *Casablanca*, was the beginning of a beautiful friendship."

"Don't get carried away," Lula cautioned. "Tolerating her company doesn't make us friends."

"But maybe the fact that she tolerates yours right back does."

"Not a lot of people in this town want to be seen keeping company with Tallulah Leonard," her grandmother noted. "Though the neighbors seem a little more tolerant of my existence since Eleanor Chandler showed up here last year."

"Why'd she come here?" Meg asked, surprised.

"Why wouldn't she?" Lula said, a slight edge to her voice. "It was her house."

"I don't understand."

"Raylan and Eleanor bought this place so that I'd be able to give my daughters a home."

"And they've been holding that over your head ever since," she surmised, though she had some difficult reconciling the kind of people who would do that with the couple she'd never known to be anything but warm and welcoming.

"Actually, they haven't," Lula admitted. "In fact, a few months ago, Eleanor showed up here again with papers transferring ownership to me. When I objected to being the recipient of more Chandler charity, Eleanor pointed out that I'd been paying the bills and maintaining the property for close to forty years, which was worth more than what they'd paid for the house when they bought it. So this house is really mine now."

"Then the hatchet has truly been buried," Meg mused.

"A good thing for Tess and Holt. And perhaps for you and Flynn, too."

She drew back, startled by the latter remark.

"Me and Flynn are friends," she reminded her grandmother.

"You keep telling yourself that," Tallulah said with a wink.

Chapter Four

Flynn awoke, sweaty and shivering, and thankfully with no memory of the nightmare that had intruded on his sleep. It took some effort to extricate himself from the blanket that was tangled around his limbs, but he finally managed to do so. Rising to his feet, he peered at the glowing numbers on the clock beside his bed: 3:12 a.m.

Of course—it was never 2:30 or 4:00, but always between 3:00 and 3:20.

His PTSD was as dependable as a freaking alarm clock.

As much as he'd hated receiving the official diagnosis, it undoubtedly explained a lot of the things he'd been dealing with since his return from overseas.

Unwanted and persistent thoughts or memories of the traumatic event? Check.

Difficulty falling asleep? Check.

Disturbing dreams that replay the traumatic event? Check.

Feeling hypervigilant, as if danger is imminent? Check.

Detached or disconnected from emotions? Unable to experience happiness or sadness? Check and check.

Increasingly irritable or angry? Check.

Guilt or shame related to the traumatic event? Check.

Congratulations, Sergeant First Class Chandler, you have PTSD.

Unfortunately, the diagnosis didn't come with any quick fix.

There was no magic prescription that could make it go away. Nothing that could lift the weight of the guilt he carried.

And the truth was, he didn't want to let go of the guilt—he didn't deserve to live without it. Not until Ellis was home.

When he'd first returned to the States, Flynn had been certain that his cousin and best friend would follow soon after. But with each day that passed, his doubts about that ever happening continued to grow.

When Colby had asked if he planned on going back to DHQ, he'd said *no*, and that was the truth. Because while DHQ might play by a different set of rules than the military, there were still rules. And if Flynn decided to go back to Azerbaijan to find Ellis—or at least some answers about what had happened to him—he'd do so on his own terms.

But whenever he thought about going back, he'd start to feel dizzy and weak, his breathing labored and his heart pounding. And as desperate as he was to find Ellis, he feared he'd have a freaking heart attack in the mountains, and then his parents would never know what happened to him, either.

He'd failed his best friend when he left him behind—and every day since that he hadn't figured out a way to bring him home. So Flynn was truly baffled by Colby's desire to hire him to work in the sheriff's office.

But he'd jumped through the hoops that had been set out for him, passing his firearms test with flying colors and achieving a low-risk designation on the psych eval. Which only proved that he'd said all the right things, not that he hadn't been lying his ass off.

It occurred to him now that it would have been just as easy to say all the wrong things and flunk the evaluation on purpose, so that Colby would have to find someone else for the job. The fact that he hadn't considered doing so made him wonder if he actually wanted to work in the sheriff's office, to perform a service to the community and feel useful again.

Megan probably had some thoughts on that. She seemed to have thoughts about most everything and wasn't usually afraid to share them.

Maybe that was why she was the only person he found it easy to be completely honest with. Because she was the only person who didn't judge him.

Lying and subterfuge had become second nature for him since he'd returned home. Lying to his family and pretending he was okay, so they wouldn't worry about him. Not that they'd been entirely convinced, which was how he'd ended up at the support group where he'd met Megan Wheeler.

At the time of their initial meeting, he hadn't known that she was also a cousin of Ellis's—a result of the fact that her mom and his dad were half siblings on the maternal side. Flynn's dad and Ellis's dad were half siblings, too, but on the paternal side, so there was no blood between them. (A fact in which he took solace, because although he and Megan were only friends, he'd definitely checked her out at that first meeting.)

But while he didn't lie to Meg, he hadn't yet found an opportunity to tell her about Colby's job offer, despite the fact that they talked or texted almost every day.

He reached for his phone and stared at the screen for several minutes, watching as the numbers changed from 3:19 to 3:20 to 3:21. Finally, at 3:22, he opened their message chain.

Hey.

He wasn't surprised that she immediately replied.

Are you still awake or did you just wake up?

Just woke up. You?

Still awake.

He knew why he had trouble sleeping—and staying asleep—but he wasn't sure what caused her to pace the floors at night. Or sit out on her porch, looking up at the stars, sometimes even in the dead of winter.

He tapped the screen to initiate a call.

"What are you doing awake at this hour?" he asked.

"Trying to come down from my sugar high," she confided. "My grandmother made cupcakes for Em to take to school tomorrow, but we each had one for dessert after dinner, and then I ate two more after she'd gone to bed."

"So now you're pacing the floor to burn the calories?" he guessed.

"Actually, I'm sitting out under the stars right now."

"It's fourteen degrees outside."

"I'm wearing a fuzzy robe and thick socks and wrapped in a blanket."

He didn't have any trouble visualizing the image, because sometimes, on nights when he didn't want to try to sleep, he'd take a drive into town. And on more than one occasion, he'd found her just as she'd described. In the warmer summer months, she'd be without the blanket, clad in a pair of boxers and a tiny T-shirt she claimed were her pajamas (and that made it more difficult than he was willing to acknowledge to keep his eyes focused on her face).

"You want company?" he asked her now.

"No," she said. "Go back to bed."

"What if I said I was already in my truck on my way into town?"

"You're not," she said. "I can always tell by the background noise when you're driving."

"Still, I could be there in twenty minutes."

"I'll be tucked into my bed in fifteen."

"Promise?"

"Promise."

"Okay," he relented.

"In the meantime, you want to tell me about your dream?"

"I honestly don't remember."

"Is that a good thing?"

"I don't know."

"Dr. Litman might have some thoughts on that."

"You know I stopped seeing her."

"Because she wouldn't sign off on you going back to DHQ."

"Because it was always the same thing."

"Well, I'm sure she'd be happy to hear from you, if you gave her a call."

"I'd rather talk to you."

"I'm not qualified to do anything more than listen," she cautioned.

"That's all I need," he assured her.

"Are you going to be able to go back to sleep now?"

"Probably. Maybe."

"There's something else on your mind," she prompted.

"I've been offered a job," Flynn confided.

"I thought you had a job."

"That's what I said."

"And yet, you're obviously considering this offer."

"I'm not sure why."

"Tell me about it," she urged. "Maybe we can figure it out together."

"Colby wants to hire me as a deputy sheriff."

"And there's the reason right there," Meg concluded.

He frowned. "Where?"

"Colby," she said. "He's family—and it's not in your nature to let down your family."

"And yet," he mused darkly.

"This is why you should be talking to Dr. Litman rather than me," she told him.

"And yet," he said again.

"Do you really want to know what I think?"

"I do."

"Complete honesty?"

"Of course."

"Okay, then," she said. "I think you should stop hiding at West River Ranch and take the job."

He scowled at that. "I'm not hiding."

"Aren't you?" she challenged. "When was the last time you ventured into town to meet with a friend or even walk up and down the aisles of the grocery store?"

"I just offered to come to town to see you," he reminded her.

"In the middle of the night, when the likelihood of you crossing paths with anyone else is approximately nil."

"And why would I waste time walking the aisles of a physical store when online ordering is so convenient?"

"To prove that you're not hiding out at the ranch."

"Maybe I'm just not a people person."

"You didn't rise to the rank of sergeant first class in the Army Rangers by shutting out others."

"Apparently you didn't get the memo," he said. "I'm not a sergeant first class anymore."

"Take the job, Flynn," she urged. "Give yourself a reason to get out of bed in the morning that has nothing to do with cattle."

He gasped. "Blasphemy—especially coming from someone I know enjoys a nice juicy steak."

She chuckled softly, but said again, "Take the job, Flynn."

"If I do, you're likely to see a lot more of me in town."

And that was the trump card Colby hadn't known he held in his hand—proximity of the job to Meg and Emma. Because if Flynn was working in town, he'd be close enough to check on his friend and her little girl more regularly, without the necessity of having to come up with excuses for his trips into town.

"Another plus," Meg told him now.

* * *

"Can we go see Auntie Tess's baby today?" Emma asked, when Meg picked her up from her parents' house Friday afternoon.

"The baby's name is Blake," Meg reminded her. Again.

"Can we go see *Blake*?"

"I don't think today's a good day for a visit," she hedged, though she was tempted to give in to her daughter's request. Tess and Blake had been discharged the day after the little guy's birth, which meant that Meg hadn't seen her best friend or her nephew since then.

"Why not?"

"Because it's been a busy week—" compounded by several sleepless nights "—and I don't feel like driving all the way out to West River Ranch."

"But tomorrow's Valentine's Day," Emma pointed out.

"That's right—and you had a party at school today, didn't you?" Meg said, hoping to deflect her daughter's attention.

Emma nodded. "We had cookies and cupcakes and gummy candy hearts and chocolate kisses."

"Translation—you had sugar and sugar and sugar and sugar," Meg noted.

"Gramma Sunny says sugar makes me hyper."

"I'm going to have to agree with Gramma Sunny on that."

"And I got valentines from everyone in my class. Well, everyone 'cept Chloe, 'cuz she wasn't there today. Act'lly, she's been away all week. Sick, Miz Riya said. But she decorated a bag to collect the valentines for Chloe, to give her when she comes back. So maybe Chloe'll give me a valentine when she comes back, but it's okay if she doesn't, 'cuz Patrick gave me three."

"Patrick gave you three valentines?"

"Uh-huh." Emma nodded. "I thought it was a mistake and tried to give some back, but he said I got three 'cuz he likes me best."

Tess had warned Meg that she probably wouldn't survive her daughter's teenage years, but there were days—like today—that Meg wondered if she'd make it to Emma's teenage years.

"Anyway, Miz Riya said everyone has to get a valentine on Valentine's Day."

"That makes sense," Meg agreed. "You wouldn't want any of your classmates to feel left out."

"And I don't want Auntie Tess's baby to feel left out."

Well, she'd walked into that one, hadn't she?

"I think Ms. Riya meant that everyone in your class should get a valentine," Meg clarified.

"But when I made valentines at Gramma Sunny's, I made one for Blake."

A heads-up from her mom in that regard would have been nice, Meg mused.

"And you can give it to Blake the next time you see him."

"I made one for Unca Flynn, too."

"You did?" she asked, taken aback by that revelation.

"Uh-huh," Emma confirmed, nodding.

"Why?"

"'Cuz I don't think he has anyone else to give him one," the little girl said matter-of-factly.

"Well, that was very thoughtful," she said.

"So…can we go to the ranch?" Emma asked.

Meg sighed and turned her vehicle in the direction of West River Ranch.

Flynn had been telling the truth when he assured Colby that he had plenty to keep him busy around the ranch—and more than enough at his own little cabin. Today, he walked out the door with a toolbox in hand, intending to fix the hinges on the back gate, when he saw Meg's SUV parked in his driveway and the woman herself—and her daughter—making her way toward him.

"What brings you all the way out here on a Friday afternoon?" he asked curiously.

"Emma made a valentine for Blake and insisted that we deliver it today."

"A valentine, huh? I guess that means it's February."

The little girl giggled. "You're funny, Unca Flynn."

"A regular comedian," Meg agreed dryly.

"So how is your new cousin?" Flynn asked Emma.

She wrinkled her nose. "Stinky."

"Emma declined to help change Blake's diaper."

He nodded at the little girl. "Good call."

"He didn't even look at my valentine," Emma told him, obviously insulted by the infant's lack of interest in her gift. "But Auntie Tess said it was really pretty."

"I'm sure it was," Flynn agreed.

Emma reached for the backpack her mom carried, then unzipped the main compartment and pulled out a pink construction-paper heart glued onto a paper doily. The heart was decorated with puffy paint, feathers, sparkly beads and glitter.

"I made one for you, too," Emma said, offering him the heart.

Flynn was taken aback. "For me?"

She nodded, her pigtails—tied with red ribbons today—bobbing.

He set down the toolbox to accept the paper heart. "But… why?"

"'Cuz it's Valentine's Day and everyone should get a valentine on Valentine's Day."

He stared at the elaborately decorated heart, not sure what to say.

"Do you like it?" Emma pressed.

"It's really pretty," he said, borrowing his sister-in-law's words.

Emma beamed. "Turn it over."

He did so and saw that she'd carefully printed her name and added "XOXO."

"Really pretty," he said again, inexplicably moved by the gesture and sentiment. "Thank you, Emma."

"You're welcome." She looked at him hopefully. "Do you have a valentine for me?"

"No." He shook his head. "I'm sorry. To be honest, I forgot it was almost Valentine's Day."

"That's okay. You can make one for me now."

"Emma," Meg admonished gently. "You can't ask someone to give you a valentine just because you gave them one."

"I'd be happy to make one," Flynn said. "But I don't have any valentine-making stuff."

"I do," Emma told him, reaching into her backpack again. "Gramma Sunny gave me the extra craft supplies."

"Well, isn't that lucky?" he said.

"Everything's in here." She pulled a plastic bag out of her pack. "But there's no more purple glitter 'cuz I used it all up."

He accepted the offering and peered inside. "I'm sure I can make do without purple glitter."

But the little girl's attention had been snagged by something in the distance.

"Buddy!" she shouted.

Responding to her call, Holt's Lab-mix rescue dog turned in her direction.

Taking advantage of the little girl's distraction, Holt said to Meg, "Everything okay?"

She forced a smile. "Sure. Why do you ask?"

"You look a little tense. More than end-of-a-long-week tense," he clarified, before she could brush off his question with that explanation.

"I guess I am," she admitted.

"Want to tell me why?"

"I yelled at one of the surgeons yesterday," she confided.

His brows lifted. "I don't know that I've ever heard you yell."

Her gaze shifted to her daughter, who was giggling as she fussed over Buddy, and a small smile curved her lips, confirming that the joyful sound lifted her heart the same way it did his own.

"I try not to," she finally responded to his comment. "But he was bullying one of the female residents—seriously berating her for the same mistake that I'd seen several male residents make in his presence that only earned them a stern correction—and she was practically in tears and…"

"Your Mama Bear instincts kicked in," he concluded when her words trailed off.

She shrugged. "I guess so."

"Sounds to me like he deserved it." And Flynn was proud of her for speaking up, aware that doing so wouldn't have been easy for a woman who'd been the target of verbal abuse—and worse—in the past.

"But he's a surgeon and I'm a nurse," she reminded him. "So now I'm waiting to see if he files a complaint, and if he does, I'm not sure I can count on the female resident to back me up, because she told me she doesn't need anyone else to fight her battles for her."

"Do you think you did the right thing?" he asked.

She nodded.

"Then you did the right thing," he said confidently.

"Even if I tanked my career?"

"You didn't tank your career."

"How do you know?" she challenged.

"Because I know that Dr. Tierney specifically asked for you when she operated on my grandfather's gunshot wound last spring," he told her. "And she wouldn't have done so if she didn't believe you were one of the best."

"Or at least one of the best on duty that day," Meg countered.

"One of the best," he said again. Firmly. "And the reason

you're one of the best is that you have a strong moral code and good instincts, and anyone who hears that you yelled at a surgeon will know that he deserved it."

She managed another small smile then. "I'm not sure that's true, but I appreciate the pep talk."

"Anytime," he said, and gave her a quick hug.

He drew back quickly when a whistle sounded in the distance, then Buddy abandoned his human playmate to race toward his own home and Emma skipped back to them.

"Can I watch TV while you're making my valentine?" the little girl asked hopefully.

"We have rules about TV," Meg reminded her daughter. "And rules about inviting ourselves into other people's homes."

"Unca Flynn isn't people," Emma said.

"And Uncle Flynn doesn't have a TV," he told her.

"You don't have a TV?" Meg asked, surprised.

"Why don't you have a TV?" Emma wanted to know.

He shrugged. "I'm not much interested in watching the news."

"I don't watch the news, either," the little girl informed him. "I watch *Bubble Guppies* and *Stella and Sam* and *My Little Pony* and *Eureka*."

"Not all of those shows every day," Meg felt compelled to clarify. "She gets two half-hour blocks of TV-watching time, *max*, on any day."

"I'm not judging," Flynn promised.

"*My Little Pony*'s my fav'rite," Emma said.

"And if we go now, we might make it home in time to watch *My Little Pony*," Meg told her.

"But Unca Flynn's gonna make a valentine for me."

"A task that will be much easier for him to accomplish if you're not hovering over him asking all kinds of questions."

"Asking questions is how you learn," Emma said.

"And that's why you'll be applying for your Mensa membership before the end of second grade."

"What's Mensa?"

"I'll explain it to you in the car," Meg promised.

And with a wave to Flynn, she ushered her daughter back to the car, buckled her into her car seat and drove off, leaving him holding the bag—literally.

Chapter Five

Eleven months earlier

Four weeks after he'd first seen her at a meeting, Flynn had yet to learn anything about the woman who'd snagged his attention that day. Though she'd attended each subsequent Wednesday afternoon meeting, she always slipped out before the session was over. The habitual disappearing act made him wonder if she had somewhere that she needed to be or if she was simply eager to avoid chitchat with the other members when the group dispersed.

And so, on week four, instead of going into the meeting room, Flynn decided to wait in the hall to catch her on her way out.

He didn't think too hard about why he was so eager to talk to her when he hadn't made an effort to strike up a conversation with anyone else in the meetings. Because he didn't know that he could articulate a reason—he only knew that her appearance at the group seemed to have awakened something that had been long dormant inside him.

"Hey," he said, when she stepped into the corridor.

She glanced up. Startled. Wary.

"I'm in the group, too." He gestured to the door of the meeting room through which she'd just exited, hoping the information would reassure her.

"I've seen you there," she acknowledged, still obviously wary.

"My name's Flynn."

She nodded. "I know who you are."

He raised his brows, surprised—and perhaps a little unnerved—by her admission.

"You're a Chandler," she noted. "You can't honestly expect to go anywhere in this town and not be recognized."

She was right, of course. Which made him realize that probably everyone in the group knew who he was, though no one else had called out his identity.

"Then you have me at a disadvantage," he told her.

"Probably not something you've ever said before."

"Probably not."

"Now if you'll excuse me," she said, ignoring his clumsy effort to learn her name. "There's somewhere I need to be."

"Where?"

"That's absolutely none of your business."

"You're right," he agreed.

An acknowledgment that apparently surprised her enough to make her pause and turn back around.

"I'm not good at this group therapy stuff," he confided. "I understand the purpose, but I don't really want a bunch of strangers watching me bleed out my trauma, like rubberneckers at the scene of a horrific crash."

"That's an interesting visual," she mused.

"Maybe we could discuss it over a cup of coffee?"

"I have no interest in watching you bleed out your trauma in the middle of a coffee shop," she said. "Especially if you think it will entitle you to watch me bleed out mine."

"Just coffee," he said. "No bleeding required."

She glanced at her watch, and he realized there really was somewhere that she needed to be.

"Alright," she relented. "But I need to make a quick call first."

"To let your husband know you'll be late?"

He didn't know why he asked the question. Why he was fishing for information about the relationship status of this woman who had yet to even share her name. Because even if she was the most beautiful female he'd crossed paths with in a long time, he wasn't looking for a relationship—or even a hookup. He had to get his own life sorted out before he could consider inviting anyone in, and he didn't hold out much hope of that happening anytime soon.

"To let my parents know I'll be late." She held his gaze, her expression almost challenging. "They're babysitting my daughter."

His surprise must have been evident, because she followed up by asking, "Still want to go for that coffee?"

He nodded.

After she made her phone call, they walked across the street to Southside Perk.

"My name's Meg," she said, when they settled across from one another in a booth by the window. "Megan Wheeler."

"It's a pleasure to meet you, Megan Wheeler."

"And a little strange that we're meeting for the first time considering our family connection," she remarked.

"We have a family connection?" he asked, surprised.

She nodded. "Through Uncle Wyatt—my mom's half brother, who's also your dad's half brother."

"Then we have met before," Flynn said to Megan now, choosing to focus on that fact rather than acknowledge that Ellis, his cousin and best friend, was her cousin, too. "At my grandparents' fiftieth anniversary party at West River Ranch."

"How long ago was that?" she wondered. "Because it's not ringing any bells for me."

"Almost fifteen years ago," he said. "And the only reason I was able to answer that question off the top of my head is that they're planning their celebration of sixty-five years in June."

"Fifteen years ago." She furrowed her brow, as if trying to

remember. "Hmm...maybe I do have a vague memory of lots of people, long tables covered with platters of food, and an enormous cake. And me and my cousin Tess sneaking off to a barn to see a litter of newborn kittens."

"I remember having to wear a tie."

She chuckled softly.

"And telling a couple of young girls who were hiding in a corner about the litter of kittens that had recently been born."

"I remember the kittens," she said. "I don't remember you."

"Ouch."

"It *was* fifteen years ago," she pointed out.

"Fair point," he acknowledged.

"Now fast forward to today and tell me why you were lurking in the hall instead of sitting in the meeting," she suggested.

"I wanted a chance to talk to you."

"Is that your MO? You troll meetings to pick up women?"

"No," he immediately denied. "Today was my first day lurking."

"So why do you go to the meetings?" she asked him now. "Because I haven't heard you say a word in any of the ones I've attended."

"Maybe I do all my talking after you leave."

"Touché."

"The truth is, my mom found the group for me. She was worried that I'd isolated myself since I got back and thought it might help if I had someone to talk to."

"Because the one person you would have talked to didn't come back with you," she realized.

"Yeah." He swallowed another mouthful of coffee.

"You and Ellis were in the army, right?"

He nodded. "Then the Army Rangers. We did a couple of tours with them, back when they were still letting the Rangers see real action. After that, we went to work for a private military contractor, doing more of the same thing.

"And now I go to meetings so that I can tell my mom I do, and it keeps her off my back."

"Not everyone is comfortable talking in front of a group," Meg noted. "You might find one-on-one counseling more helpful."

"I tried that when I was in the hospital."

"I heard that you were injured."

He nodded again. "According to the doctors, I'm lucky to be alive."

"Do you feel lucky?" she asked.

He stared into the bottom of his mug for a long minute, as if the answer to her question might be found in the brown stain there.

Did he feel lucky?

He knew that he should. He was alive, and so many—too many—others had lost their lives.

And one had simply disappeared.

But that was not something he wanted to think about now.

"You said you didn't want to watch me bleed out my trauma in the middle of a coffee shop," he reminded her.

"I'm a nurse. Maybe I can stop the bleeding."

"Thanks, but I'm not ready to rip the Band-Aid off just yet."

"Okay," she said. "But if you change your mind, I've been told I'm a pretty good listener."

"I can't talk about it," he told her. "Not because I'm not capable, but because I'm not allowed."

"I understand that you can't share any details of your missions, but you could talk about how you feel looking back at your experiences."

"Or I could just open up a vein."

"I didn't say it was easy," she acknowledged. "But it's important. Keeping things inside is how they fester."

"I'll keep that in mind," he said.

"And on that note—" she glanced at the watch on her wrist "—I really do need to be going."

"Maybe we could do this again next week," he suggested, rising from the table as she did.

Meg shook her head. "I can't."

And maybe it was wishful thinking on his part, but he thought she sounded the teensiest bit regretful.

"Afraid you might get too attached to me?" he asked, obviously teasing.

She rolled her eyes. "I'm registered for a two-day robotic surgery course next week. Tuesday is the first of those days."

"So you really are a nurse," he mused.

"Did you think I'd made that up?"

He shrugged.

"I'm a surgical nurse at Whispering Canyon Medical Center," she admitted. "Though if my life had gone according to plan, I'd be in my last year of med school right now."

"What happened to derail your plans?"

"Emma."

But she said it with a smile, leading him to ask, "That's your daughter's name?"

"It is," she confirmed.

"And how old is Emma?"

"Three-and-a-half."

"You ever think about going back to med school?"

"Every day," she said. "But right now, my daughter is my priority. Which means working to keep a roof over her head and put food in her belly."

"Her dad doesn't help at all?"

Her expression immediately shuttered, like clouds closing over the sun. "No."

And though he knew he was treading on boggy ground, Flynn felt compelled to press forward. "He has a legal obligation to support his child, and if he's balking at that, you could—"

"He's dead."

Not boggy ground, he realized, but quicksand.

And he was flailing in it.

"I'm sorry," he said.

"I'm not," Megan replied bluntly.

And didn't that response raise more questions than it answered?

"Then I'm sorry I overstepped," he told her.

She considered for a minute, then nodded. "Apology accepted."

"So how about the week after next for coffee again?" he prompted, shifting to a more neutral topic of conversation and onto more solid ground.

"Maybe."

Though her response was noncommittal, she hadn't shot down the suggestion completely, and he decided to take it as a win.

They turned in different directions then, and as Flynn made his way to his truck, he wondered why his face felt odd.

He realized then, with no small amount of surprise, that he was smiling.

Chapter Six

Meg didn't expect Flynn to do anything with the craft supplies Emma had left with him. But once again, the former Army Ranger surprised her, showing up at her door just before six o'clock Saturday night with a valentine and a large pizza.

"It's always nice to see you in town," Meg said. "And even nicer when you bring pizza."

"It turns out, I'm going to be spending a lot more time in town in the future," he said, setting a shiny badge on top of the pizza box on the table.

She smiled. "You took the job."

"I took the job," he confirmed.

"What's it say?" Emma asked, picking up the badge for a closer look.

"It says that Uncle Flynn is now a deputy sheriff," Meg said.

"Whatsa dep'ty sheriff?"

"Someone who gets to put bad guys in jail," he said.

"Really?"

He nodded.

"Can you put Scotty in jail?" she asked hopefully.

"Who's Scotty?" Flynn asked.

"A boy in her class at preschool," Meg explained.

"A bad boy," Emma told him.

"What did he do that was so bad?" her mom asked.

"He butted ahead of me in line for the slide at recess."

"That wasn't nice," Meg acknowledged. "But I'm not sure it warrants jail time."

"Unca Flynn?" Emma asked hopefully.

"I've gotta side with your mom on this one," he said.

"Did you tell Miss Riya?" Meg asked.

Emma nodded. "She put him in time-out."

"Which is kind of like the preschool equivalent of jail, don't you think?"

"But she didn't make him miss next recess," Emma complained. "He shoulda had to miss recess."

"Instead of worrying about Scotty's punishment, why don't we serve up this pizza and celebrate Uncle Flynn's new job?" Meg suggested.

Emma's eyes widened and her lips curved. "It's a cel'bration?"

"A new job is definitely cause for celebration," Meg said.

"Do we get cake?" the little girl asked.

"Sorry, no cake," Flynn said. "Just pizza."

"But cel'bration means cake," Emma insisted.

"I did put Great-Gramma Lula's leftover cupcakes in the freezer," Meg admitted.

"And ice cream?" Emma asked hopefully.

Her mom chuckled. "I think we have some ice cream, too."

"Speaking of jobs," Flynn said to Meg, as she scooped ice cream to go with the cupcakes topped with pink and red heart-shaped sprinkles. "Has there been any fallout from your altercation with the bully surgeon?"

"Not only was there no fallout, I got a text message apology from him this morning."

"Because you did the right thing."

"I shouldn't have yelled," she acknowledged, distributing the desserts around the table. "But I do think his behavior needed to be called out."

"Like Scotty's," Emma said, with a mouthful of cupcake.

"You're right. And I'm proud of you for standing up for yourself."

"Like mother, like daughter," Flynn noted.

When the little girl had eaten her fill and was excused from the table, she skipped up to her room with her valentine in hand.

"She has a magnetic whiteboard in her room, above her desk, where she puts her favorite things," Meg told Flynn. "I'll bet when I go upstairs to tuck her in, I'll find your valentine there."

"I'm not sure my lopsided heart is whiteboard worthy."

"The effort matters more than the result."

"Remember you said that when there's glitter all over her room," Flynn said.

"I have an almost-five-year-old who loves crafts," Meg pointed out. "There's glitter all over this house."

"You seemed surprised when I gave the valentine to Emma," he noted.

"I guess I was," she admitted, reaching for her wineglass only to discover that it was already empty.

"Even though I said I'd make one for her?" he pressed.

"Saying and doing are two different things," she responded lightly.

"You don't have a lot of faith that a man will keep his word, do you?"

She shrugged. "I don't have a lot of experience with a man keeping his word."

"I don't believe in making promises I can't keep," he told her. "Which is why I don't make a lot of promises, but Emma's request was a simple enough one to honor."

"And I thank you for that."

"You don't have to thank me," Flynn said. "It makes me happy to make Emma happy."

"Well, I'm grateful anyway."

"But not happy," he noted.

She frowned.

"Are you disappointed that I didn't make a valentine for you?"

"Given the choice, I'd take a hot pizza over a paper heart any day of the week—and especially on February 14."

"Not a fan of the Valentine's Day?" he asked, obviously surprised by her response.

"No." She contemplated a second glass of pinot noir, then decided that her want of liquid courage was exactly why she couldn't let herself have it. She rose from the sofa and carried her empty glass to the kitchen. "Do you want coffee?"

"Sure."

She inserted a pod and set a mug beneath the spout, then repeated the process to make a second cup. She carried both back to the living room and set one on the coaster in front of Flynn.

"Thanks."

She nodded as she settled with her own cup cradled between her palms. "I met Daymond on February 14," she confided now.

"Enough said," he told her.

She nodded and took a cautious sip of the hot coffee.

"Unless…you want to talk about it?" Flynn said.

Now she shook her head. "I'm also not a fan of walks down memory lane." Especially not when the lane was littered with memories of angry accusations, hard hands and debilitating fear.

"Okay."

She exhaled a quiet sigh of relief, grateful for his unquestioning support. "Anyway, all of that was just a lead up to saying that this was the best Valentine's Day I've had in a very long time," she said. "So thank you for that."

"You're welcome," Flynn responded, turning to smile at her at the same moment that Meg leaned forward to kiss his cheek.

Her lips landed awkwardly at the side of his mouth.

She quickly pulled back, because it *was* awkward.

It was also, unexpectedly, tingly.

Tingly?

She mentally rolled her eyes at the completely inane and totally inappropriate description.

"I'm so sorry," she said.

Her cheeks were burning with embarrassment; her body was humming with awareness. But it was easier—and much smarter—to focus on the embarrassment rather than the awareness.

"No need to apologize," Flynn said.

Though the words were casual enough, there was an uncharacteristic huskiness in his tone.

Electricity crackled in the air, making her tingle all over. Making her feel things she hadn't felt in a very long time and didn't want to be feeling now—especially not in the presence of a man who was one of her best friends.

Flynn headed into town on Sunday grateful to have a new job to focus on. Unfortunately, he was soon to discover that being a deputy in Whispering Canyon could sometimes be as challenging as watching paint dry. As a result, any hopes that he'd be too busy to think about the fact that Meg had kissed him—a thought that had preoccupied his mind as if written there in neon lights since it happened—were quickly dashed.

"Maybe we should paint the office," he said.

"It could use some sprucing up," Hillary Langley—the other new hire in the department—agreed.

Colby glanced up from the reports he was reviewing—because, as sheriff, he had real work to do. "There's no money in the budget for redecorating."

"What if we got someone to donate the paint?" Flynn asked.

"You've got more important things to do with your time than paint."

"We do?"

Colby looked up again. "Day one and you're bored already?"

"No, sir," Langley immediately denied.

At the same time Flynn said, "A little."

The sheriff looked from one deputy to the other.

Neither of them flinched.

"So go out on patrol," he suggested.

"Yes, sir." Langley was already up from her desk and snagging the keys for one of the department's official vehicles.

"But don't shoot anyone," Colby called out as they started toward the door.

"No, sir," Langley said again.

"Don't even unholster your weapon."

"No, sir."

Flynn frowned as he followed the other deputy out to the parking lot. "What's the point of having to prove our proficiency with firearms if we're not allowed to use them?"

"You're new to law enforcement, aren't you?" Langley asked.

It was a simple question, without judgment.

"Yeah," he admitted.

"Former military?" she guessed.

"Yeah," he said again.

"Well, when you're stateside and you're carrying a badge, you have to not only account for your ammunition but file a report every time you draw your weapon. If you actually discharge it, an investigation is initiated."

"The sheriff didn't tell me any of that when he gave me the badge and gun," Flynn grumbled, fastening his seat belt.

"Would it have made a difference?"

"No," he admitted.

Langley pulled out of the parking lot and onto Main Street.

"How long have you worked in law enforcement?" he asked her.

"Since I graduated from college."

"Were you annoyed Colby got the job you wanted?"

"Not really," she said. "I knew it was a long shot to hope that the people of Whispering Canyon might vote for an outsider, but I was looking for a reason to leave Howlett's Pass because my boss was a misogynistic asshole, and when Colby offered me the job here, I finally got it."

"And now you're stuck training me," he noted.

"I've got things to learn, too," she said. "Every department is different and every sheriff has his own way of doing things—and thank God for that."

"Okay, so tell me what exactly 'going out on patrol' entails," he suggested.

"Driving around town in a marked vehicle to ensure that local residents see us and feel confident that their tax dollars are being well spent."

"Doesn't seem too challenging," he noted.

"Again, it depends on the town, but I don't anticipate too many problems," she agreed. "Of course, you need to keep a lookout, too, for traffic infractions and bylaw violations, such as drivers failing to stop at posted signs and dog owners neglecting to stoop and scoop."

"Someone can go to jail for that?"

"No, they get fined for that," she said. "Although, if they rack up enough fines, they could end up in jail."

"How about pushing in front of someone in line for the slide at school—can someone go to jail for that?"

Langley chuckled. "Not likely."

"I didn't think so."

"You a dad?" she asked.

He shook his head. "An uncle."

"Community outreach is another important part of law enforcement," she told him. "We could stop at the playground one day for you to flash your badge—that usually impresses the kids and might make the line-jumper think twice next time."

"I'll keep that in mind," he said.

And while cruising the streets of Whispering Canyon with Langley didn't completely take his mind off Megan's kiss, it was at least better than sitting behind a desk and staring at paint that had finished drying long ago.

It wasn't even a kiss, Meg admonished herself as she stripped out of her protective gear after a day of thankfully routine surgeries.

A kiss required both intent and cooperation.

And okay, she had intended to kiss Flynn's cheek, so it could be argued that the intent was there.

But there had been a decided lack of cooperation, which meant it wasn't a kiss.

So why couldn't she stop thinking about the moment that her lips made contact with the corner of his mouth?

And how was it possible that, when she thought about it—*three days later*—the memory still made her lips tingle?

But that wasn't the worst of it.

No, far worse than the tingling of her lips was the heat that pulsed in her veins and flowed through her body.

It was as if her hormones, dormant for so long, had suddenly reawakened to remind her that she wasn't only a mom and a nurse but also a woman.

Or maybe she was perimenopausal.

And why, she wondered as she stepped under the spray of the shower in the locker room, was that possibility almost comforting?

She could guess the answer to that question—because menopause was an inevitable part of a woman's reproductive cycle, and though it wasn't something over which she had any control, it also wasn't connected to other people in her life.

It had nothing to do with the surprising softness of a man's lips. Or the roughness of his unshaven cheek. Or his familiar and somehow newly tantalizing masculine scent.

Menopause was just another example of Mother Nature wreaking havoc with a woman's body, as She was wont to do.

And as She was doing right now, Meg noted, wrapping a towel around her torso and making her way back to her locker.

When she was dressed, she took a long drink from her water bottle, as if the liquid might cool the heat in her veins. And then, with the stainless steel pressed against her cheek, she pulled out her phone and sent a text message to Tess.

Is twenty-nine too young for hot flashes?

Her phone immediately vibrated in her hand and she glanced at the screen to see Tess was calling.

"Are you seriously having hot flashes? Because if you are, you should make an appointment to see your doctor to rule out hyperthyroidism or POI."

"How did I forget that you have a tendency to go straight to the worst-case scenario whenever we discuss medical issues?"

Tess huffed out a breath. "So the hot flashes aren't real?"

"They're probably not real hot flashes," Meg allowed.

"Tell me more about your symptoms," her friend demanded.

"There's nothing really to tell," she hedged. "It's just that there have been a couple times, in recent days, that I've felt… warm. Almost flushed. Even a little…tingly."

"Until you got to the tingly part, I was thinking you might have the flu."

"Maybe it *is* the flu. There's definitely something going through Emma's preschool classroom," she noted. "And that's more likely than perimenopause, right?"

"Where are you right now?" Tess asked curiously.

"The hospital. Why?"

"Any chance you were in surgery with Dr. Delicious today?"

"I really wish you wouldn't call him that," Meg said, grateful that the locker room was almost empty and that no one was close enough to overhear their conversation.

"Everyone at the hospital calls him that," her friend pointed out. "And with good reason."

Meg couldn't argue that point. Not that anyone could tell how ridiculously good-looking Nathan Duchesne was when he was masked and gowned for surgery, but of course the staff all knew that he was. And almost all of them turned to watch him walk down the hall, because anyone who'd studied anatomy had learned to appreciate a well-built body.

Meg was no different than her colleagues, though the truth was, she was even more impressed by his surgical abilities. He had a brilliant mind, technical know-how and good communication skills that made it clear he was leading the team while also being part of it. And, of course, he had seriously amazing hands—precise and steady, even under immense pressure.

But she'd never found herself looking at those hands and wondering if he could get a woman out of her clothes as seemingly effortlessly as he disposed of a troublesome blood clot. And even deliberately steering her thoughts in that direction now didn't cause any kind of visceral reaction, except mild discomfort that she was objectifying a colleague in such a blatantly sexual way.

"As a matter of fact, I did work with Dr. Duchesne today," she confirmed now.

"Well, there you have it," her friend concluded. "Working in close proximity with Dr. Delicious would make any woman hot and tingly."

"Maybe you're right," Meg allowed, preferring to let Tess think that the uncomfortable "hot flashes" were caused by the doctor rather than a sudden and inexplicable attraction to her brother-in-law.

Not that she couldn't imagine another woman being attracted to Flynn. Like the rest of the Chandlers, he was undeniably and incredibly attractive. Add to that the fact that the Chandlers were one of the wealthiest ranching families in the state, and it was actually a little surprising that he didn't have women throwing themselves at him whenever he went into town.

But it was inexplicable that Meg would suddenly find herself attracted to him when she hadn't met anyone else who'd stirred her interest since her divorce. And if she was suddenly going to show an interest in someone, it shouldn't be a man whom she considered a friend.

And definitely not a man who was also a friend of Emma's—and one of the best examples of a good man in the life of a little girl who hadn't known too many.

No way was Meg going to jeopardize Emma's relationship with Flynn just because her hormones seemed to have awakened from a long period of hibernation.

"Can you come out to the ranch next Saturday?" Tess asked, apparently having solved the issue of her friend's hot flashes and ready to move on to another topic of conversation. "I want to start making plans for Blake's christening."

"I'd love to help with the planning—and to see you and Blake, but Emma has her usual appointment with Dr. Halstead that day," Meg said, naming the child psychologist her daughter had been seeing for almost two years now—since they'd moved back to Whispering Canyon.

"I thought her sessions were once a month now."

"They are," Meg confirmed. "But next week is her next session."

"What time is the appointment?"

"Eleven o'clock."

"Can you come after? I'm sure Willow would be happy to put something together for lunch."

Meg recognized "Willow" as the name of Raylan and Eleanor's longtime housekeeper. "Then this isn't an informal brainstorming session but a family meeting at the big house," she realized.

Tess laughed. "Most of us refer to it as the main house, to avoid any negative connotations."

"But it *is* big. And scary."

"It's big," her friend agreed. "But *not* scary."

"My mom took me and Nicole there once—or maybe twice—when we were kids. I don't remember why, but I do remember being told to take our shoes off as soon as we walked through the door, to remember our manners, sit still, be quiet and not touch anything."

"I think that memory says more about your mom than it does about Mrs. Chandler."

"Probably," Meg acknowledged. Or maybe what she was really afraid of was the prospect of crossing paths with Flynn at West River Ranch and making a bigger fool of herself than she'd already done.

"Anyway, you're not a kid anymore," Tess noted.

"But I have a kid—and I'm going to have to tell her to take her shoes off, remember her manners, sit still, be quiet and not touch anything."

"You have a great kid," Tess pointed out. "So maybe you just tell her that you're going to have lunch at a friend's house."

"Maybe," Meg said dubiously.

And while their conversation hadn't resolved her concerns about the uncomfortable feelings recently stirred up by Flynn's presence, Meg at least had a lunch date with her friend to look forward to now.

Chapter Seven

After ten days, Flynn decided that patrol was his favorite part of his new job. He liked to know that he was maintaining public safety, deterring crime and building community relationships simply by driving along the streets of Whispering Canyon.

And if his route happened to take him down Walnut Street more frequently than some of the town's other roads, he didn't think anyone noticed. Especially not in the early hours of the morning.

He cruised past the strip mall on Winterberry, saw an old man folding his clothes inside the twenty-four-hour coin laundry. The illuminated Open sign in the window of the pizza place adjacent to the laundromat went dark, followed by the interior lights as the manager headed out.

It was 2:45 a.m. when he turned onto Oakridge Drive and saw Selena Alamilla—a bartender at Denim & Diamonds—pull into her driveway. Flynn had gone out with Selena a few times in high school, double dates with Ellis and Caitlyn, and he idled at the curb for a minute to ensure she made it inside safely. Then he continued along the road, turning onto Beechwood Road.

Half an hour later, he found himself on Walnut Street, looking toward Meg's house. There was often a barely visible glow from a second-floor window that he knew was Emma's bedroom. A night-light to help keep her bad dreams at bay. The third level, where Tess Barrett used to live, had been empty since Meg's cousin and best friend married Flynn's brother Holt the previous summer.

He saw a shadow on the porch and immediately eased over to the curb, touching a hand to his holster to confirm his gun was where it was supposed to be, in case he needed it. Flynn hoped like hell he wouldn't need it—and not only because of Langley's warning about the paperwork.

He'd passed the fire range testing without difficulty, but it was easy to focus on and shoot at a target. Not so easy when you had to look into a person's eyes and make the split-second decision to pull the trigger. He hoped he never had to make that decision again, but he also knew that he wouldn't hesitate if the circumstances warranted.

If you hesitate, you're dead.

Or maybe you just disappeared, which might be an even worse fate than death—at least for the people left behind.

"I've got a .38 in my hand and I'm not afraid to use it." Meg's voice was low and steady.

"Do you have a license for that .38?" he asked.

"Flynn?" she asked, a hint of surprise in her tone.

"Yeah." He stepped into the faint halo from the streetlight.

"If I'd actually had a gun, I might have killed you," she noted.

"I wasn't worried."

"You have that much faith in your Kevlar vest?" She was obviously teasing, but as soon as the words were out of her mouth, her expression changed—regret chasing any hint of amusement from her face. "I'm sorry."

He waved away her apology. "It's fine."

"It's not," she said. "I wasn't thinking. Obviously."

"Forget it," he told her.

"If I thought you could forget it, I would, too."

She was referring to what had happened in Azerbaijan and the fact that the ceramic plates the team leader had insisted they add to their body armor before heading out had saved his life—and nearly killed him in the process. Because while the rounds hadn't penetrated the plates, there had been significant backface deformation, the blunt force trauma causing secondary internal injuries—including broken ribs, pulmonary contusions and atrial valve damage. Thankfully the doctors at LRMC had managed to repair his heart and, within a few months, he'd completely recovered—at least from his physical injuries.

"Actually, I meant I wasn't worried because I know you wouldn't keep a firearm in the house with Emma," he said, steering their conversation back on track.

"You're right," she admitted. "Now tell me what you're doing skulking around my porch at—" she glanced at the time displayed on her phone screen "—3:29?"

"Wanting to see who was skulking around your porch at 3:29," he said.

She managed a smile.

He didn't wait for an invitation but climbed the few steps to the porch and settled into the Adirondack chair beside hers.

"Why are you up? Did Emma have a night terror?"

After a brief hesitation, she nodded.

Then she sighed and shook her head. "No. The truth is, she's been sleeping really well the last several months."

"You, not so much?" he guessed.

Now she shrugged.

"Did it ever occur to you that you've been so focused on helping Emma deal with her trauma that it's held you back from dealing with your own?"

"My abusive ex-husband died. I promise you, I was not traumatized by the news."

"I was referring to the trauma of your marriage."

"Oh."

"A man who promised to love and cherish you deliberately inflicted pain on you."

"Forty percent of women experience some form of intimate partner violence in their lifetime," she told him.

"The statistics don't diminish your personal pain."

"No, but that was my past and I'm focused on living in the present now. Speaking of," she said, in an obvious effort to shift the topic of conversation, "how's your new job working out?"

"The job's fine, I guess. It's the accommodations that I'm having trouble adjusting to."

"Accommodations?"

"I've been crashing on a cot in the lounge at the sheriff's department when I'm on night shift—or trying to."

"A cot?" she echoed dubiously.

"I've slept in plenty of worse places," he acknowledged. "Much worse places. But it's hard to get real sleep when other people are walking in and out at all hours. And obviously going back to my cabin isn't an option, as the distance from West River Ranch would prevent me from responding to calls in a timely manner."

"So that's why you're driving around town," she guessed.

"I'm usually awake around this time, anyway," he reminded her.

"I don't know that anyone who puts in a call to the sheriff's department wants a sleep-deprived deputy responding."

"I don't need a lot of sleep."

"Even so, I feel compelled to remind you that Tess's old room is just sitting there, empty, if you ever want to crash in it."

"Really?"

"Sure."

"I thought you were going to put a sign up at the hospital, advertising the room for rent."

"I changed my mind about that. While the loft has an outside entrance, it also has inside access to the rest of the house, so anyone who rented that room would essentially be living with us and I didn't like the idea of a stranger in close proximity to my daughter."

"But you think you can trust the sheriff's newest deputy?" he asked, teasing.

"I trust him with my life," she said. "And, even more significant, with Emma's life."

He was quiet for a moment, taking in how much faith she was willing to place in him. In their friendship. "I appreciate the offer. Sincerely."

"I'll stop by the hardware store tomorrow to get a key cut for you," she told him.

"And I'm happy to pay whatever Tess was paying—or whatever you think is fair," he amended, considering that her best friend and cousin had likely paid a discounted rate.

"I'm not going to ask you to pay rent," Meg protested, sounding horrified at the thought.

"Why not? Tess did."

"Because she lived here full-time."

And he knew that when Tess moved out, she'd worried that Megan would struggle to make the mortgage payments without the additional income from renting the upper unit.

"Even if I'm not here full-time, your offer to let me stay here on occasion means that you can't rent it to someone else."

"Which I'd already decided I wasn't going to do."

"Because you weren't comfortable with the idea of a stranger sleeping under the same roof as your daughter, not because you don't need the money."

"Thanks for pointing that out," she said dryly.

"If I wanted to crash at The Outlaw Inn, they wouldn't give me a key without first running my credit card."

"You already buy pizza for us at least once a month," she argued.

"Because I sponge homemade meals off you at least twice as often," he countered.

"And you bring treats or gifts for Emma far more often than you should."

He shrugged. "She pays me in hugs."

"You wouldn't even let me cover the cost of the new tap that you put in the powder room last month."

"It wasn't very expensive," he assured her.

"That's not the point."

"What is the point?"

"That I'm not going to let you pay rent for sleeping in Tess's old room a few nights a week," she said. "But I will encourage you to bring your toolbox the next time you come over."

Of course, after Flynn had gone, Meg had second thoughts about the wisdom of her offer. While there had been no more awkward moments between them since the Valentine's Day not-quite-kiss, she couldn't help but worry that spending too much time in his company might tempt fate.

But she knew that Flynn struggled to sleep at the best of times—and that bunking on a cot in the sheriff's lounge was not the best of times—and if giving him a quiet place to lay his head might help, she could at least do that. So far, he'd taken her up on the offer only once, showing up after she'd gone to bed and disappearing again before she was up in the morning.

In fact, if not for Ramona Martin's questions about the vehicle parked in her driveway overnight—and the empty coffee mug in the sink—Meg might not have even realized he'd been there. Her neighbor, a retired librarian, seemed to have taken to spinning elaborate stories about her neighbors now that she was away from the books that had surrounded her for so many years. Meg wasn't usually bothered by her questions, as the woman was more curious than critical, but she wasn't happy to be ambushed by Ramona when she was already running behind schedule and trying to get her daughter to preschool in the morning.

In any event, more than a week had passed since then, and though Flynn had made use of the spare bedroom twice more, their paths hadn't crossed during his visits. But he'd taken her at her word about bringing his toolbox, because after his second stay, she noticed that the cupboard above the microwave, the one that had never closed properly, was closed properly. And after his third stay, the burned-out lightbulb in the walk-in pantry had been replaced. Clearly the man was determined to earn his keep—and was doing so.

Now it was Saturday, and she and Emma were headed to West River Ranch to meet Tess and Mrs. Chandler at the big house for lunch.

"Are we there yet?" Emma asked from the back seat.

"Not yet," Meg said, repeating the same answer she'd given each of the last five times her daughter had asked the same question in the past ten minutes.

"How much longer?"

"Probably another ten minutes."

"But I'm hungry *now*."

"Then you should have taken the granola bar I offered when we were on our way to Dr. Halstead's office."

"Can I have it now?"

"No, because then you won't be hungry for lunch."

"I will be hungry," Emma insisted. "'Cuz I'm *starving* now."

"We'll be there soon."

"Maybe lunch will be macaroni and cheese. Or chicken fingers!"

"I wouldn't count on it," Meg cautioned.

"But they're my fav'rites."

"I thought spaghetti and meatballs was your favorite. And pizza. And Great-Gramma Lula's brownies."

"I have lotsa fav'rites," Emma said.

"Well, whatever Mrs. Chandler serves for lunch today, you're going to pretend it's your favorite."

"How come?"

"Because it's the polite thing to do when you're eating at someone else's house."

"But what if it's a fish with the head and tail on it?"

"I don't think you need to worry about that," she said, shuddering at the thought. "And where would you even come up with such an idea?"

"Scotty said they went to a fancy restaurant for dinner and his daddy ordered fish and when it came, it had a head and tail and was sitting up on the plate, almost like it was swimming."

"I think that might be a tall tale," Meg said.

"Nuh-uh." Emma shook her head. "He said his mama took a picture of it."

"This is the same Scotty who jumped ahead of you in line for the slide?"

Now the little girl nodded. "There's only one Scotty in my class. But two—" she held up two fingers "—Sophias and three—" she added a third finger "—Emmas. There's a Emma B., a Emma K. and a Emma W. That's me."

"I'm aware," Meg said, as she turned onto the long winding road that passed beneath the ornate wooden sign that proclaimed the property as West River Ranch.

"Are we there *now*?" Emma asked.

"Getting close," Meg promised.

"Why does Auntie Tess have to live so far away?" the little girl grumbled.

"That's a question you can ask her," Meg said.

"Is that the house?" Emma asked, pointing.

"That's *a* house—in fact, I think it might be where Uncle Holt's mom and dad live—but it's not where we're going."

"Is *that* where we're going?" Emma asked, pointing again.

"No, it's not that one, either."

The big house—or main house, as Tess called it—truly was a grand structure of wood and stone, with lots of windows and a wide, covered porch. What had originally started as a simple two-story farmhouse had undergone numerous updates and renovations over the years as the family that lived inside it had similarly grown and changed.

The house in its current form was a testament to the success of West River Ranch and the wealth of its owners, and its stature and history were a little intimidating to a single mother who essentially lived paycheck to paycheck, even if her own mother had spent several years living under that roof while she was growing up.

Raylan and Eleanor continued to live in the main house, along with their eldest son, Clayton, his wife, Laura, and Raylan and Eleanor's longtime housekeeper, Willow—whose husband had also worked on the ranch before his passing.

As Emma had noted, there were several other homes on the property, making it seem as if West River Ranch was more a compound than a ranch. There were also barns and stables, silos and sheds for sheltering the animals and storing equipment, feed and supplies; a bunkhouse for the hired hands; and a handful of old cabins, some of which had been renovated and updated, including the one that Holt and Tess called home.

In the distance, Meg could see a herd of cattle gathered around the feeders that were used when there was too much snow—as there was now—for them to forage. A little further along, she spotted a solitary figure on horseback—a man wearing a leather jacket open over a flannel shirt and blue jeans, with a Stetson and cowboy boots. Not an uncommon sight on a cattle ranch in Wyoming, and though he was too far away for Meg to be certain of his identity, she knew it was Flynn.

She knew because that distant glimpse was enough to heat the blood in her veins.

Or maybe she was having another hot flash.

"Is *that* the house?" Emma asked again, yanking her mother's attention back to the present.

"That's the house," she confirmed.

"Yay! We can eat."

Meg sighed. "Please remember your manners."

"I will, Mama."

And, for the most part, she did.

She said *hello* to Mrs. Chandler and Willow and let her mom help remove her coat and her boots rather than just dump them on the floor like she did at home. When Tess appeared in the entranceway, after putting the baby down for a nap, Emma forgot herself for a minute, launching herself at "Auntie Tess."

"How's my favorite girl?" Tess asked, lifting Emma into her arms for a hug.

"I'm *starving*," she replied.

Meg felt her face grow warm, but their hostess only chuckled.

"Come on into the dining room then, so that Willow can serve lunch," Eleanor said, offering her hand to the child when Tess set her back on her feet.

Emma took it happily and skipped along beside her.

"Do you remember when she was shy and quiet?" Meg asked her friend.

"Shy and quiet and scared of her own shadow," Tess recalled. "This is much better."

"You're right," she agreed. "I just hope there isn't any fish on the menu."

And there wasn't.

The adults started with a homemade roasted red-pepper soup with crème fraîche, followed by chicken Florentine with Parmesan herb orzo and sautéed baby broccoli, and finished off with flaky lemon tarts dusted with powdered sugar.

Emma, who tried very hard not to make a face when she saw the bowls of soup being placed around the table, was thrilled to discover that she had an entirely different menu. She was served a cup of macaroni and cheese, then chicken fingers with waffle fries (and barbecue sauce and ketchup in fancy glass cups for dipping) followed by an ice cream sundae, complete with chocolate sauce, sprinkles, whipped cream and a cherry.

"I got to eat all my fav'rite foods today," Emma said, dipping her spoon into her ice cream again.

"I hoped they might be," Eleanor said.

"How did you guess?" Meg asked.

"I have two grandsons of a similar age, so I have some experience with the preschool palate."

"She'd eat chicken fingers at every meal if I let her," the little girl's mom confided. "But you really shouldn't have gone to so much trouble."

"It was all Willow," Eleanor told her.

"And it was my pleasure," the housekeeper said, as she cleared the dessert plates from the table. "I don't often get to make anything fancier than soup and sandwiches. Or, in the summer months, salad and sandwiches."

"Because if I ate like this every day, Zelda wouldn't be happy," Eleanor pointed out.

"Who's Zelda?" Emma asked around a mouthful of ice cream.

"My horse."

The little girl's eyes grew wide. "You have a horse?"

"We've got a few of them here on the ranch," Eleanor told her. "Do you like horses?"

Emma nodded.

"She likes cartoon horses," Meg clarified. "She's never seen a horse up close."

"Well, maybe after we finish making plans for your cousin's christening, we can change that," Eleanor said.

"And then can we go see Unca Flynn?" Emma asked her mom.

"Uncle Flynn might be working in town today," Meg cautioned.

"I don't think he is," Tess said. "Because he went out early this morning, with Holt and Austin, to feed the cattle."

"Or Uncle Flynn might be busy with ranch chores," Meg amended.

"Even if he is, I'm sure he'd be happy to make time for both of you," Eleanor chimed in with a knowing smile.

Though what Flynn's grandmother thought she knew Meg couldn't imagine—or maybe didn't want to acknowledge.

Chapter Eight

The planning didn't take nearly as long as Meg had anticipated. Tess already knew what she wanted for the christening at the United church with a family celebration to follow at West River Ranch and only required Eleanor and Meg to nod their heads in agreement as she shared the order of events for the day, thoughts on décor and menu ideas. And while Tess kiboshed most of Emma's suggestions for the party—a bouncy castle, a pinata, balloon animals and pizza—she did so in such a way that the little girl believed the final decisions had been made possible as a result of her contributions. Especially as Tess did agree that cake was an essential element of any celebration.

During their discussions, Meg had mostly focused on cuddling her best friend's baby and lamenting the fact that she'd had little time to do the same when Emma was an infant. Water under the bridge, obviously, and if she had regrets about some things that had happened in the past—and she did—she could find solace in the fact that her daughter was thriving now.

"The last thing we need to pin down—and which probably should have been the first—is the date." Tess opened the calendar app on her tablet. "You're going to need to look at your schedule, too, Meg."

"Can't," she said unapologetically. "My hands are full."

Tess rolled her eyes. "Emma, can you get your mom's phone?"

"Where is it?"

"In the zippered front pocket of my backpack," Meg told her.

"Which I saw Willow put in the closet," Eleanor said, leading the little girl back to the entranceway.

"He's going to want to eat soon," Tess told Meg, her eyes softening as she looked at her baby in her friend's arms, his mouth moving in his sleep.

"And I'll have to give him back then," Meg acknowledged. "But I'm not giving him back a minute sooner."

"You should have another one of your own—or two or three," Tess suggested.

"Yeah, I don't see that happening."

"I remember when you were pregnant with Em," her friend said now. "How excited you were planning not only for her arrival but for a houseful of kids."

"Plans change," Meg responded lightly, unwilling to let her melancholy cast a shadow over the day.

"I have a lot of reasons to hate Daymond, but one of the biggest is that he took that dream from you."

"Hating a dead man is an exercise in futility," Meg said, a statement of fact that was in no way meant to imply she didn't feel the same way. "You should focus on all the good stuff in your life instead."

"I know how lucky I am," Tess assured her. "Especially to have a best friend like you."

"Well, *obviously*."

Meg's attempt to lighten the mood proved successful when Tess chuckled softly.

Then Emma and Eleanor returned with Meg's phone, but she still didn't give up the baby, instead scrolling with one hand while she continued to hold Blake in her other arm, close to her aching heart.

As they discussed dates, the infant's eyelids flickered and opened. He stared at Meg for a long minute, his big blue eyes fixed on her face, then his forehead crinkled and he turned his head to the side. Looking for his mom, she guessed.

"I'm here," Tess murmured, moving into his line of sight.

Immediately, the crinkle in his brow relaxed.

"And that's my cue," Meg said, reluctantly returning the baby to his mom.

Tess was already reaching inside her top to unfasten the cup of her nursing bra to feed her baby.

"And maybe a good time for us to go see some horses?" Eleanor suggested to Emma, as Blake began rooting at his mother's breast.

"Yes, please."

Meg followed them out of the room.

Emma was bouncing with excitement at the prospect of seeing a "real" horse, so it took some doing to wrangle her into her coat and the fancy shoes she'd insisted on wearing because they were going to a fancy lunch. Shoes that Meg felt compelled to warn her daughter, once again, wouldn't provide much traction on the snowy ground.

They were heading toward the stable—"Where the horses live," as Eleanor explained to the little girl—when Emma stopped in mid-stride, her eyes growing wide.

"Look, Mama, look," she urged, pointing to the animal in a nearby paddock.

"I'm looking," Meg assured her.

"That's Bandit," Eleanor said, changing direction to lead them to the enclosure.

Raylan, who was walking the pony, guided Bandit over to meet them on the other side of the fence.

"Is he a real horse?" Emma asked.

"Actually, he's a Welsh pony."

"A pony," the little girl echoed reverently.

"Come on over and meet him," Raylan invited.

Emma looked at her mom, as if for permission.

Meg picked her up and carried her closer to the fence for the introductions.

"Bandit, this is Emma," Raylan said. "Can you say *hello* to Emma?"

The little girl giggled. "Ponies can't talk."

And, of course, Bandit didn't, but he blew out his breath and gave a shake of his head, the action making her start.

"Ponies can't talk like you and I talk," Raylan confirmed. "But they have their own ways of communicating, and that was his way of saying *hello* to you."

"Now it's your turn to say *hello* to Bandit," Meg told her.

"Hello," Emma said dutifully, albeit a little cautiously.

Bandit nodded his big head, seeming to acknowledge her greeting.

"Would you like to pet him?" Eleanor asked Emma now.

The little girl's already wide eyes somehow grew wider. "Can I?"

"If your mom says so."

Emma's head swiveled to look at her mom.

Meg nodded but cautioned, "Be gentle."

"Like this," Raylan said, demonstrating by rubbing his hand down the pony's neck.

She lifted a hand and tentatively reached toward the animal, rubbing his neck as the old man had done.

Bandit nickered softly.

"What's he saying now?" she asked.

"He's saying that he likes you."

Emma looked at her mom again, her smile wide. "He likes me."

"I can see that," Meg confirmed.

"And what do you think of Bandit?" Eleanor prompted.

"I love him so much."

Her enthusiastic declaration made Raylan grin.

"You ever been on a pony?" he asked her.

Emma shook her head.

"No," Meg said, confirming her daughter's reply. "And no," she said again. Firmly.

Raylan frowned at her obviously preemptive response. "He's gentle as a kitten, Megan. I promise."

"I've never seen a kitten that stands—" she eyed the horse "—four feet tall."

"We use hands to describe a horse's height," the old man told her. "And he's eleven-and-a-half hands, about forty-six inches, so your four feet was a good guesstimate."

"And a lot bigger than a kitten," she pointed out.

"I bought him for Gage and Zane—Boone's boys—so that they could learn to ride."

"Gage and Zane go to school with me," Emma announced.

"Is that right?" Raylan said to her.

She nodded. "Gage is in the yellow group for activity stations and Zane is in the red group, same as me, but sometimes they switch and Miz Riya doesn't even know."

"How do you know they switch?" Meg wondered.

"'Cuz Gage has red laces in his shoes and Zane's are blue," her daughter replied matter-of-factly.

"You'd think that's a detail the teacher might have picked up on," Meg mused.

"And one that I'll suggest Boone bring to her attention, to avoid future shenanigans by my great-grandsons," Raylan said.

"How are they doing with their riding lessons?" Meg asked, circling back to the original topic of conversation.

"They're Chandlers, so they sit in the saddle like they were born there," Raylan said proudly. "The biggest challenge is ensuring they each have the same amount of time for their lessons, because they'll certainly let me know if they suspect otherwise."

"I imagine they do," she agreed with a smile.

"But they've been under the weather for most of the week, which means that Bandit hasn't gotten much exercise, so I thought I'd at least get him out for some fresh air and a walk around the paddock.

"Of course, he'd like that walk a lot more if he had a saddle and a rider on his back," Raylan continued.

"Then you should saddle him up and take him for a ride," Meg said, refusing the bait he dangled.

"A little pony like this needs a little rider," the rancher insisted.

Emma waved her hand in the air, like she would before answering a question at school. "I'm a little rider."

"Hmm." Raylan rubbed his chin, as if considering. "You probably would be just about the right size."

"I said *no*," Meg reminded him.

"I'll be right beside her the whole time," he promised.

"Raylan," his wife admonished.

"What?" he asked, with feigned innocence.

"Megan is the one who gets to decide what is and isn't appropriate for her daughter," Eleanor reminded him.

"But I wanna ride Bandit," Emma chimed in.

"What's going on here?" Flynn asked, joining them by the paddock.

"I wanna ride Bandit," Emma said again.

"Well, of course you do," Flynn said. "Bandit's an awesome pony."

"Mama said *no*," Emma told him now, pouting.

"Oh." He looked at the little girl's mom then, only slightly chagrined. "Well, I'm sure your mama has valid reasons for not wanting to put you on the back of a sweet, gentle pony like Bandit."

Meg narrowed her gaze on him. "I don't need any reasons, other than that I'm the mom."

"No, of course not," he agreed.

But Emma wasn't willing to relent so easily. "*Pleeease*, Mama, can I go for a ride?"

And, not wanting to seem completely unreasonable, she found herself searching for an excuse that would support her position. “I don’t think those fancy shoes are appropriate for a pony ride,” she hedged.

“I’ll bet I can find a pair of boots in the tack room that’ll fit her,” Raylan chimed in, trying to be helpful.

Eleanor just shook her head.

“I seem to be running out of arguments,” Meg acknowledged ruefully.

“Is that a *yes*?” Flynn prompted.

“Pleeease.” Emma folded her hands and tucked them under her chin, looking at her mom beseechingly. “Pretty, pretty, pretty *pleeease*.”

“A slow turn around the paddock,” she relented. “*If* Mr. Chandler can find boots for you.”

“Yay!” Emma clapped her hands together.

“And a helmet,” Meg added, as Flynn offered his hand to lead her to the stables.

Raylan followed with the pony, to get him ready.

“There really isn’t any need to worry,” Eleanor promised. “Raylan would never let her get hurt.”

“You’re a mother, so you should know that having no reason doesn’t necessarily stop the worry.”

“True enough,” the family matriarch agreed. “Not for a mother, grandmother or even great-grandmother.”

“And being a single parent is like being stuck on a never-ending carousel of self-doubt and second-guessing.”

“I’m sorry for that,” Eleanor said. “But for what it’s worth, you’re doing a wonderful job as a mother.”

“I’m trying. But I’m also not doing it on my own. My parents provide after-school care—and occasional full day care—and they have a wonderful relationship with her.”

Eleanor obviously heard what she didn’t say as clearly as

what she did, because she asked gently, "And how is your relationship with your parents?"

"Things are great with my dad—a little strained with my mom," she confided. "She seemed to take it as a personal affront that I got pregnant out of wedlock."

"Sunny always did hold herself to very high standards," Eleanor noted.

"High and rigid," Meg said. "And I know that probably goes back to her own childhood and her determination to be a better mother to me and Nicole than she had."

"Tallulah had some struggles," Eleanor acknowledged. "Perhaps even some failings, but not loving her children wasn't one of them."

"Gramma Lula's fond of saying, 'If you can't be a good example, be a horrible warning.'"

Eleanor managed a smile. "I can hear your grandmother saying exactly that—which doesn't mean she doesn't regret some of the mistakes she made along the way."

"I know," Meg agreed.

"But she wasn't the only one who made mistakes. I can't tell you how many times I've wondered if Raylan and I made one when we decided to bring Abby and Sunny here with Wyatt, to live with us."

"You shouldn't wonder about that," Meg said. "It was what was best for all of them, and if Tallulah couldn't see it at the time, she acknowledges it now."

A chime sounded from the vicinity of Eleanor's coat pocket.

"That's a reminder that I've got a Teams meeting with the Whispering Canyon Historical Society," she said. "I'm sorry to abandon you, but if I'm late, Sheila Hartford will never let me hear the end of it."

"Then you don't want to be late," she agreed.

"It was really lovely to see you again, Megan, and to spend some time with you and your daughter."

"To see you, too," Meg replied. "And thank you so much for the delicious meal."

"Please come back anytime. I know Willow would be happy to create something completely different but equally delicious."

As Eleanor made her way back to the main house, Meg saw the door of the stables slide open and watched as Emma strutted out—there really was no other word to describe her gait—kicking her cowboy-boot-clad feet ahead of her.

"Look at me, Mama."

"I see you," Meg assured her.

"I gots cowboy boots."

"You're *borrowing* cowboy boots," she reminded her daughter.

And, she was relieved to see, a riding helmet, too.

"I'm gonna ride Bandit."

"You hold on tight," Meg said, ignoring the knots in her stomach. "And do exactly what Mr. Chandler tells you to do."

"He told me to call him 'Gramps,'" Emma said.

She purposely kept her expression neutral, not letting her daughter or Raylan know that such familiarity made her uneasy. Notwithstanding—or maybe because of—the fact that her mother had lived at West River Ranch for a number of years, had slept in Raylan and Eleanor's home and eaten at their table.

"Then you do exactly what Gramps tells you," she said.

"I will," the little girl promised.

"Ready?" Raylan asked.

"Ready," she confirmed.

The old man effortlessly lifted her into the saddle, then guided her feet into the stirrups and showed her how to hold the reins.

"She looks good up there," Flynn said, rejoining Meg at the fence. "You, on the other hand, look like you want to throw up."

"Maybe because my not-yet-five-year-old daughter is precariously balanced on the back of a horse."

"Bandit's a pony," he reminded her. "And I promise there is nothing precarious about her situation. In fact, I'd argue she's safer on the back of that pony with my grandfather by her side than she is at the playground at school."

"Not helpful."

"So don't listen to me," Flynn said. "Look at her. Look at the smile on her face."

"I am," Meg admitted. "It's the reason I only look like I want to throw up and am not actually doing so."

Though Emma was generally an easygoing child, her demeanor was often serious, a testament to the fact that she learned at far too early an age that the world—or at least the people in it—could be cruel. But she was smiling now, and the smile was in more than just the curve of her lips, it was in the pink of her cheeks and the sparkle in her eyes.

"I think that's two turns around the paddock," Meg said, when Raylan brought the pony toward them again.

"One more?" Emma asked hopefully.

"You've already had one more," she pointed out. "Now say thank you to Bandit—and Mr. Chandler—for the ride."

"Thank you, Bandit," she said, leaning forward to wrap her arms around the pony's neck.

And when Raylan lifted her out of the saddle, she hugged him, too. "Thank you, Mr. Chandler."

"I thought you were gonna call me Gramps."

"Thank you, Gramps."

"You're very welcome, sweetheart. And if you ever wanna ride Bandit again, I'm sure he'd be happy to oblige."

"Whatsa blige?" the little girl asked.

"*Oblige*," Meg enunciated. "It means he'd let you."

"Oh."

"Of course, your mama's gotta say it's okay, too," Raylan said now.

Meg nodded, acknowledging and appreciating the clarification.

"There's plenty of horses for you to choose from, too," the rancher told her. "Anytime you want to ride, you're welcome here."

"Thank you," she said, not bothering to explain why she was unlikely to ever take him up on the offer.

"Come on, Emma," Flynn said, lifting the little girl out of his grandfather's arms and into his own. "Let's go see if we can remember where we put your fancy shoes."

"I 'member," she told him. "I'll show you."

Meg was smiling as she watched the cowboy and her little girl head back into the stables.

"And now it's my turn to thank you," Raylan said to Meg.

"Me?" she asked, surprised. "What are you thanking me for?"

"Giving me and Eleanor back at least one of the grandsons we lost overseas." There was an uncharacteristic gruffness to his tone, evidence of his raw emotions.

"I wish I could take credit, but I really didn't do anything," Meg told him.

Raylan looked at her, warmth in his gaze. "You gave him acceptance of who he is, and that is a rare and precious gift."

"She's going to be talking about this at preschool on Monday," Meg remarked, when Emma and Flynn returned from the stables.

"I hafta tell Emma K.," her daughter confirmed.

"Emma K. had a pony at her recent birthday party," Meg explained to the men.

"And I din't get to go," Emma said unhappily.

"Because Keeley's party was the same day and you'd already promised to go to her party."

"But she din't have a pony."

"Them's the breaks," Meg said, not unsympathetically.

"Can we have a pony at my birthday?" Emma asked hopefully.

"Sorry, honey. Our backyard isn't big enough for a puppy, never mind a pony."

Emma pouted.

"Maybe you could have her birthday party here," Flynn suggested.

"Here?" Emma echoed, another smile spreading across her face again as both Meg and Raylan looked at him in surprise.

Flynn shrugged. "Why not?"

"I can't think of any reason," Raylan decided.

"That's a generous offer," Meg said. "But Emma told me last week that she wants a princess party this year."

"But now I wanna pony party," Emma decided.

"Emma," her mom said, an unmistakable note of warning in her voice.

"*Pleeeease*," the little girl said, undeterred.

Meg sighed. "Apparently it's time to go home."

"No! I don't wanna go home!"

"Past time," she amended.

"No!" Emma said again, stomping her foot on the ground.

"Don't you sass your mama," Raylan said, speaking calmly but firmly to the little girl.

She blinked, taken aback by his admonishment.

The old man knelt to look Emma in the eye. "I know your mama is very busy taking care of you and working at her own job, and if she can make the time, she'll bring you back to ride Bandit. Okay?"

Emma nodded, and Raylan smiled at her as he stood.

To Meg, he said, "Just think about the party. We'd be happy to do whatever we can to help make it happen. If—" he glanced at the little girl again "—you'd be comfortable with that."

“I’ll think about it,” she said, then followed as Flynn carried Emma to her vehicle and buckled her into her car seat.

“I heard my grandfather tell you that you’re welcome to come out any time to go for a ride,” he remarked.

“Your grandparents are both kind and generous people,” she said sincerely.

“You should take him up on his offer,” Flynn told her.

“And I probably would—if I knew how to ride.”

He looked taken aback. “You don’t know how to ride?”

“That’s what I said.”

“How did I not know that about you?” he wondered aloud.

She shrugged. “It’s not really the kind of thing that comes up in everyday conversation.”

“Did you never want to learn?”

“I was desperate to learn,” she confided. “But my mom kept me busy with other activities, hoping I’d give up asking for riding lessons—and eventually I did.”

“There’s no reason you couldn’t learn now,” he told her.

“Haven’t you heard the saying ‘you can’t teach an old dog new tricks’?”

He held up his hands. “I’m not going to touch that analogy with a ten-foot pole. But I will assure you that a smart, strong woman like you can master horseback riding—and maybe even learn to enjoy it.”

“A tempting prospect,” she said. “But I don’t have time to take lessons.”

“We’ll fit them into your schedule.”

She arched a brow. “You’re offering to teach me?”

“Why not?”

“Because you don’t have any more free time than I do,” she said. “And even less now that you’re a deputy sheriff.”

“I’ve learned to make times for the things that matter.”

“Why does this matter to you?” she wondered aloud.

It was a good question, and one Flynn considered for a long

minute before responding. "When I came back from…overseas, the physical limitations imposed by my injuries at that time made me feel…trapped. I felt trapped in this town, in the hospital bed in my parents' house, even in my own skin.

"It was a relief when I was finally able to get around again, but it wasn't until I was strong enough to ride that I started to feel better. Because it was when I was riding that I was able to escape the weight of my thoughts and feelings, when I was able to feel any sense of peace. And I guess…I want that peace for you," he concluded.

It was the most information he'd ever shared about his feelings and his recovery at any one time, and she was grateful for his trust and humbled by his offer. "Well, then, I guess you're going to have to teach me to ride, cowboy."

Chapter Nine

Meg didn't hear from Flynn again until Saturday morning.

Early Saturday morning.

She was cutting a toaster waffle into sticks for Emma when her phone rang.

Stifling a yawn, she connected the call. "Nobody I know would call this early on a Saturday morning."

"It's eight o'clock."

"On. A. Sat-ur-day," she said again, setting the waffle in front of Emma and reaching for the mug of French roast that had just finished brewing.

"Should I call back after you've had your coffee?"

"It's in my hand now."

"Good. And when you're sufficiently caffeinated, you can get dressed into something appropriate for riding."

"Why?"

"Emma has a lesson with Gramps today, doesn't she?"

"She does." After their visit to West River Ranch, Emma hadn't stopped asking when she could ride again, and so Meg had called Raylan and they'd set up a schedule of weekly lessons for her daughter.

"And since you're going to be at the ranch and I don't have to work, I figured it was a good opportunity for you to have a lesson, too."

As she drove the ranch with Emma—dressed in appropriate riding attire, per Flynn's direction—she was mostly excited about the prospect of getting on the back of the horse but a little bit apprehensive, too.

Her apprehension increased when Flynn took her to meet her mount.

"Maybe I should start with a pony," she said.

"There's nothing to be afraid of, Megan. You might be new at this, but Wilma's a pro."

She eyed the bareback mare dubiously. "Doesn't Wilma need a saddle?"

"Yes, she does. And you're going to put it on her."

"I am?"

"Part of learning to ride is learning to take care of your mount," he explained.

"Emma didn't have to saddle Bandit."

"Emma's four and her saddle probably weighs half as much as she does right now. But I promise you, if she keeps up with her lessons, Gramps will teach her to groom and tack, too."

Since she couldn't argue with that, she paid close attention as he walked her through the steps, from brushing the horse to checking the equipment, then placing the blanket and saddle, attaching and adjusting the girth, adjusting the stirrups, placing the reins, then finally the bit and the bridle.

"I'm never going to remember all of this," she told him.

"Don't worry—the test isn't until week three."

"There's a test?"

"I'm joking."

"You're not funny."

"And you *will* remember all this," he promised. "Once you've done it often enough, it'll become second nature. Something you can do almost without thinking—like scrubbing up for surgery."

"*In*," she told him. "You scrub *in* for surgery."

"And now, Miss Smarty Pants, you're going to put your butt *in* the saddle," he said.

She glanced at her watch. "Emma's lesson is probably almost over by now."

"Get on the horse, Megan."

Still, she hesitated.

"Gramps won't tie her to the front gate with a For Sale sign hanging around her neck if we're not back when her lesson's finished," he promised.

"I know," she said.

"So why are you balking?"

"I just don't think I'm ready."

"You're ready."

He put his hands on her waist, and she squawked.

Actually squawked.

She felt her cheeks grow warm as the corners of his mouth twitched in obvious amusement.

The hint of movement drew her attention to his lips.

His surprisingly soft lips.

At the same time, she was aware of his hands—big and strong—on her torso.

She swallowed. "What are you doing?"

She'd meant to sound indignant. Instead, she sounded… breathless.

"Giving you a boost," he said easily.

Wilma stood motionless beside her, patiently waiting for her rider to mount.

Meg's heart was pounding, but she was no longer sure if it was fear of getting up on the horse or awareness of Flynn's proximity that was responsible for the acceleration.

He held her gaze. "You can do this," he asserted confidently. "Be brave."

She licked her suddenly dry lips. "I'm not that brave."

"One of the bravest people I know," he told her.

And with his encouragement, she not only got up on the horse but enjoyed a leisurely ride through a green meadow dotted with yellow and orange wildflowers. But the whole time she was in the saddle, she lamented not being courageous enough to breach the distance between them and *really* kiss him.

There was no way Meg could make a trip to West River Ranch and not stop by to see Tess. And after half an hour on horseback, she figured she deserved the reward of baby cuddles.

When her friend led her into her living room, she sank gratefully into the sofa and exhaled a weary sigh. Buddy—Holt's rescued canine companion, part Lab, part hound and part retriever with possibly other parts mixed in—trotted over and dropped his head onto Meg's knee. Perhaps offering sympathy, more likely seeking attention.

She lifted a hand to scratch behind his ears.

"Sore butt?" Tess asked sympathetically.

Meg nodded.

"It'll hurt even more tomorrow," her friend warned.

"Yay—something to look forward to."

"But the more you ride, the easier it gets."

"That's what Emma told me."

Because her daughter, with two lessons under her belt compared to Meg's one, considered herself the voice of experience.

"Speaking of—where's my favorite girl?" Tess asked.

"She wanted to hang out with Boone's boys for a while, which gave me an excuse to come and see you."

"As if you need an excuse."

Meg held out her hands to her friend and Tess, correctly interpreting the wordless request, handed over the baby.

"I can't believe how much he's grown in a few weeks," she murmured.

"I'm not surprised he's growing fast—it seems as if he's constantly eating."

"Who's constantly eating?" Holt asked, walking into the room with a sandwich in his hand.

"It would seem he comes by his appetite honestly," Meg remarked, her tone tinged with amusement.

Her cousin's husband grinned. "Hey, Meg. When did you get here?"

"About two minutes ago."

"We saw you out riding with Flynn. First lesson?"

"Was it that obvious?"

"You'll get the hang of it," he said confidently.

"In the meantime," Tess said to her husband, "my BFF and I have some catching up to do."

"You're kicking me out?"

"I'm setting you free to go play with one of your brothers," she said.

"You're kicking me out," he said again, but it was a statement rather than a question this time.

"Do you want to stay and listen to us compare childbirth stories and breastfeeding woes and—"

He bent his head to silence her with a kiss. "Do you need anything before I go?"

"I wouldn't mind a glass of iced tea."

"Meg?"

"Iced tea sounds good."

He returned with two tall glasses and set them within reach of the women.

"Come on, Buddy," he said, and the dog trotted happily after him.

Tess smiled as she watched her husband walk out of the room.

"Men are so predictable," she said, but with obvious and sincere affection.

Not all of them, Meg thought. And not all of the time.

But she shoved those memories aside, unwilling to let them intrude on this day.

"So, tell me what's on your mind," Tess urged, when Holt and Buddy were gone.

"Nothing that warranted kicking your husband out," she told her friend.

"I'll be the one who decides that—now spill."

Meg picked up her glass and swallowed a mouthful of iced tea. "I kissed Flynn."

Tess bobbled her drink, nearly spilling it. "As in my brother-in-law Flynn?"

"Yeah," she admitted. "Except it was more of an accident than a kiss."

Her friend's brows rose. "How do you accidentally kiss someone?"

"Well, I meant to kiss him," she clarified. "But it was supposed to be a kiss on the cheek—a gesture of appreciation—but he turned his head as I leaned forward and my lips landed on the side of his mouth."

"And then?" Tess prompted.

"And then nothing. That was it."

"So far this story isn't very interesting," her friend lamented.

"But ever since, I've been feeling..."

"Sexual urges that you mistook for hot flashes?" her friend guessed.

"Yeah," she admitted.

"So...are you going to go for it?"

"No!"

"Why not?"

"Because it's *Flynn*. And, anyway, this isn't really about him—it's about me trying to decide if I want to put myself out there and start dating again."

"Of course, you should," Tess said.

"I don't know," she hedged. "Considering my track record with men, I'm probably better off alone."

"We've all made some regrettable choices in the past, and thinking of Daymond as anything more than that gives him power that he doesn't deserve."

"You're right," Meg acknowledged. "I know you're right. Still, I can't help but think that a handheld toy might be the best choice for me."

"That might get the job done, but it's not going to keep you warm afterward."

"So I'll put an extra blanket on the bed."

Tess shook her head despairingly. "When was the last time you were on a date?"

"It was August." Meg counted on her fingers. "Seven months ago."

"And that was…Cameron?"

Meg nodded. "The one who wanted revenge sex." A brother of one of her coworkers who'd asked his sister to get Meg's contact information for him. She'd been flattered and, because she liked Candace, consented to the release of her number.

After they'd exchanged a few text messages, they arranged to meet for coffee—where she was bluntly propositioned. Because Cameron had recently broken up with a girlfriend who'd cheated on him, and though she was sorry and eager to reconcile, he felt he needed to sleep with someone else first to even the score.

Meg had politely declined to assist him in that endeavor.

"And before Cameron?" Tess prompted.

"James. The avocado guy." She'd met him in the produce department. He'd wanted to make guacamole for a get-together with friends and asked Meg if she could help him find ripe avocados. Instead, she'd shown him where to find the ready-made dip in the deli section, and he'd offered to buy her dinner.

It was only when they were at the restaurant that he told her the get-together was for March Madness, which was why he'd spent the entire meal checking basketball scores on his phone.

"Not my worst first date, but definitely not one that warranted a follow-up, either," Meg decided.

"What about…Heath? Wasn't that the name of the first guy you dated after you moved back to Whispering Canyon?"

"It was," she confirmed.

She'd crossed paths with Heath at the Mug Shot Café and decided there was no harm in enjoying a meal with a handsome man. At lunch, he'd continued to be charming and interesting—and interested in Meg. Another mark in his favor, he hadn't seemed at all put off to learn that she had a two-and-a-half-year-old daughter, which was how old Emma had been at the time.

"I liked him," Tess said now.

"I did, too," Meg agreed. "But the whole time we were having dinner, I couldn't help but compare him to Daymond."

"He was nothing like Daymond."

"But Daymond was charming, too, when we first met—and for a long time after."

"Until he wasn't," Tess said darkly.

"Yeah," Meg agreed, not wanting to say much more on the topic of her ex-husband, aware it was a bit of a sore subject for Tess, who'd been hurt by the discovery that her best friend had hidden the truth about her abusive marriage until it was over.

"So that's it? Three dates in the past two years?"

"I guess so."

"Wait—you forgot about the guy with the ugly dog."

"Thomas," she said. "Aka the reporter."

Tess winced. "Right."

Meg *had* forgotten—perhaps deliberately—about Thomas.

He'd been walking his dog in the park and she'd been watching Emma play on the climber. It was the dog that had caused Meg to let her guard down. Some kind of mixed breed that had taken all of the ugliest parts and mashed them together, but incredibly sweet and friendly. And when the dog's owner asked her to go out, she'd decided that a man who could love an animal like that had to be a good guy, and she'd said *yes*.

It was only when they were at dinner, offering the usual bits of information that were typically shared on a first date, that her radar started to hum. Because his get-to-know-you questions were more intrusive than inquisitive. She'd skirted around the ones she didn't want to answer, but then he'd circle back again. At the park, he'd confided that he was a writer with dreams of penning the great American novel. It was only over dinner that she'd learned he was working as a reporter for the *Powell Tribune* in the interim, making her radar shift from humming to screaming. And then, as she was dipping her spoon into her crème brûlée, he'd asked if they could talk about the night her husband died.

Meg responded by setting down the utensil, picking up her purse and walking out of the restaurant.

"He was a snake," Tess said now.

"Yeah, but even before I saw him slithering through the grass, I didn't feel the slightest stirring of attraction."

"So why'd you go out with him?"

"The same reason I went out with Heath and James and Cameron," Meg admitted. "Because I was trying to convince you and Nicole and my parents and Gramma Lula that I was ready to move on with my life."

"You might have had more luck convincing us if you'd actually gone on a second date with any one of them."

"Maybe my experience with Daymond cured me of any romantic notions or amorous feelings."

"Until you kissed Flynn."

"It wasn't even really a kiss," Meg said again.

"And doesn't that tell you everything you need to know?" Tess mused smugly.

Flynn was chopping wood when his middle brother wandered across the field Saturday afternoon, Buddy trotting along beside him. He hefted the axe into the air again and brought it down hard, splitting the log in two, then repeating the process to split each half again.

"You look like you could use a break—and a beer," Holt said as Flynn tossed the pieces aside.

He wiped the sweat off his forehead with his sleeve. "What time is it?"

"It's gotta be five o'clock somewhere."

"Go on in and grab a couple beers then," Flynn said.

While he waited for his brother to return, he stacked the wood he'd chopped, adding it to the pile beside the shed, then refastened the buttons of his Henley, covering the scar that bisected his chest.

"Stocking up for the winter?" Holt asked, tongue-in-cheek, as he offered his brother one of the bottles and tossed to his dog a biscuit he'd pilfered from the box Flynn kept on hand for his visits.

Buddy crunched down on his treat and Flynn lifted his beer to his lips. "Just had some excess energy I wanted to burn off."

"Something happen with you and Meg?"

"What? No." He scowled. "Why would you ask me that? Did she say something happened?"

"That was a lot of answers to one simple question," Holt remarked.

"It was a strange question," he said in his defense. "Why would you ask me about Megan?"

"Because I saw you out riding with her earlier."

Flynn didn't want to think about earlier. Didn't want to remember the temptation of being close to Megan. So close he could smell the scent of her shampoo. So close he could see the rapid beat of her pulse at the base of her jaw. So close he'd almost given in to the temptation to kiss her breathless.

He pushed all that aside and responded, "So?"

"So…nothing, I guess," Holt said.

"Exactly." Flynn swallowed another mouthful of beer then pushed back his sleeve to check the time on his watch. "It really is almost five o'clock. Maybe I should grab a quick shower and head into town for a bite to eat."

"Maybe you should see a doctor while you're there, too, because you're obviously not feeling like yourself."

"Ha," Flynn said, aware that his brother was referring to the long months immediately following his return during which he'd been reluctant to leave the sanctuary of West River Ranch. "It so happens that I go into town almost every day now."

"To work," Holt acknowledged.

"And occasionally when I need groceries. Which I do. But a trip to the grocery store would still require me to figure out what I want for dinner and cook it, whereas if I go into town to eat, I skip all those other steps."

"Tess has a roast in the slow cooker, if you want to join us for dinner."

"I'll pass, thanks."

"And Mom would no doubt be happy to set another place at the table."

"Another pass," Flynn said. "Weekly Sunday night dinners are the extent of my quota."

"So maybe you're not just heading into town for a meal but to have a meal with a certain single mom and her daughter," Holt mused aloud. "Because I still say there's a definite vibe when the two of you are together."

"There's one big hole in *that* theory," Flynn pointed out to his brother.

Holt frowned. "What is it?"

"Meg isn't in town—she's at your place."

"Oh. Right."

"Are *you* okay?" Flynn asked, wondering how his brother could have forgotten a detail he'd shared with him only a few minutes earlier.

"Yeah. Just a little sleep deprived. I swear Blake is up every two hours in the night, which means that Tess and I are up every two hours in the night."

"That's rough."

Holt nodded. "She's suggested that I go sleep in the den—or even at the main house with Grams and Gramps—but as tempting as that might be, it wouldn't be fair to make her responsible for dealing with all of the little guy's needs."

"Well, she is the only one who can feed him," he pointed out reasonably.

"Yeah, but I can burp him and change him."

Flynn felt a smile tugging at the corners of his mouth. "I never thought I'd see the day that my little brother was volunteering for diaper duty."

"Neither did I," Holt admitted. "But being a dad has a way of changing one's perspectives on a lot of things."

"I imagine it does."

"Anyway, I'm trying to talk Tess into pumping, so that I can help with feeding, but she's worried about something called nipple confusion and wants to stick with what's working right now—even if she's exhausted."

"She's lucky to have you," he said, and meant it.

"I'm the lucky one," Holt insisted, and Flynn knew he meant it, too.

He took the now-empty bottle from his brother's hand. "Go on home to your wife and baby," he said. "And give them both a kiss for me."

"And if Meg's still there—should I give her a kiss from you, too?"

He pointedly ignored his brother's question. "Thanks for stopping by."

Then he turned and made his way into the cabin, trying not to think about Holt's teasing remark—and the kiss that wasn't really a kiss that Megan had given him on Valentine's Day and his own growing curiosity about how she might respond if *he* kissed *her*.

Because while he knew she hadn't intended her kiss to be

anything more than a friendly gesture, it had created a new awareness between them.

Or maybe an awakening.

She'd felt it, too. There was no denying that. He'd seen the flicker in the depths of those warm whiskey-colored eyes. A flicker followed by a definite flare of heat.

The same heat he felt within himself.

Heat that threatened to set him on fire, turning his unexpected desire into something fierce and intense that tempted him to haul her into his arms and kiss her until they were both breathless.

But he knew that would be a mistake. Because they were friends, and he valued her friendship too much to risk it for a moment of pleasure.

He'd been a soldier, so he understood that there were times to advance and times to retreat. This was definitely a time to retreat.

Of course, it was possible that what he was feeling for Megan wasn't about her so much as the fact that she was a woman and it had been a long time since he'd been with a woman. A long time since he'd wanted to be, having decided that he wasn't interested in the trade-off of half an hour of meaningless chitchat for thirty minutes of meaningless sex.

Sex with Megan wouldn't be meaningless.

It couldn't be. They knew one another too well.

Sex with Megan would mean something—and he wasn't ready for that. And he didn't think she was, either. They both had a lot more healing to do before they'd be ready for a relationship.

But apparently he was ready for sex. At least, his body was indicating a willingness to indulge in some mindless pleasure. Mindless pleasure that could definitely not be found with Megan.

Chapter Ten

Ten months earlier

After their second coffee meeting—Meg didn't dare let herself think of it as a coffee date, as she'd sworn off any kind of dating—they exchanged phone numbers. After their third meeting, she found herself sitting on the porch one night, long after Emma had gone to bed, staring at Flynn's name in her list of contacts.

She opened the messaging app and started to compose a text without any intention of actually sending it. Her thumbs moved over the keys, spilling out all the secrets she'd never been able to tell him in person. It was therapeutic and harmless, because as soon as she was done, she could delete the message without Flynn ever knowing she'd wanted to reach out when she needed someone to talk to in the middle of the night.

But she'd barely started to put down her thoughts when a message from Flynn came through to her.

Are we ever actually going to use the contact info we exchanged last week?

She hastily deleted everything she'd written so far and responded:

Apparently we are.

I didn't expect you'd be awake.

You thought I'd be sleeping at 3 am?

I did.

Which only proves you don't know me at all.

And you don't know me, which might make it easier to talk about things you don't usually talk about.

It might.

You could call me, if you want to actually talk.

It's easier to delete written words than spoken ones.

Your call. Or text.

She responded to that with an eyeroll emoji.

I started going to the meetings because Emma has night terrors. I'm hoping to learn strategies to help her deal with them.

I don't know a lot about night terrors.
Aren't they a sleep disorder that kids eventually outgrow?

They can be. Or they can result from PTSD.

Your 3-yr-old has PTSD?

I guess that takes me out of the running for mom of the year, huh?

Whatever trauma she experienced, I don't believe for a minute that it was your fault.

You can't know that, because you don't know me.

So tell me.

And so she took a deep breath and pressed the button to initiate a call, because no way could she text everything she suddenly wanted to say. Because somehow she knew that Flynn was someone she could really talk to—and when he answered, she started talking.

"I got married too young and without knowing my future husband very well, because I was pregnant and naively optimistic about building a life with the father of my baby. And everything was mostly okay until Emma was born, but only a few weeks later, Daymond lost his job as a bank manager. He blamed company cutbacks and I trusted that he'd be able to get another job soon enough, but it didn't happen. The longer he was unemployed, the more frustrated he got, and he started taking his frustrations out on me.

"I knew it wasn't a healthy situation for me or Emma, but I didn't know how to get out of it. Especially as we were living outside of Cheyenne at the time, far away from my family, which meant there wasn't anyone around to help with the baby. No one but Daymond.

"And as much as I hated leaving Emma with him, I had no choice. I had to work because he'd lost his job and we had rent to pay and a child to take care of. And of course, when I came home after a ten-hour shift, he'd accuse me of abandoning my baby and somehow make me responsible for the fact that she was crying and hungry, even though he'd been with her all day.

"I don't think I've slept through the night since before Emma was born," she confided. "Because babies don't sleep through the night, and by the time she was doing so, our home situation was so precarious that I slept with one ear open, to ensure that

I could respond to the slightest peep from my daughter's room rather than risk my husband's wrath if his sleep was disturbed."

"Explain to me what you mean by wrath," he demanded.

"Daymond was abusive," she admitted, and discovered it was a relief to say the words out loud. "Verbally. Emotionally. Physically. That's why I finally left him.

"Unfortunately, I didn't leave soon enough, and Emma witnessed some things that...I wish she hadn't. Things that made her afraid of him even though he never—as far as I know—laid a finger on her.

"And then, when we moved to Whispering Canyon, Emma was dealing with a lot of major life changes—including a new home and new routines—and continuing to have bad dreams and night terrors that didn't wake her but definitely woke—and terrified—me."

She finally ran out of breath and stopped talking, a little embarrassed to realize that she'd dumped so much of her emotional baggage at his feet.

But Flynn didn't seem bothered by the fact. And he didn't offer meaningless platitudes or false promises that everything would get better. Instead he only said, "It's no wonder you can't sleep."

It was a simple statement filled with understanding, and somehow, his words made Meg feel infinitely better. Almost normal, even.

"Do you want to tell me now why you're awake at 3:00 a.m.?" she asked him, hoping she might be able to return the favor.

"Considering that it's now almost four and I suspect you have to work in a few hours, why don't we save that for next time?" he suggested.

"I'm going to hold you to that," she said.

And she did—and he did—and that was the real beginning of their friendship.

Chapter Eleven

Flynn was getting used to his job as deputy sheriff. So far this week, he'd been called out to take a report about the broken window of a vehicle parked in the owner's driveway; a complaint from a woman who believed her husband's suspected cheating was somehow a police matter; and the misappropriation of a plastic snowman from the front porch of a local senior.

In the first incident, he'd managed to identify the vandals after reviewing the homeowners' security camera footage and doing some reconnaissance at the local middle school; in the second, he'd suggested the allegedly scorned spouse hire a private investigator—and possibly a divorce attorney; and in the third, during his initial interview of the complainant, the daughter of the elderly man stopped by to have coffee with her dad and confessed…to moving the snowman into the garage. ("Because it's March, Dad," she'd responded to the baffled man's question.)

Flynn might have been amused by the exchange between father and daughter if not for the fact that he still had to write up an incident report. Langley had been right about that—the job required an inordinate amount of paperwork, even without ever pulling his weapon.

Now he was looking ahead to a weekend off, but instead of immediately heading back to West River Ranch and hoping to find something to eat in a refrigerator that he still hadn't bothered to restock, he decided to stop by The Bootlegger to grab a bite.

There were a handful of decent restaurants in town, but Flynn had always been partial to this one, known for its casual atmosphere with good food and friendly service. He bypassed the dining room in favor of the bar, and took a minute to scan the counter, looking for a vacant seat. And there was one—next to Megan, who was absently sipping a glass of diet Coke and sneaking occasional peeks at her phone. She was casually dressed in a soft knit sweater and dark jeans with low-heeled boots on her feet, but the way that sweater and those jeans hugged her feminine curves hit him like a punch in the gut, taking his breath away.

He took a moment to draw air into his lungs again, reminding himself that while she might be one of the most beautiful women he'd ever seen, she was also one of his best friends and he had no business ogling her—as no less than half a dozen other men at the bar were doing, though she seemed oblivious to their stares.

"I can't imagine any man in this town would be a fool enough to stand you up," Flynn said, settling onto the empty stool beside her.

Meg's gaze shifted and the small smile that curved her lips indicated that she was pleased to see him—and made him the envy of the half dozen other men who'd failed to catch her attention. "What did you say?"

"The way you were looking at your phone, I thought you might be waiting to hear from a waylaid date."

"Ha," she responded, as if amused by the thought. "I'm waiting for a call or text from my parents."

Her response eased some of the inexplicable tension inside him. "Regarding something specific?" he asked. "Or just a random communication?"

"Specifically, a request to pick up Emma."

He glanced at his watch. "Isn't she usually in bed by this time?"

Now Meg nodded. "And she's supposed to be in bed at their place tonight."

"Her first sleepover?" he guessed.

"Actually, the first one was a few weeks ago," she told him.

"And how did that go?"

"Surprisingly well," Meg confided.

The bartender interjected then to tell Meg that her chicken burger and fries would be up in a few minutes and pour the beer Flynn requested.

"So why are you anticipating a problem tonight?" Flynn asked, when the bartender had moved on to other customers.

"Because every time I let down my guard, every time I let myself think that maybe her night terrors are in the past, reality slaps me in the face."

"How long has it been since she's woken up screaming?"

"She doesn't usually wake up," Meg reminded him. "She only wakes me up. If there's a silver lining, it's that she doesn't have any memory of the terrors."

"Here's an idea," he said, leaning closer as if to share his thought in confidence. "Trust that your mom and dad will deal with any problems that might arise and let yourself enjoy some rare time to yourself."

"That's what I'm hoping to do," she told him. "I'm just waiting for my food, then I'm going home to eat in front of the television, watching *The Masked Singer*."

"Isn't that on Wednesday nights?"

She arched a brow. "Is it possible that a man who claims to not even have a TV is a closet *TMS* fan?"

"No," he assured her. "And I really don't have a TV. I only know the show's on Wednesday nights because it's all Langley talks about on Thursday mornings."

"New episodes release on Wednesdays," Meg confirmed. "But Emma has Tiny Tumblers then, so I DVR it to watch later."

"If I order my food to go, too, can I watch it with you?"

"You *are* a closet *TMS* fan," she said accusingly.

"No," he said again. "Just curious to see what all the fuss is about. Also, I wouldn't mind some company while I eat."

"Alright," she agreed. "You can come over. But fair warning—I sing along."

"That's something I definitely have to hear."

In all the time that she'd known him, Meg had never been uncomfortable around Flynn. She'd been wary at first—as likely any woman would be when confronted by a guy apparently waiting for her outside of a support group meeting—but she'd never been uncomfortable.

Their friendship had evolved naturally and easily as they got to know one another. Perhaps it was because they'd met at a support group—or at least as a consequence of their attendance at the same group—that neither of them had tried to pretend that everything was right in their world.

By contrast, when a couple of random strangers crossed paths and decided to strike up a conversation, each one usually measured their words and actions, wanting to put their best foot forward. But Meg and Flynn were random strangers who'd met because they were both survivors of trauma, which meant that, right from the beginning, they knew stuff about one another.

Not any of the details, of course, but the simple fact that they'd each lived through stuff with which they were now struggling. As a result, they were less concerned about putting their best foot forward than they were about simply putting one foot in front of the other to move on to the next day.

It gave them common ground: two wounded souls looking not necessarily for healing but acceptance. Searching for someone who might see and acknowledge them as they were, including their flaws and imperfections.

Still, Meg had never intended to introduce Flynn to her then-three-year-old daughter. She didn't need to know the details of his military experience to know that the former Army Ranger was suffering from PTSD, and Emma already had enough reasons to be distrustful of men without forcing her to interact with one who might remind her of those reasons.

Then they were at the local toy store one day, because Meg had implemented a reward system in which her daughter earned stickers for picking up her toys/going to bed on time/taking turns at preschool/being polite and respectful—and quiet when Gramma Sunny was on the phone (that one required fairly frequent reminders as she was accustomed to being the center of attention and tended to object when that status quo was interfered with), and when Emma accumulated a specific number of stickers on her chart, she earned a reward. She usually wanted to go to the bookstore, but one of the kids in her preschool class had taken a new My Little Pony character to school, inspiring her to ask if she could have a toy instead of a book this time.

Of all the places that Meg might have imagined bumping into Flynn, Half Acre Wood was not one of them. But that day, while Emma was trying to decide between Sunny Starscout and Izzy Moonbow, Flynn walked by with two readily recognizable yellow-and-black boxes, one tucked under each arm.

He spotted her first and halted in mid-stride, obviously as taken aback to see her as she was to see him. "Megan—hi."

"Hello, Flynn."

Emma immediately took cover behind her mother's legs, as she was in the habit of doing around unfamiliar people. Flynn didn't smile, as a lot of grown-ups did in an effort to put a child at ease—although, to be honest, Meg wasn't sure she'd ever seen him smile—but respected the little girl's desire to be unobtrusive and kept his gaze focused on her mom.

"Reliving your childhood?" Meg asked, nodding toward the boxes under his arms.

"Birthday presents for my nephews," he explained. "Twins."

"Gage and Zane are twins," Emma chimed in, surprising her mom by volunteering information to a stranger.

"They're in Emma's preschool class," Meg told him.

"And my nephews," he said.

Which she might have guessed, if she'd thought about it, because she knew their surname was Chandler.

Then he tipped his cowboy hat to the little girl, who was still peeking curiously out from behind her mom's legs, and said, "You must be Emma."

She nodded.

"It's a pleasure to meet you."

"Are you…a cowboy?" she ventured to ask.

"I suppose I am," he agreed.

"Do you ride horses?"

"I do."

"Emma's recently discovered a show called *My Little Pony* and is trying to decide which character she wants to buy," Meg explained.

"Hmm… What are your options?" Flynn asked.

The little girl showed him the toys in her hands.

He set down the boxes he'd been holding—an excavator and front loader—and squatted so he was at eye level with her for a closer look.

"I've never seen a horse with a horn sticking out of its head like that before," Flynn confided. "Although, to be fair, I've never seen a purple horse with a blue mane and tail, either."

"That's Izzy Moonbow," Emma said. "She's a unicorn."

"That would explain the horn," he noted.

"This is Sunny Starscout," she said, gesturing with the other toy—an orange-bodied pony with a bright pink mane and tail.

"And you have to decide which one you want to take home and which one you're going to leave in the store for someone else?"

Emma nodded.

"What's your favorite color?"

She answered without hesitation. "Pink."

And with that in mind, she handed Sunny Starscout to her mom.

Meg was dubious that her daughter—always painstakingly slow to decide how she wanted to redeem her sticker rewards—had made a final choice. "Are you sure? Are we safe to go check out now?"

Emma nodded and, with one last wistful glance, placed Izzy Moonbow back on the shelf.

"Thank you," Meg said to Flynn. "Sincerely."

He picked up the Tonka boxes again and they walked to the cash register together.

Emma was mostly quiet while they made their purchases, but she stood beside rather than hiding behind her mom while Meg continued to chat with Flynn.

It was a surprisingly positive (albeit limited) interaction for a little girl who'd borne witness to her dad's abusive behavior. And though Meg wanted to believe her daughter didn't have any solid memories from those early years, certain impressions and fears lingered, making her instinctively—and understandably—fearful of most of the men she met.

Meg didn't know what it was about Flynn that made him different, at least in Emma's eyes, and she didn't care. What mattered was that her little girl had quickly taken a liking to the cowboy and—this was perhaps the bigger surprise—the stoic Army Ranger liked her, too.

Meg enjoyed watching them together, pleased to see how genuine Flynn was in his interactions with her daughter and thrilled to watch Emma's innate shyness disappear around the cowboy. And whenever the three of them were together, it was easy and comfortable.

But now she'd invited Flynn into her home when her daughter wouldn't be there to act as a buffer between them, notwithstanding the fact that she was still feeling a little uneasy as a result of the Valentine's Day incident. (As she was now referring to it, since "kiss" really was a misnomer.)

Well, the truth was that he'd invited himself, but she hadn't objected because she'd taken it as a good sign that he wanted to hang out. Proof that he wasn't the least bit uncomfortable with her in the wake of that awkward incident—and the second almost-incident in the stables at West River Ranch the previous weekend.

"Can you give me an idea of what to expect?"

Flynn's question, as he followed her into the house, drew Meg back to the present. But it took her another second to refocus her thoughts and realize he was asking her about the show they were planning to watch.

"It's an elimination-style competition," she told him. "A certain number of costumed singers—usually between four and six—are judged by the panel and audience members to determine who moves on and who goes home."

"And you try to guess who's behind the mask?"

"That's part of it," she agreed, picking up the remote to turn on the TV.

"Just by their voices?"

"No, there are other clues, but they're deliberately cryptic and usually not much help at all. Of course, when the mask is removed and the singer's identity is revealed, it all makes sense."

As he settled on the sofa with his food, she went to the kitchen and returned with a Coke for Flynn and a diet Coke for herself.

"Are they all singers?" he asked, as she lowered herself onto the opposite end of the sofa.

"No. I'd guess that most of them are—and usually the winner is a recognizable name in the music industry." As she spoke, she scrolled through the listings to find the recording she wanted. "But they've also showcased professional athletes, sitcom stars, game show hosts, social media influencers and even former politicians."

She started the playback.

"What else do I need to know?" he asked.

"That if you talk during the show, you'll be banished to the kitchen."

He mimed zipping his lips.

For the next forty-odd minutes, they sat eating their meals out of takeout containers and watching the show.

And when Meg finished her dinner, she sang along to the songs she knew, as promised.

"What did you think?" she asked, when the credits were rolling.

He took a minute to consider his response before he said, "The opening song was really good."

"The theme song?" she guessed.

He nodded. "I'm a big fan of The Who."

She rolled her eyes. "After watching an entire episode, that's all you have to say?"

"That and the costumes were…creative."

"The costume designer is a genius," she agreed.

He set his empty takeout container on the coffee table and picked up his Coke.

"Anything else?" she prompted.

"Nope, that about sums it up."

"You're holding something back."

"Please don't make me say it."

"Say it," she urged.

He sighed. "You really can't carry a tune."

Meg gasped, as if offended by his remark. But she knew he was only speaking the truth, and she was actually reassured by his honest response, because it confirmed that he would always tell her the truth, even when it was an uncomfortable truth. So whatever feelings might have been stirred by that Valentine's

Day incident were her problem to deal with—their friendship had not been affected, and that was a big relief to her. (And also, perhaps, a tiny disappointment.)

"I'm sorry," he said now. "But it's true. And if a friend ever invites you to karaoke, make an excuse. Do. Not. Go. Because that person isn't really your friend. Or perhaps a friend who has just never heard you sing."

She had to laugh as she gathered their empty containers. "I'll keep that in mind."

"So this is how you spend your Friday nights, huh?" he asked, following her to the kitchen.

She shrugged, feigning a casualness she no longer felt because her usually spacious kitchen suddenly felt crowded with Flynn standing close. So close she could see the individual hairs that made up the dark stubble on his jaw. So close she could smell the clean masculine scent of his soap. So close she could tip her head back and—

She abruptly severed that thought.

"We all have our vices," she finally responded to his question.

"If you consider that a vice, you need to get out more."

Meg nodded. "I've been thinking the same thing."

Meg had not slept well.

That in and of itself wasn't uncommon, but lately she'd been dreaming, which was out of the ordinary. And though she didn't remember any of the details of her dreams, she had an uneasy feeling that Flynn was playing a starring role in her nighttime imaginings.

So when she walked into her kitchen the following Thursday morning and found him standing beside the coffeemaker, she halted in mid-stride, not entirely certain she wasn't still dreaming.

"Good morning," he said, in a husky morning voice that skimmed over her like a physical caress.

"Good morning," she echoed.

He removed the mug of coffee from beneath the spout of her single-serve brewer and offered it to her.

She blinked.

A sexy man offering her coffee?

Definitely still dreaming.

"You made this for me?" She lifted the mug to her lips for that first essential jolt of caffeine.

"I made it for me," he admitted. "But I can just as easily make another one."

"So why did you give it to me?" she asked.

"Just following instructions," he said, his gaze dropping for a second and a flush of color darkening his cheeks before he turned his attention to the brewer.

"Huh?" Clearly the caffeine had yet to kick in.

He gestured, a little awkwardly, to the T-shirt she wore over lime-green boxer shorts.

On the front was an image of Garfield holding out a coffee mug inscribed with the words "Give me coffee and no one gets hurt."

It was an old T-shirt, the picture faded as a result of countless washing. Of course, those countless washings had also worn the fabric thin, so that it did absolutely nothing to hide the fact that her nipples were currently standing at attention.

And she couldn't even pretend he hadn't noticed, because he'd been reading the words printed on her shirt, right between her breasts. And the awareness that he'd been looking at—or at least in the vicinity of—her nipples, churned up her hormones all over again.

She cleared her throat.

"Good call," she said, picking up the thread of the conversation—and folding her arms over her chest to hide her traitorous nipples. “Thank you.”

“You’re welcome,” he said, then cleared his throat, too, his gaze focused intently on his own mug as he lifted it to his lips.

Her mind scrambled, desperately searching for a way to shift the conversation—and found it as she swallowed another mouthful of coffee. “Why does this taste different?”

“You mean better?” he suggested, sounding as grateful as she was for the change of topic.

She took another cautious sip. “Maybe.”

“Because you were almost out of pods, so I picked up a box at the Mug Shot the other day.”

She frowned. “Their pods are expensive.”

“Because their coffee is better than the generic stuff you get at the grocery store.”

She couldn’t disagree, but the fact was, the generic stuff was a much better fit for her budget.

“You have to stop buying my groceries,” she said admonishingly.

“I’m not sure a box of coffee pods qualifies as groceries.”

“The coffee’s only the latest thing. Last week, I was sure I was almost out of bread, and then I came home to find a whole loaf on the counter. And a dozen eggs in the refrigerator.”

“Because I’d used your last egg that morning. And made toast,” he told her. “And since you won’t let me pay to sleep in your house, the least I can do is pick up a few essentials now and again.”

“Emma’s favorite fruit snacks aren’t an essential.”

“They are to Emma.”

“You also paid when we went to Pasquale’s for dinner the other night.”

“Food is definitely essential.”

“And Disney Plus?” she prompted.

He swallowed another mouthful of coffee. "I didn't know you had Disney Plus."

"We didn't," she told him. "And now, suddenly, we do."

"Maybe it's some kind of free promotion," he suggested.

"Or maybe you bought the subscription and told Emma not to tell me."

His wince confirmed that he'd been busted.

"I didn't tell her not to tell you—I just told her that it could be our secret."

"Obviously you didn't know that we have a rule," Meg explained to him. "Which is that if someone tells her to keep a secret—especially if that someone is an adult and specifically if that someone tells her not to tell her mom—then she has to tell me so that we can decide together if it's a safe or unsafe secret."

"A good rule," he acknowledged.

"So you'll cancel the subscription?"

"I already paid for the year."

She sighed.

"There's a new *Moana* movie coming out that I really want to see."

"You mean that Emma really wants to see? And that she'll probably talk me into taking her to the theater to see long before it's available on Disney Plus?"

"Speaking of Emma—" He glanced at the time displayed on the stove. "Shouldn't she be up and getting ready for preschool?"

"Yes, but don't think that distraction gets you off the hook," Meg cautioned, taking her coffee with her on her way out of the room.

And though she was grateful for the opportunity to make her escape, she was also beginning to accept that she and Flynn wouldn't be able to tiptoe around the tension between them forever. Sooner or later, there was going to be a reckoning.

Chapter Twelve

"You seem a little out of sorts today," Langley remarked to Flynn, as they were heading back to the sheriff's office after a safety presentation at the local elementary school.

"Maybe because you made me wear the ridiculous Deputy Dog costume."

"That was the sheriff's decision."

"Because you bribed him with donuts," he said accusingly.

"Because I have a naturally pleasant demeanor that doesn't scare impressionable children," she countered easily.

He scowled at her.

"Thank you for proving my point."

He pulled up in front of the Mug Shot Café.

"I guess it's coffee break time," she said.

He opened the door of the café for her.

"Even out of sorts, your manners are ingrained," she noted.

"Order your coffee," he said.

"I'll have a latte," she told the barista behind the counter.

"Ceramic cup or paper?"

She glanced over her shoulder at Flynn. "Are we staying or going?"

"We can stay," he said. "But get the paper cup, anyway. Just in case."

The barista punched in the order.

"And for you, sir?"

"Regular coffee. Black."

"Is that everything?"

"Yeah."

"No," Langley decided. "Give us a chocolate-glazed donut, too."

Flynn shook his head. "Such a cliché."

"Maybe. But the cliché is for you."

"Why?"

She tapped her card to pay for their order. "I thought your mood might be linked to the fact that all the donuts were gone by the time you showed up this morning."

"I was on time for my shift."

"I didn't say you weren't."

They took their cups—and the one donut—to a table by the window.

"For future reference, apple fritters are my favorite."

"I know," she said. "I got the chocolate-glazed because I suspect you might stubbornly refuse to accept my peace offering and leave the donut untouched. And then I, reluctant to see good carbohydrates go to waste, would have to eat it—a much more palatable sacrifice when it's a chocolate-glazed."

"So you bought me your favorite kind of donut?"

She shrugged.

"Thanks." He lifted it off the plate and took a big bite.

The corners of her mouth twitched. "You take pleasure in being contrary, don't you?"

"Nope."

The smile spread as she lifted her cup to her lips.

He polished off the donut in two more bites.

"Feel better now?" she asked him.

"I felt fine before."

"I know we're not actually partners, but there will be occasions—like today—when the sheriff assigns us to work together, and it might help those assignments go more smoothly if we developed something of a camaraderie."

"You think so?"

"I'll start," she said. "I'm thirty-seven years old, twice divorced, no kids. You already know that I previously worked as a deputy sheriff in Howlett's Pass, and so far, I have no regrets about the move to Whispering Canyon. Though I've experienced a little pushback from some residents who seem to be holding a grudge over the fact that I dared to run against one of the town's favorite sons for the top law enforcement job, I'm confident that my competence and charm will win them over."

"An interesting synopsis," he remarked.

"Now it's your turn."

"Pass."

"Contrary," she said again.

"Maybe I just don't like talking about myself."

"The newspaper calls you a hero."

He scowled. "You've been reading some really old newspapers."

"The online archives of *The Canyon Whisperer*."

"Don't believe everything you read," he cautioned. "The staff of the biweekly publication aren't exactly hard-hitting journalists."

"Are you denying that you played a part in the rescue of five hostages—humanitarian aid workers—from an unnamed country somewhere overseas?"

"A very small part."

"And nearly lost your life, as a result."

"But here I am, very much alive and kicking."

She sipped her coffee, considering. "Relationship status?" she prompted.

His brows lifted. "Are you hitting on me?"

She sputtered. "Ohmygod—*no*! I would never…that would be completely inappropriate. I shouldn't have… I didn't mean—"

"Relax, Langley. I was joking."

"Oh." She exhaled an audible sigh, then eyed him across the

table. "I was actually trying to determine, in a roundabout way, if your mood this morning is a sign of relationship trouble."

"No relationship, therefore, no trouble."

It wasn't only better that way, it was necessary—because he had a lot of work to do to put his life back together before he could share it with anyone else. (And if an image of Megan and Emma flickered in his mind when he thought of anyone else, that was for him to deal with.)

"Really?" Langley seemed surprised by his response. "So the woman and little girl I saw you with at Pasquale's the other night are…?"

"Friends," he answered the unfinished question for her.

And reminded himself.

"I thought I might find you baking a big cake for the christening," Meg said, when she entered her grandmother's kitchen and found her…chopping vegetables?

"I offered, but I've been informed that Miranda has ordered a fancy cake from Hart Cakes," Tallulah said, as she removed the seeds from the inside of a yellow pepper. "A huge cake with layers of chocolate, vanilla and red-velvet sponge."

"Well, not everyone loves cake, anyway," Meg said, in an obvious effort to soothe what she assumed were her grandmother's hurt feelings.

Lula slid her a look as she picked up a knife and began slicing the pepper into strips. "I don't know anyone who doesn't love cake, but I made brownies, pecan tarts, lemon bars and macaroons so that guests would have other options."

"Your pecan tarts are my favorite," Meg told her.

"And Emma likes my brownies even more than my cupcakes." Tallulah scraped the pepper strips off the cutting board into a bowl, then wiped her hands on a tea towel. "Do you want a cup of coffee?"

"Sometimes I think it's caffeine that flows through my veins."

Her grandmother interpreted her response as a *yes* and set a mug under the spout of her single-serve coffeemaker.

"What's on your mind?" she asked, when they were seated at the table with their drinks.

"Maybe I just came for your pecan tarts," Meg said, selecting one from the plate of goodies in the middle of the table.

"You're not in the habit of dropping by on the off chance I might have made some."

"Maybe I should make it a habit, because they're definitely worth the trip."

But her grandmother wasn't fooled for a minute by her circular response. "Boy trouble?" she guessed.

Meg had to smile at that, unable to imagine a man more inaccurately described as a boy than Flynn Chandler. "I'm not entirely sure."

"Sounds like boy trouble to me," Tallulah said. "There's nothing that can twist a girl up inside like a boy—even a smart girl like you."

"After Daymond, I didn't think I'd ever be attracted to a man again," she confided. "I didn't want to be."

"And then you met Flynn," her grandmother concluded.

Meg frowned. "How do you know I'm talking about Flynn?"

"Because I know you—and it seems to be an undeniable fact that Leonard women have a weakness for Chandler men."

"But we're friends," she said. "Even if being around him has started to make me feel things I don't want to be feeling."

And maybe the feelings that were churning inside her now had more to do with timing than the man. Maybe she hadn't been ready when she went out with Heath or James or Cameron, but now it was spring and her body was awakening again.

"You're a young woman," Lula noted. "Surely you didn't expect your hormones to stay in hibernation forever."

"I don't know if I expected it, but I kind of hoped they would."

"And now that you know you were wrong?"

"Maybe the best thing to do is nothing and hope the feelings go away." Because there were all kinds of reasons that Flynn Chandler was the absolute last man she should be attracted to. "His friendship means a lot to me, and I don't want to risk losing it."

"You have other friends," her grandmother said easily.

"No one who understands me like he does. Plus, he's become not only an important part of my life but of Emma's life, too. Aside from my dad, she hasn't had a lot of positive male role models in her life, but he's one of them. And if we decided to see if this...chemistry—if that's what it is—could lead to anything else, she's the one who could end up getting hurt."

"She is going to get hurt," Tallulah pointed out in a matter-of-fact tone. "As much as you might want to, you can't protect her from everything all the time."

"Maybe not," Meg allowed. "But I can do a better job protecting her now than I did in the past. I *need* to do a better job."

"It's not your fault that her dad was a bully."

"No," she agreed. "But shouldn't I have figured that out before I married him?"

"You were young and pregnant and didn't want to struggle as a single mom to raise your child."

"And look at me now," she mused.

"Look at you," Tallulah agreed. "You're a strong, smart woman with an impressive career, your own home and an amazing little girl."

Meg smiled. "She is pretty amazing, isn't she?"

Lula reached across the table to give her hand a gentle squeeze. "Takes after her mom," she said with pride and affection.

For the most part, Meg worked regular hours that allowed her to take Emma to preschool every morning and be home for dinner with her every night. It was rare that she was asked to work a night-time shift, but extended hours weren't uncommon, which was why she knew she was fortunate to have her parents available to step in and take care of Emma when such occasions arose.

But this week, her parents were in Alaska visiting her sister—a trip they'd made every few months since Nicole had accepted a teaching position in the northernmost state—requiring Meg to make alternative arrangements for Emma. Doing so had never been an issue when Tess was living with them, but her BFF had a husband and a baby of her own now and lived thirty miles outside of town. So Meg could hardly expect her friend to bundle up her infant son and trek into town to pick up Emma from preschool, though she had no doubt Tess would do so if she was asked.

Instead, Meg reached out to Gramma Lula, who grumbled—predictably—about being too old to chase after an active preschooler. But the haste with which she'd accepted the assignment assured Meg that Tallulah was secretly pleased to have been asked. And it was for a couple of hours, anyway, because Meg agreed that anything more would likely be too much for her almost-eighty-year-old grandmother.

But at four o'clock, before she scrubbed in for another surgery, she slipped into the locker room to call home and tell Tallulah she was going to be late. She didn't have time to go into detail, and she wouldn't have done so if she did, knowing the shockwaves of the tragic accident would be felt throughout town soon enough.

A group of teenage boys—most of them due to graduate from Howlett's Pass High School in a few weeks—had been crammed into a pickup on their way back to school after their lunch break when the driver took a corner too fast and the truck rolled. That driver and the two passengers belted into the cab walked away from the crash, but their friends—seven of them—

riding in the bed of the truck were thrown from the vehicle, some of them suffering catastrophic injuries.

The first responders to arrive at the scene immediately radioed to Whispering Canyon for additional support. One teen was pronounced dead at the scene, two others deemed especially critical were airlifted to outside trauma centers, while three ambulances raced to WCMC, lights flashing and sirens screaming.

Meg had assisted Dr. Duchesne with one of the emergency surgeries—a seventeen-year-old male with a ruptured spleen and internal bleeding. (He also suffered numerous gashes and contusions and several cracked ribs, but the priority was to repair the spleen and stop the bleeding.) At the same time, Dr. Howard—WCMC's top orthopedic surgeon—was dealing with a compound femur fracture and Dr. Reece was handling the unenviable task of discussing organ donation with the parents of a sixteen-year-old who'd suffered a stroke en route to the hospital as a consequence of an intracranial hemorrhage.

When Meg finally got home, just after six o'clock, she was physically and mentally exhausted. So much so that she didn't take note of the vehicle parked in front of the house until she saw Flynn seated across from Emma at the kitchen table.

They were each focused on the cards in their respective hands, but Emma spotted her first and lifted her head, a smile spreading across her face. "Mama! You're home!"

"I'm home," she confirmed, dropping a kiss on the top of her daughter's head and taking a moment to breathe in the familiar soothing scent of baby shampoo and little girl. "But what have you done to poor Great-Gramma Lula? You've run her so ragged, she doesn't look anything like herself."

Emma giggled. "That's not Great-Gramma Lula. That's Unca Flynn."

"Silly me," Meg remarked.

"I stopped by to replace the drum belt in your dryer and your grandmother tagged me to take over so that she could get ready for her weekly bingo game."

"First I've heard of a weekly bingo game," she noted.

Flynn just shrugged. "I'm not working today, so it wasn't a problem."

"Got any sea turtles?" Emma asked, turning her attention back to the game at hand.

Her conscripted babysitter sighed and handed two cards from his hand.

The little girl beamed as she combined them with another two in her hand and set the four of a kind aside.

"I hope you're not playing for money," Meg said lightly.

"If we were, your daughter's college fund would be flush," Flynn told her.

"It's your turn, Unca Flynn," Emma pointed out.

He glanced at the cards in his hand. "Got any seahorses?"

"Go Fish!"

He drew a card from the deck in the center of the table.

"Got any clown fish?"

He again handed over two cards.

"There are chicken fingers and salad in the fridge, if you're hungry," Flynn said to Meg. "Or I could scramble you some eggs."

"Chicken fingers, huh? Who would have guessed that Emma would have asked for chicken fingers for dinner?"

"They're my fav'rite," the little girl reminded her mom.

"Probably the most favorite of all your favorites," Meg agreed.

She couldn't remember when she'd last eaten, and though she was more tired than hungry, she knew that she should eat something to fuel her body and keep her awake until her daughter's bedtime. She opened the cupboard and pulled out a package of Oreo cookies.

"Got any sharks?"

Emma sighed and handed over a single card.

"That's hardly an appropriate meal," Flynn chided Meg.

"It'll do," she said, shoving a cookie into her mouth.

He responded to Emma's request for narwhals with "Go Fish." She did so, taking the final card from the now-depleted pile in the center of the table.

Of course, she drew the requested card and smiled widely as she displayed another group of four on the table. "I win."

"Yes, you do," he confirmed. "Again."

"Can we play one more time?" Emma asked.

He glanced at Meg.

She shook her head. "Not tonight, Em," she said. "You have to get ready for Tiny Tumblers."

"I'm ready," her daughter replied.

"You plan on wearing that dress to your gym class?"

The little girl nodded. "Great-Gramma Lula said I look bee-yoo-ti-ful."

"And you do," Meg confirmed. "But the skirt might get tangled around your legs when you're rolling on the mats."

"Oh." Emma pouted, unhappy that she hadn't considered that possibility.

"Why don't you go put on a pair of leggings and a T-shirt and hang up your dress to wear another day?"

"Okay," she agreed, and skipped up the stairs to her bedroom to change.

"I should change, too," Meg said, glancing down at the clean scrubs she'd donned after her shower at the hospital, hoping the hot spray might help wash away the fatigue that had seeped into her bones.

Obviously it hadn't worked, as evidenced by Flynn's remark after his gaze skimmed over her. "You look exhausted."

"You really have to stop with the flattery," she told him, turning to reach into the cupboard over the sink for a bottle of Tylenol. "You're going to turn my head."

He let her struggle with the childproof cap for a moment before he took the bottle from her, uncapped it and dispensed two pills into her hand.

"Thank you."

He nodded. "Why don't you go have a nap?"

"Because I have to take Emma to Tiny Tumblers."

"At the community center?"

"Yeah."

"I happen to know where that is," he said. "I can take her."

"You can't just drop her off," Meg protested. "You have to stay and watch."

"I'm capable of that, too," he assured her.

She was exhausted—and more than a little tempted to let him carry the weight of her responsibilities for a little while. (And immediately felt guilty for thinking of her daughter—the center of her world and source of all her joy—as a responsibility.)

"So now the question is—are you capable of accepting help from a friend?" Flynn asked.

"I am," she told him, willing to be convinced that accepting help wasn't the same as abdicating responsibility or neglecting her child, who would likely be thrilled to spend more time with Uncle Flynn.

"Then you need to say, 'Thank you, Flynn. I'd appreciate that.'"

"Before I do, I feel compelled to point out that a lot of parents of the kids in Tiny Tumblers first met at a play group specifically for single parents."

"So?" he prompted.

"So you're likely to be the only man in the midst of a bunch of women. Unmarried women," she clarified.

"Is that supposed to scare me off?"

"I just want you to know what you're getting yourself into," she said.

"I'm more concerned about getting you into bed," he told her.

He was obviously referring to her state of exhaustion, not propositioning her, but the air was crackling again.

"I appreciate the thought," she responded lightly, in an effort to defuse the sudden tension, "but you should know by now that I'm not that kind of girl."

"I do know," he confirmed. "And yet, I still hang around."

"Why is that?" she wondered aloud.

"I'm head over heels for your kid."

"She's a pretty great kid."

"There are times her mom isn't so bad, either," he said.

"Yeah?"

"And there are other times—like now—when she's stubborn and uncooperative and unwilling to accept help when it's offered."

"Thank you, Flynn," she intoned. "I'd appreciate you taking Emma to Tiny Tumblers tonight."

"There you go," he said approvingly. "That wasn't really so hard, was it?"

"No," she admitted. "But we'll see what your answer is to the same question when you get back."

Chapter Thirteen

There were about a dozen kids already in the gym when Flynn and Emma arrived, and their moms—and yes, they were all moms—were in groups of two or three, standing against the wall or seated on the narrow benches where they could watch the activities when they got underway. Flynn helped Emma take off her coat and boots, then she placed them in the storage cubby before hurrying to the center of the room to join her playmates.

Two more kids showed up a few minutes later, and the instructor gathered them around her in a circle to check their names off a list. After that, she led them through a series of gentle stretches, explaining the importance of warming up their muscles, before letting them loose on what was essentially an obstacle course of physical activities: mats to roll across, mini trampolines to jump on, traffic cones to weave around, hoops to spin around their arms, foam shapes to climb over and pop-up tunnels to crawl through.

"It's like a preschool version of *American Ninja Warrior*—but without the water hazards."

He hadn't realized he'd spoken aloud until the woman seated closest to him responded, "That's what I said when Duncan came to his first class."

And suddenly Flynn found himself stuck in the middle of a conversation he'd never meant to start.

"Which one is Duncan?" he asked politely.

"The one with the red hair sticking up in every direction."

She tossed her long tresses of the same color over her shoulder. "He comes by the color honestly—and perhaps the wildness, too," she added with a wink. "Ainsley Tate."

"Flynn Chandler," he said, shaking her proffered hand before refocusing his attention on the obstacle course.

He winced as one of the kids threw herself over a foam triangle and did a face-plant on the mat.

Beside him, Ainsley tittered. "I shouldn't laugh, but honestly, that Epiphaneia has absolutely no coordination."

Epiphaneia?

The poor kid never had a chance, having been saddled with a clumsy name like that.

Aloud he only said, "As long as she's having fun."

Emma looked up and, seeing that he was watching, lifted her hand to wave.

"You brought Emma," Ainsley noted.

"Yeah."

"You're a friend of Meg's then?" she guessed.

He nodded.

"Me, too," she said, as if both of them knowing Emma's mom somehow created a connection between them.

Meg had warned him that it was unusual for a man to show up at Tiny Tumblers; a fact made evident when the other women, having realized he was talking to the redhead seated beside him, started to gravitate in their direction, showing more interest in the rare male specimen in their midst than what their kids were doing.

It's only a sixty-minute class, he reminded himself, resisting the urge to put his elbows up and regain some rapidly dwindling space.

When all the kids had made their way through the course several times, they moved back to the circle in the center of the room and the instructor put on some music. She took them through the motions of the "Hokey Pokey," "Head Shoulders

Knees and Toes," "Up and Down," then encouraged them to do their own thing to "Freeze Dance" and ended with a song that seemed to require them to flap their arms and wiggle their bottoms.

Flynn was certain that sixty minutes in a 110-degree desert with a thirty-pound pack on his back and the sun beating down had never lasted so long as Emma's Tiny Tumblers class.

Finally, the music stopped and the instructor blew out an exaggerated breath.

"Wow, you guys really brought your energy tonight," she said. "Thanks for your enthusiastic participation. Now go find your moms before they wander off without appropriate child supervision.

"Mom *or* dad," she amended, with an apologetic glance at Flynn.

"Uncle," he clarified, as Emma raced over to him.

She smiled. "I'm glad you were able to bring Emma out tonight—she adds so much joy and enthusiasm to the class."

"It was my pleasure," he told her, a polite response more than a sincere one. To Emma, he said, "Go get your coat and boots."

She scampered off to retrieve her belongings.

"Did you see me twirl, Unca Flynn?" she asked, after she'd returned and he was zipping up her coat.

"I saw you twirl *and* jump *and* roll *and* spin," he assured her.

"And flap my wings?"

"If your arms are wings, then yeah," he said. "But why were you doing that?"

"It's the chicken dance!"

"I'm not familiar with that one."

"I could teach you," she said. "It goes like this."

She opened and closed her hands—pretending they were beaks?—then flapped her arms, followed by twisting her torso while bending her knees before straightening up again and clapping her hands.

"Now you try," she urged.

"Another time maybe."

She sighed. "That's what Mama says when she means *no*."

"When I mean *no*, I say *no*," Flynn told her.

"Mama says that, too."

The boy with the wild red hair ran up to Emma then and whispered something in her ear before racing back to his mom.

"What was that about?" Flynn asked her.

"Duncan said his mom's taking him to Scoops for ice cream."

"Why was he telling you?"

"'Cuz sometimes Mama takes me for ice cream after Tiny Tumblers, too."

"She didn't say anything to me about ice cream."

"Pleeease."

And maybe her mom could resist such a plea, but Flynn had no defenses against the little girl's big blue eyes.

"A kiddie cone," he agreed.

She rewarded his acquiescence with a beaming smile.

And that was how Flynn found himself at Scoops, the local ice cream parlor, with several of the moms from the Tiny Tumblers group.

But at least he had Emma as a safeguard here.

Or so he thought, until he handed her the cone he'd promised and she scampered off to a booth with her friends.

"I haven't seen you at the gym with Emma before."

Flynn glanced at the woman who'd squeezed onto the end of the bench seat beside him, forcing him to squeeze closer to the woman on his other side—the redhead whose name he couldn't remember. Aubrey? Ashley?

"Tonight was my first time," he admitted.

"I heard Emma call you Uncle Flynn," a woman across the table noted.

"It's just an honorary title."

"And you and Meg are…?" She deliberately let the words trail off, leaving the question unfinished.

"Friends," he answered. Again.

Her smile widened then.

"I don't see a ring on your hand," a woman with short dark hair noted.

"Subtle, Lana."

"We're all busy moms—who has time for subtlety?" she challenged.

"Not all married men wear rings," Lana's friend pointed out.

"And even some who do wear them choose not to wear them all of the time."

There was an unmistakable note of bitterness in Lana's tone, leading Flynn to believe that she had some experience with a man who fell into the latter category.

"In some jobs, a ring can be a safety hazard," he pointed out.

"You said your last name was Chandler," Ashley—no, it was, Ainsley, he remembered now—commented. "As in West River Ranch?"

"That's the family business," he confirmed. "And while I still work at the ranch, I'm also a deputy with the sheriff's department."

"I don't know what's hotter—a man on horseback or a man in uniform," Lana mused.

"A man on horseback," the short-haired brunette declared.

At the same time Ainsley said, "A man in uniform."

Meg owed him *big-time* for this—never mind that he'd volunteered to take Emma to the class; he had *not* signed up to be studied like a newly discovered specimen under a microscope.

He glanced at his watch. "Is that the time already? I almost forgot that I've got a meeting tonight, and if I don't get Emma home right away, I'll be late."

"I do hope we'll see you again," Ainsley said.

"I'm sure our paths will cross."

He managed to extricate himself from the group in the booth and make his way to where Emma was seated. She poked out her tongue for another lick of her ice cream.

He'd only bought her a kiddie cone—how was it possible that she hadn't finished it already?

"We have to go," he told her.

"But I'm not finished my ice cream," she protested.

"You can finish it in the car."

She shook her head. "Mama doesn't let me eat ice cream in the car."

"And in your mama's car, you have to follow her rules," he agreed. "But we came in my truck tonight. Remember? I moved your car seat from her vehicle to mine."

Her brow furrowed, a gesture that made her look so like her mom, he might have smiled if he wasn't focused on making his escape. "But why do we hafta go?"

"Because I said so."

"That's not a good reason," she admonished.

A fair point, but he had no desire to stay there a single minute longer arguing with a not-yet-five-year-old. "Are you bringing the ice cream or not?" he asked instead.

She brought the ice cream.

Meg wasn't accustomed to shirking her duties, and she'd felt more than a twinge of guilt as she waved goodbye to Flynn and Emma. What kind of mom abdicated her responsibilities just because she'd had a rough day at work?

But today had admittedly been rougher than most—tragedies involving kids were always a gut-punch—and the senselessness of this one only made it worse.

So many lives forever changed as a consequence of one poor decision.

But whose poor decision had it been?

Right now, most people were likely pointing fingers at the

young driver, speculating that he'd been showing off, driving too fast, being reckless. And maybe it was true. Or maybe his friends in the cab of the truck were urging him to go faster, so they wouldn't be late back to school. Or perhaps the passengers in the back were fooling around, distracting him with their antics.

And then there was the owner of the truck. The driver's dad, who'd given his son the keys.

What if he'd just said no?

Of course, none of the speculation would change what had happened today. Nothing could undo the damage that had been done. And Meg knew from personal experience that what-ifs were an exercise in futility.

What if I'd known him better before I let him talk me into bed?

What if I'd been strong/brave enough to trust I could raise my child on my own and rejected his marriage proposal?

What if I'd walked away the first time I caught a glimpse of his temper?

Those were her own demons, and ones she still wrestled with on occasion, because no matter how determined she was to move forward, there were still pieces of the past that she carried with her. But she wasn't letting those pieces weigh her down. Not anymore.

More important, they didn't seem to be weighing Emma down. Dr. Halstead assured Meg that her daughter was doing great, exhibiting all the normal behaviors of an almost-five-year-old. Yes, Emma could be a little shy at times, but a lot of children were shy. If her moods sometimes changed abruptly, that was simply because children need to learn to regulate their emotions. And it had been almost six months since she'd woken Meg up with her screaming, suggesting that her night terrors were finally in the rearview mirror.

Meg desperately wanted her daughter to be okay. To be normal. And so, she was trying to give her more of the freedoms that other kids her age enjoyed. And that included going to playdates and activities without her mom having to be there every minute.

Still, it was one thing to have Gramma or Grampa pick up Emma at preschool and a completely different thing to let Flynn take her to Tiny Tumblers. And while she appreciated that he'd made the offer because he was concerned about Meg, she didn't feel right taking the time to nap when there were so many things that needed to be done around the house.

At the top of the list: a dishwasher full of clean dishes to be put away and a hamper full of dirty clothes to be washed.

She stifled a yawn as she made her way upstairs to get the laundry and found herself reconsidering Flynn's advice to take advantage of the quiet and close her eyes for thirty minutes.

And since her bed was right there, she stretched out and closed her eyes—and crashed hard.

When Flynn and Emma got back to the house, they found it in darkness. There was no sign of Meg on the main level and no response when Emma called out to her.

"She's prob'ly upstairs," the little girl said, kicking off her boots and dropping her coat in the entranceway.

"Wait," he said, when she started toward the staircase. "Before you go racing up there, put your coat and boots where they belong so your mom doesn't trip over them later."

Emma sighed but dutifully returned to hang her coat on a hook in the closet and set her boots in the tray.

"And try to be quiet, in case your mom's sleeping," he urged, following her up the stairs.

"She *is* sleeping," Emma said, when they discovered Meg sprawled on top of the covers of her bed, still dressed in the scrubs she'd worn home from the hospital and obviously out for the count.

He touched a finger to his lips, silently communicating for Emma to be quiet, before turning her around and steering her down the hall.

"Your mom had a really busy day at work today, so we're going to let her sleep," Flynn told her, keeping his voice low so as not to disturb the little girl's sleeping mother.

"But who's gonna give me my bath and help me brush my teeth and tuck me into bed?" Emma wanted to know.

"I think you're going to have to skip the bath tonight," he said. "But I'll help with the other stuff."

"Mama says if I don't have a bath after gym class I'll get stinky."

He leaned his head toward her and gave an exaggerated sniff. "You don't smell too stinky."

"You hafta smell my pits," she said, lifting her arms over her head and high into the air.

He obliged, sniffing first one, then the other.

"Not too stinky," he assured her. "And if your mom disagrees, she can deal with your stinky self in the morning."

"Okay."

"Now go get your jammies on, then we'll brush your teeth."

"Okay," she said again.

But somehow, between changing into her pajamas and making her way to the bathroom, her happy demeanor seemed to have gotten lost. She handed him her toothbrush and toothpaste, and he helped clean her teeth, then gave her a paper cup of water to rinse and spit.

"What's next?" he asked.

"Story time," she said unhappily.

"I don't think so."

She scowled at him.

"It can't be story time," he told her. "Because the Emma W. I know loves story time too much to ever announce it with a frowny face."

"I don't have a frowny face."

He lifted her up to the mirror so she could see for herself.

"That's my sad face," she told him.

"My mistake," he said, sitting her on the counter so that she was closer to his eye level. "Do you want to tell me why you're sad?"

"'Cuz I don't have a daddy."

Which was hardly a new revelation, leading him to believe that something had happened recently to remind her of the fact.

Now would be a good time for Megan to wake up and take over, he mused, because talking to a preschooler about her family situation seemed like something that was above his pay grade. But as he hadn't heard a peep from the little girl's mom, he had no choice but to deal with it—or at least to tiptoe carefully around the subject so as not cause Emma any further distress.

"You don't have a dad," he acknowledged. "But you're a very lucky girl, because you have the best mom in the world."

"But it's not fair," Emma said, sniffling. "Emma B. has three dads and I don't even have one."

"Three dads?" he echoed dubiously.

She nodded. "Her mommy and daddy got a 'vorce and then they got married to new daddies."

Way above his pay grade.

"Is Emma B. in your Tiny Tumblers group?"

She shook her head. "She goes to preschool with me."

"So, what made you think about this now?" he wondered aloud.

"Keeley asked if you were my dad."

"Keeley's in Tiny Tumblers?"

Now Em nodded.

"Ah." So maybe he hadn't done Meg any favors by taking her daughter to her gym class and laying the groundwork for this conversation.

"I told her that I don't have a daddy, and her sister Kasey said that I'd get a new daddy if my mom got married again."

"What makes Kasey an expert on the subject?" he asked her.

"She's in first grade and really smart." Emma sniffled. "Could you marry Mama and be my daddy?"

So far above his pay grade.

"I don't think your mom's looking to get married again," he said gently. "And besides, I like being your uncle."

"But if you were my daddy, you could live with us and read me bedtime stories every night," Emma said.

It was hard to refute the child's logic, he mused.

And harder still not to be tempted by the picture she painted.

Flynn had never given much thought to having a family. Probably because he'd barely been eighteen when he enlisted and focused on serving his country to the exclusion of all else. But if he'd taken the time to think about it, he likely would have imagined his life taking a turn down the traditional "marriage and kids" path at some future point in time.

But when he came home, it was all he could do to go through the motions from one day to the next. He'd had no thoughts of a future—no right to aspire to any of the usual milestones when his cousin had been deprived of opportunities for the same.

His therapist had offered some resources and strategies to help him process his grief and guilt and move on, but he couldn't imagine any woman wanting to build a life with someone as screwed up as he was.

Then he'd met Meg—and through Meg, Emma. And spending time with the single mom and her little girl somehow helped quiet the noise around him and even, occasionally, allowed him to find pleasure in the moment. Still, he knew it would be a mistake to let himself believe he could ever have anything more than what he had right now, to hope he could be what they needed when he was still so entangled in his own guilt and grief.

"I'm here now," he pointed out to Emma. "And happy to read you a story—maybe even two stories."

"*Two* stories?" she echoed, and the hint of pleasure in her voice was like a glimpse of the sun through the clouds.

"Do you think you can stay awake for two stories?"

She nodded her head.

"Then go ahead and pick out two books," he told her.

"You hafta come, too, Unca Flynn. To read in the story chair."

"I'm right behind you," he promised.

Chapter Fourteen

Meg was dreaming about Flynn. *Again.*

This dream seemed to be a mash-up of fact and fantasy that started at West River Ranch. (Apparently she had some latent cowboy fantasies of which she'd previously been unaware, and perhaps it made sense that Flynn would play the starring role, as she knew for a fact that he looked damn good on horseback.) He effortlessly boosted her into the saddle, and Meg put her feet in the stirrups and took hold of the reins. Then they were galloping—confirmation that this was a dream as Meg had balked at the prospect of trotting—across the fields.

The sun was shining down on them, her hair streaming out behind her, laughter dancing on the breeze. When they stopped to rest the horses, Flynn spread a blanket out on green grass dotted with yellow wildflowers. She stretched out on the blanket, staring up at the blue sky, and started to protest when he leaned over her, blocking the sun. Then his mouth brushed over hers and her eyes drifted shut on a sigh.

"Megan?"

Most of her friends and family called her Meg. Only Flynn regularly used the longer form of her name, and she liked the way it sounded from his lips.

"Mmm," she responded, wishing he would kiss her again.

"Can I get you anything?"

"More."

There was a pause before he said, "More what?"

But obviously he knew, because suddenly he was kissing her again. And then, even more suddenly, they were both naked. She let her hands roam over his body as freely as his roamed over hers, but the image in her mind was fuzzy, like a camera lens not quite in focus.

But of course she couldn't get all the details right, because she'd never seen Flynn naked. And she shouldn't be dreaming about him naked now.

Maybe she would have been embarrassed to realize that she was having a sex dream about a man who was one of her best friends—and surprised that she could be inspired to have a sex dream at all when her recent intimate experiences had been anything but satisfactory—but it was only a dream.

Instead, she exhaled another blissful sigh and slipped deeper into the fantasy.

Flynn quietly closed Meg's bedroom door, to ensure she wouldn't be disturbed by his reading aloud to Emma. He was a little concerned that the little girl's mom had been out for so long, but he decided to leave her be and focus on her daughter's bedtime routine.

"Did you pick out two books?" he asked Emma.

She held them up.

The Day the Crayons Quit and *Grumpy Monkey.*

"And which one do you want to start with?"

She looked back and forth between the two books in her hand, then handed him the one about the crayons.

He settled in the "story chair"—an old-fashioned wooden rocker in the corner of her room—and Emma crawled into his lap, her favorite stuffy—a mottled pink bunny with long ears—tucked under one arm and leaned her head back against his shoulder.

He opened the cover of the book and began to read, immediately charmed by the concept of the story. (Though he realized, as he enumerated the complaints of red crayon, the title should have been a pretty big clue.)

"This is a long book," Flynn remarked, realizing they were only about halfway through. Probably because Emma interjected with her own stories about what she used each color for, which made the telling take much longer than it was meant to. "I don't think you're going to be able to stay awake for the second one."

"I'll be awake," she said confidently, rubbing her eyes with the back of her hand.

She fell asleep before the second story was finished, but he continued reading to the end, wanting to know if Jim Panzee would ever recognize that he was, in fact, a grumpy monkey. (Spoiler alert: He did. And, more important, he realized that it was okay to be grumpy sometimes.)

Then Flynn set the books aside and carried Emma the short distance to her bed. Beside her bed was a child's desk and, above the desk, the magnetic whiteboard Meg had told him about. And sure enough, there was the paper valentine he'd made for her, along with a "Happy Helper" certificate from her preschool, a My Little Pony coloring page and a photo of Emma with her mom in front of a Christmas tree.

The little girl stirred as he settled her on her pillow and tucked the covers around her, her eyelids flickering. "Unca Flynn?"

"What do you need, sweetie?"

"Nothin'," she said. "I just wanted to say g'night."

"Good night," he echoed.

"Love you."

He touched his lips to her forehead. "Love you more."

She was smiling as she drifted off to sleep again.

He tiptoed out of the room, marveling that the first female he'd ever said those words to since Angela Davey in tenth grade was a sassy preschooler.

But the truth was, his affection for Emma was a lot deeper and more real than anything he'd felt for his tenth-grade girlfriend. He'd only said the words to Angela because she'd said them first and because he wanted to get into her pants. And yeah, he knew that was crass and crude, but sixteen-year-old boys had a tendency to think with their hormones rather than their brains.

There had been other girls—and women—after Angela, but he'd never again invoked the L-word, because he hadn't felt comfortable using it when he wasn't certain he felt it. Anyway, he'd gone straight into the military after high school graduation. Army training had changed him, mentally even more than physically, but it was the hard body that women noticed when he came home. (He'd already been strong, as a result of working on the ranch for so many years, but it was his military training that packed on the muscle.) That made the ones who'd given him a pass in high school now take a second look.

He'd hooked up with Angela again. Not because he'd loved her but because he'd wanted to thank her for not being one of those girls. And by the time he went back to Georgia, she'd been thoroughly convinced of his gratitude.

The next time he came home, Angela was engaged. And so, when he caught some of those other girls looking, he sometimes looked back—and sometimes the looking led to more.

Of course, the first stop Ellis always made on his trips home was to see Caitlyn Blackstone. He'd fallen head over heels for Caitlyn in seventh grade and never looked back. Flynn used to tell his friend that he didn't know what he was missing out on—that the world offered up a smorgasbord of beautiful, willing women and he was still filling his plate at the salad bar. (Not that Flynn didn't think Caitlyn was great—because she was. He just couldn't fathom, especially at that age, the idea of being with only one woman for the rest of his life.)

Ellis was never bothered by his teasing—or the least bit

tempted by any other woman. For him, it had always been Caitlyn. So he told Flynn to enjoy the smorgasbord, because while a sample of this and a bit of that might seem appealing, when he finally met the right woman, he'd know how much more fulfilling it was to be with someone he loved and who loved him back.

Flynn had been skeptical that the happily-ever-after kind of love even existed, but Ellis and Caitlyn certainly presented a solid argument in its favor—at least for a while. And now Holt and Tess made another compelling case.

But maybe Flynn wasn't capable of that depth of emotion—at least not in a romantic context. Or maybe he'd simply lost interest in playing the games that men and women played, because he hadn't been involved with a woman since his return. Of course, in the early days, he hadn't been able to get himself out of bed so the idea of seducing a woman into one had been way down his list of priorities.

When he'd recovered enough to be out and about, he caught some of those familiar lingering looks. But he wasn't sixteen anymore—or even eighteen or twenty. He was thirty-three now and felt twice that age some days.

Physically, he was healed. Mentally and emotionally, he was still very much a work in progress—a fact that his mother had recognized long before he did and the reason she'd pushed him to attend the support group where he'd met Megan.

The concept of "a safe and supportive gathering place for survivors of trauma" was good but almost too broad in scope to offer real help to anyone in need of it. Talking to Meg had done more for Flynn than all the sessions he'd attended before they met. And being with Emma had lifted enough of the clouds to bring color back into his gray world.

The little girl loved so freely it was impossible not to love her back; Flynn's feelings for Emma's mom weren't nearly as simple.

Megan was one of his best friends. Someone he could talk

to about almost anything but also someone that he could simply be with without feeling the need to talk. With Megan, silence could be comfortable, even comforting.

Until the kiss that wasn't really a kiss.

Since then, he'd been feeling other things that didn't strictly fall under the heading of friendship. Since then, every touch—however casual or innocent—seemed to reverberate through his system.

He'd always known and appreciated that she was beautiful, smart, sexy, kind and caring. But while those had previously been characteristics of his friend, they were now attributes of the woman he couldn't get out of his mind.

They'd been friends for a long time, so why was he looking at her differently now? Why was his body suddenly achingly aware of the fact that she was a desirable woman?

He didn't know the answers to any of those questions.

What he did know was that it was a difficult juggling act, pretending that nothing had changed when it felt as if everything had. And he didn't know how long he could keep the balls in the air before they all came crashing down.

Meg jolted awake—startled to discover sunlight streaming into the room through her open curtains. Obviously, she'd forgotten to close them before she'd gone to bed the night before. And apparently forgotten to change into her pajamas, too, as she was still wearing her hospital scrubs.

She squinted at the glowing numbers on the clock beside her bed: 7:12.

Not only had she slept through the night—she'd slept more than twelve hours. And during that time, she'd had some interesting dreams...but she didn't have time to wonder about those dreams now—there was only one thought in her mind:

Emma.

She threw back the covers and darted across the hall to her

daughter's room, her heart rate accelerating even more when she found the little girl's bed was empty.

"Emma!" She raced down the stairs. "Emma!"

Flynn stepped out of the kitchen, a spatula in hand. "Breathe, Megan."

"Emma," she said again.

"She's at the table having her breakfast," he said, gesturing with the utensil.

Meg paused for a brief moment to press a hand against her chest, where her heart was pounding so hard it threatened to break through her ribs. She started to move past him, needing to see for herself that Emma was there. Safe.

But Flynn shifted to block her path.

"Give yourself a minute," he urged softly. "If you go storming in there looking panicked, you're going to scare her."

"You're right." She drew in a long, deep breath. Exhaled slowly. Emma had endured enough scary things in her short life—she didn't need her mom to be one of them. "I didn't realize you were here. I didn't expect… Did you stay? Or did you come back?"

"I stayed," he admitted. "You were sawing logs so loudly when we got back from Tiny Tumblers, I wasn't sure you'd hear Em in the night if she woke up and needed anything."

"I was *snoring*?" she asked, appalled.

"Sawing logs might have been an exaggeration," he allowed. "But when I checked on you, I heard some soft sighs and murmurs that made me think you were in the middle of an interesting dream."

"I don't dream."

"Then why are your cheeks red?"

"My cheeks aren't red," she denied, though she could feel them burning.

His gaze narrowed thoughtfully. "Megan Wheeler…did you have a *sex dream* last night?"

"No!"

"I think you did."

"Well, if I did, I don't remember," she told him. "I don't remember anything from the minute my head hit the pillow. I didn't even hear you guys leave—or come back."

"You obviously needed the sleep."

"I did," she agreed. "But even so, I shouldn't have imposed on you to take care of my daughter."

"You didn't impose, I offered," he reminded her.

"Still."

"And it would have been okay if you'd asked. Being a single mom doesn't mean you have to do every single thing on your own."

"Yes, it does," she said. "Because as soon as I start to rely on anyone else, they let me down."

His brows lifted. "Surely you're not including Tess in that collective?"

She flushed. "Of course not."

But maybe she was. Although her friend certainly had valid—and wonderful—reasons for not being available to Meg these days, it was an undeniable fact that Meg had relied on Tess to be there to help out and now she was gone. And, of course, she understood why, but perhaps there was a tiny part of her that felt abandoned nonetheless.

"Can I see my daughter now?"

Flynn stepped aside so that she could enter the kitchen.

"Good morning," Meg said, greeting her daughter in a singsong voice.

"Mama!" The little girl's enthusiastic response and bright smile smoothed the last of her ruffled edges. "Are you feeling better today?"

"Much better." She dropped a kiss on the top of her daughter's head, then glanced at her plate. "What have you got there?"

"Unca Flynn made teddy bear pancakes."

"Teddy bear pancakes, huh?" She looked at the creative arrangement on her daughter's plate—a big circle for the head, two smaller circles for the ears and a third small circle in the middle of the head to represent the snout, with the eyes and nose/mouth details drawn on with chocolate sauce.

"Clever," she said.

"Google can teach you how to do almost anything," Flynn said modestly.

"Apparently," she agreed, before shifting her attention back to Emma. "But your teddy bear seems to be missing an ear."

"'Cuz I ate it!"

"Do you want a teddy bear pancake?" Flynn asked Meg.

"Thanks, but I'm fine," she said, taking a seat at the table across from her daughter.

Flynn made a cup of coffee for her. And poured a glass of juice. Then he set a plate of pancakes—an unassembled teddy bear—in front of her.

"Eat," he said.

"I don't need you to take care of me, Flynn."

"I know. But you do need to eat because you didn't last night."

Because it was true—and the fluffy golden pancakes smelled as good as they looked—she picked up her knife and fork.

And when she'd all but licked her plate clean, Flynn loaded it up again.

"You skipped dinner," he reminded her, when she sent him a quizzical look.

"And you slept on that tiny sofa," she said, as she poured syrup over the second stack of pancakes.

"I've slept in worse places," he pointed out.

"But why wouldn't you sleep in the bed upstairs?"

"Because I wasn't sure that I'd be able to hear Emma from up there, if she woke up and needed something."

He brought his mug of coffee to the table and sat down across from her.

"Aren't you having pancakes?"

"I ate already," he said.

"And will use that as an excuse to stock my refrigerator," she guessed.

"You are low on milk. And cheese. And completely out of bacon. I made a list," he explained. "I'll stop by the grocery store this morning."

"I should insist on doing my own shopping, but what's the point?"

"Are you always this agreeable after twelve hours of sleep?"

"I wouldn't know." She pushed away from the table and loaded her dishes in the dishwasher.

Flynn added his now-empty mug to the top rack.

After what happened last time, Meg didn't dare attempt to kiss his cheek. But she wanted to show her appreciation and decided that a hug would be safe.

"Thank you," she said, and stepped forward to put her arms around him, as he'd put his arms around her a few weeks earlier when she'd confessed to yelling at the surgeon.

He hugged her back—"You're welcome."—and gave her an extra squeeze that had the effect of bringing their bodies into alignment, from shoulders to thighs and all the erogenous zones in between.

When they drew apart, the air was crackling again.

Note to self: hugs are not *safe.*

Meg took a single step back, then another. Cleared her throat. "I really do appreciate…everything."

He nodded. "I'm not usually one to keep score, but after last night, I think maybe you do owe me one."

She eagerly jumped at the opportunity to steer the conversation onto safer ground. "Were the moms a little much?"

"Let's just say I won't be volunteering to take Emma to Tiny Tumblers again anytime soon."

"How many numbers did you get?"

"They weren't *that* obvious."

She had to smile at that. "I need to get ready for work and get Emma ready for school, but you should check your pockets," she told him.

Though dubious, Flynn did as she'd suggested and found two business cards and a receipt from Scoops with a name and number scrawled on the back.

He tossed them in the trash.

He already had the only number he wanted.

Chapter Fifteen

Ten months earlier

"We'd been warned that we'd be going in dark. Literally and figuratively," Flynn said. "Our squad leader received the intel about the hostages too late to go through the proper channels and secure the required permissions for the mission, which we're required to do in absence of a formal bilateral agreement or treaty. It's a pain in the ass to jump through political hoops, but it's essential to respect the sovereignty of the host country and avoid taking any action that might be construed as aggression."

He and Megan were having another of their late-night telephone conversations and he was finally telling her—as much as he could—about his last mission in a country he identified only as "foreign territory."

"But if we were going to rescue the hostages—and we were determined to do so—then we needed to act fast, before they were moved again."

"Can you tell me who the hostages were?" she asked. "POWs? Political prisoners?"

"Nothing like that," he said. "Just five humanitarian aid workers who'd been delivering food and medicine to a village ravaged by civil war when they were kidnapped by guerillas who planned to ransom them to fund their insurrection."

"I guess the guerillas didn't know that most governments don't negotiate with terrorists," she mused.

"No," he agreed. "But we knew that if the negotiations stalled at any point, they'd kill the hostages without blinking an eye.

"That's why we were going in dark—without the use of any communication devices—to eliminate the possibility of interception by either the guerillas or the host country—and under the cover of darkness—to increase our chances of getting in and out without being discovered.

"And that was why the extraction team, while waiting for night to fall, was sitting around twiddling our thumbs—and secretly praying that the kidnappers didn't get itchy trigger fingers.

"Wolf was passing the time reading, and seemed to be about midway through a battered paperback that he'd been carrying in his pocket for the better part of a year; Ghost was whittling, attempting to turn a piece of wood into a facsimile of a dog with his combat knife; Striker was having a nap, or at least pretending to; and me and Ellis were playing Go Fish."

"Go Fish?" she echoed curiously.

He shrugged. "A lot of the cards had gone missing from the deck, so it wasn't good for much else," he explained. And then, thinking of the adorable little girl he'd met at the toy store a few weeks earlier, he asked, "Does Emma know how to play?"

"She's just starting to learn."

"Anyway, that's what we were doing when Ellis told me he was done—that our current mission was going to be his last," Flynn said. "I wasn't surprised. Over the past several months, I'd started to suspect that he was leaning in that direction, that he'd only stayed with Bravo Group as long as he had because the money was decent.

"I teased him about wanting to go home to buy the house that Caitlyn sent him pictures of and start a family with her, and he confirmed that was his plan.

"It was a good plan," he acknowledged now. "And I told him so. He'd expected me to be mad—or maybe disappointed—that he was bailing on the team, but I assured him that I might want to go home, too, if I had someone like Caitlyn to go home to. I even suggested that maybe she could set me up with one of her friends, and he reminded me that she'd tried that once."

He smiled a little at the memory of Selena Alamilla—a pretty brunette with dark eyes and perky breasts. Flynn had enjoyed her company and appreciated her sassy attitude, even when she'd bluntly told him that she had no intention of sleeping with a guy who was fool enough to sign up to be target practice for terrorists in a foreign country.

"Obviously that set-up didn't work out," Megan remarked lightly.

"No," Flynn agreed. "But Ellis promised that if I ever did find a woman who made me believe in happily-ever-after, he'd be the best man at my wedding. Just like I—"

"Promised to be his?" Megan guessed, when he abruptly severed his comment.

"Yeah," he agreed, aware that he'd already said too much.

But she was so easy to talk to—that rare person who listened and offered support without judgment. Still there were some things he couldn't tell her. Some secrets that weren't his to share.

Chapter Sixteen

With each day that passed—every text message they exchanged, every late-night conversation they had, every cup of coffee they shared—it was getting harder and harder for Meg to deny that she had feelings for Flynn.

The problem—and she felt guilty even thinking about it as a problem—was that Flynn had been around a lot lately. Since he'd started working for the sheriff's department, he was in town more days than not and usually found a reason to stop by. And Emma, who absolutely adored him, was always thrilled by his visits, which meant there was no way Meg could ask him to stop coming around. Especially now that she'd given him a key.

Not to mention that she'd miss him, too, if she didn't see him. She just needed to stop thinking about his deliciously kissable lips and tightly muscled body—and block from her mind the far too tempting image of the sexiest man she'd ever known standing in her kitchen making pancakes.

The best way to do that, she decided, was to turn the attention of her reawakened hormones in a different direction. Because it was possible—probable even—that her sudden awareness of Flynn wasn't about him specifically so much as proximity to a healthy, virile man.

With that thought in mind, she'd resolved that the next time Emma went for a sleepover at her grandparents' house, she'd get dressed up and go out and be open to whatever might happen.

That was the reason she was rifling through her closet now,

looking for something appropriate to wear. Which, for a night at Denim & Diamonds, meant something inappropriate.

When was the last time she'd worn something inappropriate? she wondered, as she considered and discarded one article of clothing after another.

No doubt it was before Emma was born.

In fact, it was most likely the night her daughter was conceived.

At the back of her closet, she found a denim skirt from those long-ago days.

A very short denim skirt.

Meg eyed it dubiously, but as her options were limited, she discarded her jeans and pulled on the skirt, more than a little surprised to discover that it still fit. (Perhaps "fit" was a bit of a misnomer, but she was able to squeeze herself into it and tug the zipper into place.) And when she paired the skirt with a cute little cropped sweater with a deep V-neck, then slid her feet into also-very-old cowboy boots, she looked as if she might fit right in at the local honkytonk. And that was the point, wasn't it?

She nibbled on her lip as she stared at her reflection in the mirror.

Could she really pull this off?

She was a mother of an almost-five-year-old daughter—didn't that prove she was too old to be wearing a miniskirt?

But the number of hours she spent on her feet in the hospital helped keep her in shape, and she'd been blessed with good genes—for which she knew she should thank her maternal grandmother. At seventy-nine, Tallulah Leonard was slim and toned and could easily pass for a woman twenty years younger.

After double-checking her reflection in the mirror, Meg decided that while the outfit was suitably inappropriate, her hair and face needed some attention. Because the habitual ponytail and moisturizing lip gloss that worked for a quick trip to the grocery store weren't going to help her stand out from the crowd at Denim & Diamonds.

Half an hour later, her hair spilled down her back in loose waves and her face was made up with shimmer on her eyelids, mascara on her lashes, a touch of blush to highlight her cheekbones and a lip tint called "Seductress" on her mouth. She'd chosen the color in the hope it might bolster her courage to follow through with her evening plans, but she feared the knots already twisting in her belly would have the opposite effect.

In any event, she was ready—or as ready as she'd ever be—so she put some cash, a credit card and ID into a slim cardholder, tucked that into the front pocket of her skirt, and reached into the closet for her coat. She considered driving to the bar but immediately dismissed the idea. Not because she planned to overindulge but because she knew the parking lot filled up quickly and she wasn't confident that she'd be able to get her vehicle out later in the night.

Though Denim & Diamonds wasn't a far walk, it was a rather chilly night, so she passed on that plan, too, instead opening her rideshare app and crossing her fingers. The mayor had heralded the arrival of Uber in Whispering Canyon as a sign of the town's growing stature and status, but at last count, there were only four drivers in the area. So it was a pleasant surprise to get a response that "Trevor" was available, and Meg quickly tapped the screen to book the ride. Ten minutes later, she stepped out of the silver Toyota and made her way to the front doors of Denim & Diamonds.

There was always a cover charge on weekends to pay for the musical entertainment, and according to the flyers plastered on the boards outside, tonight it was a Canyon Creek Trio cover band that would be playing. It didn't seem so long ago that the original Canyon Creek Trio had played here, Meg mused. Now they had half a dozen albums, numerous industry awards, and were playing sold-out tours across the country and inspiring other musicians.

She presented her ID and the requisite ten dollars to the heavily muscled bouncer. He glanced at the photo on her driver's license, his expression changing from one of boredom to one of interest as his eyes moved slowly down the length of her body and back up again.

Perhaps she should have felt flattered. Instead, Meg felt mildly ill and honestly considered turning around and walking out the door again.

"What time does the band go on?" she asked in a conversational tone, pretending she wasn't unnerved by the intensity of his stare.

"First set is at ten."

She glanced at her watch, saw that it was barely nine o'clock.

"You're an early bird tonight," the bouncer noted.

"The early bird gets the worm," she responded lightly.

"Maybe. But if you're looking for something a lot more substantial than a worm—" he wiggled his thick brows suggestively "—I clock out at two."

"I'll keep that in mind," she said, and made her escape.

Early bird, indeed, she mused, noting that there were barely a handful of patrons in a room that would be bursting at the seams by midnight.

Back in the day, she and her friends wouldn't have headed out until ten o'clock, sometimes later. But they'd all been a lot younger then. Young and carefree with no responsibilities.

She wasn't that person anymore—and she wasn't sorry. She loved her life—her daughter, her career, her family and friends.

So why wasn't she satisfied?

Why was she there?

Going to a bar to pick up a man to scratch an inconvenient itch wasn't like her. But maybe that was because it had been a long time since she'd felt that itch, and she blamed Flynn for the one that she was dealing with now.

And *that* was why she was there. To find someone else—*anyone else*—to help her forget about the man who suddenly preoccupied far too many of her thoughts.

She maneuvered herself onto a stool at the bar—not an easy task in the short skirt—and asked the female bartender for a Sierra Nevada Pale Ale. Meg wasn't much of a beer drinker—or much of a drinker at all—but she suspected it was smarter to drink from a bottle than to trust the cleanliness of a glass.

She'd taken a first sip when a group of reasonably attractive men came in and settled at a table near the edge of the dance floor.

Regulars, she guessed, as the bartender was already filling a pitcher from one of the taps. One of the men draped his jacket over the back of a chair before making his way over to collect the pitcher and half a dozen glasses, proving that he and his buddies were braver than Meg.

Firefighters, she noted, recognizing the insignia embroidered on the navy T-shirt that stretched across his broad chest. Men who risked their lives in burning buildings weren't likely to be daunted by the prospect of some bacterial E. coli or viral hepatitis.

Of course, thinking of firefighters risking their lives reminded her of the brave young man who'd lost his in the OR a few weeks earlier and made her decide to look elsewhere for companionship. Even if the admittedly hunky man with the pitcher and glasses caught her eye and winked at her.

Meg was too startled to immediately respond, and by the time she managed to curve her lips into a smile, he was already back at his table, pouring beer for his friends.

She sighed. "Maybe this was a bad idea."

"It usually is," the bartender agreed, as she sliced a lime into narrow wedges.

"I've got an almost-five-year-old daughter at home," she said, and immediately felt self-conscious for blurting out the information as if it was a guilty confession.

"With a babysitter, I hope."

Meg couldn't help but laugh at the other woman's dry tone. "Actually, she's at her grandparents' house tonight."

Another lime was sacrificed to the knife. "Then you've got nothing to worry about."

"Nothing…except that I don't do things like this."

"Have a beer in a bar on a Friday night?"

"That, too," Meg agreed, lifting the bottle to her lips.

The wedges of fruit were dumped into a plastic container. "Whatever your reasons for being here tonight, remember that you're the only one who gets to make decisions for you. Whether the question is 'Can I buy you a drink?' or 'Do you want to dance?' or 'Your place or mine?'"

Meg nodded. "I'll remember."

"And if anyone makes you feel uncomfortable, you let me know."

"Okay. Thanks."

"I'm Selena, by the way."

"Megan," she said.

"For what it's worth, Garry's a good guy," Selena told her.

"Who?"

"The cute firefighter who winked at you. He's an outrageous flirt but loyal to his wife, so if you're looking for more than a flirtation, you'd be better off with Caleb or Marco."

"I don't know what I'm looking for," Meg hedged.

"No one comes here unless they know what they're looking for," the bartender chided.

She felt her cheeks flush. "You're right. But I'm really out of practice."

"It won't matter," Selena assured her, as she popped the caps on three vodka coolers for the trio of women who made their way to the bar in a cloud of hairspray and perfume. "Just sit tight and let them come to you—and they will."

Meg took another sip of her beer.

"Sooner rather than later, I'd bet," the bartender mused as an extremely handsome—and very young-looking—guy sidled up to the bar beside Meg. He wore a plaid flannel shirt tucked into well-worn Levi's with an oversized silver buckle on his belt, black-leather cowboy boots on his feet and a matching hat on his head.

He lifted a finger to tip up the brim of his hat—perhaps a gesture of greeting or perhaps to ensure she had an unobstructed view of his deep blue eyes and megawatt smile. Seriously, the man looked like he'd walked right out of central casting to fill the role of "handsome cowboy" on a movie set. So much so, it was impossible not to appreciate how good-looking he was, even if his nearness didn't elicit any tingles.

"Howdy," he said to her now.

"Howdy," she responded, trying not to giggle.

"Can I buy you a drink?"

"Are you even old enough to buy the drink you're offering?" she wondered aloud.

A hint of color tinged the cowboy's sharp cheekbones. "I'm twenty-five."

"Let's see the ID," Selena suggested.

"I already showed it at the door."

"And I'm asking you to show it again."

Grumbling a little, he retrieved his wallet from a back pocket, then pulled out a card.

"A bona fide state-issued driver's license that shows your age as…twenty-four," the bartender noted.

"I'll be twenty-five in a few months," he said.

"If ten months is a few," Selena agreed.

To Meg, she said, "Old enough to buy you another beer, anyway—if you want."

"I'm not even half finished with this one," Meg noted. "But you're welcome to buy a drink for yourself and keep me company, cowboy."

He grinned and settled on the stool beside her, and she tried not to think about the fact that this seemingly very young man was the same age she'd been when she had Emma.

And though she was only twenty-nine now, she couldn't help but feel that she had a lot more life experience than the cowboy sitting next to her—and not only because she'd been married and had a child.

"I'll have a bourbon," he said to the bartender.

"Rocks or neat?" she asked.

He looked at Selena blankly.

"Ice or no ice?" she clarified for him.

"Uh…ice?"

She dropped three cubes into a glass, then added a splash of the requested whiskey.

"So…what do you do?" Meg asked, picking up the dropped thread of their conversation.

"You mean for a job?"

"Yes, for a job," she confirmed, as Selena set his drink on a paper coaster.

"I'm a cowboy."

As he picked up the glass, Meg found herself wondering if he could handle his alcohol. Daymond had usually stayed pretty mellow when he was drinking beer, but when he hit the harder stuff, he got mean.

She pushed those dark memories to the back of her mind and refocused her attention on the cowboy beside her. "Ranch hand or wrangler or rodeo?"

"I worked on a few different ranches—starting in Nevada, then Idaho, Montana and Wyoming. But I'm on the circuit now." He lifted his glass to his lips, swallowed a mouthful of the bourbon, then gasped and sputtered as the whiskey burned his throat.

Meg lifted her bottle to her lips, so he wouldn't see the smile that tugged at her lips.

"Are you from Nevada then?" she asked, when he stopped sputtering.

"California, actually." He cleared his throat. "You?"

"Born and raised in Wyoming," she told him. "Right here in Whispering Canyon, as a matter of fact."

"And what do you do—for a job?"

"I'm a nurse."

"For real?"

"For real," she confirmed.

He wiggled his eyebrows. "Wanna play doctor?"

She resisted—barely—the urge to roll her eyes. "That's like asking a sous chef to take charge of the kitchen on her day off."

"Huh?"

"Never mind," she said. "Where'd you work in Wyoming?"

"Outside of Cody. A place called The Square Peg," he told her. "That's where I met a couple of guys who talked me into trying out the rodeo circuit."

She was glad he hadn't said West River Ranch. It would be weird if he'd worked alongside Flynn.

Even as the idea formed in her mind, she shoved it aside, unwilling to spare even a peripheral thought to the deputy tonight.

"Do you come here often?" the cowboy asked her now.

"No."

"It's my first time," he said. "I mean, my first time in the bar. Not my first time with a girl. I've been with lots of girls. Well, lots of times with one girl—Darla Reynolds, from high school. Then we broke up, and I've been with lots of girls since. Not at the same time, though. Just one at a time. Most of the time."

"I have no idea how to respond to that," Meg admitted.

"Then let me say that you're the prettiest girl I've seen in my travels across three states."

"I'm flattered, but I'm not going to sleep with you."

"I don't want to sleep with you," he said. "I just want to have sex with you."

"Well, that's not going to happen, either," she told him.

"You sure?"

"One hundred percent."

He frowned at that, and she wondered if it was possible the man had never struck out with a woman before.

Judging by his looks, she decided it was possible. Judging by his conversational skills, on the other hand, it was possible he was simply unaware of it.

"Did you ever tell me your name?" she asked the cowboy now.

"Bucky," he said. "You know—like Bucky Barnes, the Winter Soldier."

Someone else approached from Bucky's other side and slapped him on the back, a little too hard to be considered a strictly friendly gesture. "Or like a cowboy who can't stay on the back of a bronc for eight seconds without getting bucked off."

And Bucky's cheekbones turned pink again.

"I'm Cash," the newcomer said to Meg, propping his elbow on the bar to lean close to her. "Because I always finish with the purse, and also because that's the name my mama gave me. She was a big fan of The Man in Black."

"You don't say," Meg replied.

"So...you wanna dance?" Cash asked, clearly unconcerned that he was hitting on a woman who'd been chatting with his friend.

"Actually, I do," she said. "With Bucky."

The annoyance on the young cowboy's face lifted then, and he sent a triumphant look in Cash's direction before he followed Meg to the dance floor.

Flynn spotted her the minute he walked through the door.

Not that he recognized her straight away.

No, what he spotted was a curvy blonde in a short skirt that hugged her shapely butt and emphasized her long, toned legs. As his gaze skimmed over her, his blood heated and his body tightened in a way that surprised him.

He hadn't had such an immediate and visceral reaction to a woman in a very long time. Well, disregarding his unexpected response to Megan's even more unexpected kiss. It was as if that kiss had been a lighted match to a candle, igniting desires he'd started to think had gone MIA in Azerbaijan.

Which was the reason he was there.

The fact that he was responding to another woman—a stranger—reassured him that coming to Denim & Diamonds had been the right decision. He would talk to and flirt with women who weren't off-limits and maybe, if he was lucky, he wouldn't go home alone tonight.

He continued to watch the blonde move, admiring the way she rocked her hips and stomped her feet. She was flanked by two men, but the nature of line dancing made it difficult to tell if she was with either of them. He decided that if she left the dance floor alone, it meant the path was clear for him to make a move. If he remembered how to make a move.

Then the line of dancers pivoted, and he got his first glimpse of the blonde's face. His jaw hit the floor and a single word—a profanity that had once earned him a mouthful of soap when his grandmother heard him use it—echoed inside his head.

Because it was Megan.

Of course the woman he'd come there to forget was the same one who'd immediately snagged his attention.

But what was she doing there?

The answer was obvious—she was there for the same reason he was, the same reason that most people showed up at Denim & Diamonds—to find someone to hook up with.

Of course, it was possible she was there for the live music. Maybe she was friends with someone in the band. But the way she was dancing and flirting with the guys around her seemed to dispel that theory. And watching her dance and flirt with those other guys made him feel…

The truth was, he wasn't sure what he was feeling.

Or maybe he was reluctant to put a label on his feelings.

In any event, she shouldn't be there. She was a hardworking and devoted single mom to an adorable little girl. She wasn't the type of woman who hooked up with a stranger in a bar.

Was she?

The truth was, even with all the time he'd been spending at her place lately, helping out with odd jobs or with Emma, he really didn't know much about Megan's personal life, and the little that he did know was only what she'd told him. Which was that she hadn't dated much since her marriage had fallen apart and only two of the guys she'd gone out with had made it as far as her front door at the end of the night—and none beyond that threshold. All of which had led him to conclude that Megan didn't do casual hookups.

So what was she doing at the local country bar renowned for its hookup culture as much as its cheap beer?

And why did he want to drag her out of the bar and hide her away from the leering eyes and grasping hands of every other man in attendance?

Away somewhere that he could have her for himself.

Because apparently he wasn't just feeling protective but proprietary, even if he knew that he had no right. That she could never be his—because he didn't want the responsibility of a relationship with a woman like Megan. A woman with a kind and caring heart that, if she ever offered it to him, he'd only break. Because he didn't know how to do anything else.

And the last thing he ever wanted to do was hurt Megan.

But he couldn't deny that he wanted her.

Or maybe he just needed an outlet for the sexual frustration that had plagued him of late—ever since that awkward almost-kiss on Valentine's Day. A sexual frustration further exacerbated by the not-at-all-awkward hug they'd shared after teddy bear pancakes that had made him marvel at how good she'd felt pressed against him. Almost as if she was meant to be in his arms.

Which was bullshit, of course.

Or maybe it wasn't.

Maybe he was simply too much of a coward to admit that in his arms was exactly where she was meant to be.

And then, as if he needed more proof of his cowardice, he tore his gaze away from Megan and made his way to the far side of the room to watch the band set up.

Chapter Seventeen

It didn't take Meg long to realize that Bucky knew as much about dancing as he did about whiskey. He shuffled along as he watched her move to the music, performing a basic grapevine step that seemed beyond his comprehension. With a look of apology to the man on her other side, Meg nudged Bucky out of the line to demonstrate the simple moves where he wouldn't step on or elbow anyone.

"Start with your feet together and your arms relaxed at your sides."

He shuffled his feet closer together but didn't look relaxed.

"Now step out with your right foot."

She demonstrated, facing him, and he copied.

"Your *right* foot," she said again, tapping his leg just above the knee.

"Right. Sorry." He pulled his left foot back into position and stepped out with his right.

"Now you're going to move your left foot behind your right foot."

As he did so, he caught the toe of his left boot on the heel of his right and stumbled.

"I thought line dancing was supposed to be easy," he grumbled.

"Once you get the hang of the basic steps, it *is* easy."

"I've got a better idea," he said. "How 'bout we forget the stupid dance and go out to my truck?"

"The dance is easy," she told him. "I'm not."

"C'mon, darlin'." His tone was cajoling, his smile confident.

"Did you forget the part of our earlier conversation where I said I wasn't going to have sex with you?"

"No," he said. "But that was before you asked me to dance."

"And you thought 'dance' was code for 'sex'?"

He shrugged. "Most women I meet want to have sex with me."

"Then you should feel confident you'll find someone else who does," she said, and walked away.

"I didn't think that was going to last," Selena said, when Meg returned to her previous seat at the bar.

"Guys like that are why I don't date."

"Maybe not the sharpest knife in the drawer, but certainly a pleasure to look at."

"I can't argue with that," Meg agreed. "But—and this might be a character flaw on my part—I generally prefer to keep company with men I can actually have a conversation with."

"A rare breed," Selena said. "But this might be your lucky day, because one of those walked through the door about five minutes ago."

"Really?" Meg turned her head in the direction the bartender was looking—and winced. "Deputy Chandler?"

"One of the truly good guys," Selena confirmed.

"Do you know him well?" she asked curiously.

"I was head over heels in love with him for about five minutes in high school."

"Five minutes, huh? That would dispel any romantic illusions."

The bartender laughed. "That's not what I meant."

"What did you mean?"

"His best friend dated my best friend, so we spent a fair amount of time together. But even then, he'd been clear about his plans to join the army, and I had no intention of being one of those girls who waited at home, wringing her hands and waiting for her guy to return. Or worse—who willingly sacrificed her virtue for a guy just because he was willing to sacrifice his life.

"Caitlyn never shared my concerns. Or maybe she was too far gone over Ellis to pull back." Selena shrugged. "Anyway, a few days after graduation, the boys shipped off to basic training. A few months after that, they deployed to I-have-no-idea-where and, if Caitlyn knew, she didn't tell me. In any event, I'd already moved on.

"Flynn came back…maybe a year and a half ago? But Ellis didn't come with him. I don't think Caitlyn has moved on, but she did move to Riverton, to be closer to her family." The bartender continued her story as she filled a glass with ice, then topped it with Coke from the soda dispenser and passed it across the bar to a customer. "We keep in touch, though, which is how I know Flynn still checks in with her periodically, too, to make sure she's okay."

"A rare breed, indeed," Meg mused.

"I'd be happy to make an introduction, if you want," Selena said.

"No, thanks."

And perhaps her response was a little too quick—or vehement—because the bartender gave her a quizzical look.

"I mean, maybe later." She smiled at Cash when he sidled up to the bar again. "Right now, I owe this cowboy a dance."

Flynn waited until Meg returned to the dance floor to make his way to the bar.

"Hey, stranger," Selena said. "Haven't seen you around here in a while."

"Haven't been here in a while," he told her.

"What's it been—two years? Three?"

"Close to three." He glanced at the labels on the taps.

"Anything catch your eye?" she asked with a playful wink.

"I'll have a Teton Amber Ale," he decided.

She tipped a glass beneath the spout. "Rumor has it that you're taking down bad guys here at home now."

"Just the other day, I thwarted a crime in progress—*and* got a sobbing confession from the criminal."

"Yeah, I heard you caught nine-year-old Parker Kent stealing a pack of gum and made him cry."

"All in a day's work," he said.

"And the citizens of Whispering Canyon appreciate your dedicated service."

He handed her a ten-dollar bill in exchange for the beer she set in front of him.

"I've seen you cruising down Oakridge—oftentimes when I'm getting home from a late shift. Looking out for me, Deputy?"

"Part of the job," he said. "Is it true your parents moved to Puget Sound?"

"Yep. They live on a boat now."

"It's nice that you stayed in the house."

"I thought about selling it." She continued to pour drinks while they chatted. "Picking out curtains and planting flowers aren't really my thing, but apparently I have a nostalgic streak I never knew about until I was walking through the house with the real estate agent."

"Memories of the past can tug pretty hard on the heartstrings," he noted.

She nodded as she counted out change for another customer, her expression sympathetic. "I was sorry to hear about Ellis."

Most people he crossed paths with around town didn't dare speak his cousin's name, not even to offer tentative hope for his return or express condolences for his absence. And if it had been anyone else, Flynn would have abruptly shut the conversation down.

But Selena had known Ellis, and he knew she was being sincere. That she understood how deeply he felt the loss. So instead of snapping that he didn't want or need her sympathy, he simply said, "Thank you," and settled back with his beer to watch the crowd.

The tempo of the music changed. Slowed.

Megan was still out there—or maybe out there again—but she turned now, as if to leave the floor. The man beside her touched a hand to her arm, pausing her retreat. Though Flynn could only see the back of the man's head, it seemed evident he was asking her to dance and, after a brief pause, she nodded.

He'd been so focused on Megan—or trying not to focus on Megan—he hadn't paid any attention to the men around her.

Only now, when she stepped into the arms of her dance partner, did Flynn recognize Cash Walton. Cash was a local ranch hand who'd even worked at West River Ranch for a while, until Austin discovered his employee was in the resale business. As in, he'd take anything he thought might be of value—from the equipment shed, tack room or supply cupboard—and sell it to someone else, with the money going directly into his own pocket.

Austin had urged his grandfather to press charges, but Raylan was concerned that the man had a wife and child to support and wouldn't be able to do so from jail.

Abandoning his beer, Flynn made his way to the dance floor.

"There you are, darlin'," he said, lifting Megan's hand from Walton's shoulder and pulling her into his arms.

"What the hell do you think you're doing, Chandler?" the other man growled.

"Dancing with my girl," he said, giving Megan what he hoped might pass for a look of affection.

"*Your* girl?" Walton glanced at her, as if for confirmation.

"There's no ring on my finger," she assured him.

"A touchy subject, I know, darlin'," Flynn said. "But we'll get there."

Whether or not Walton was convinced, he walked off, muttering something that sounded like, "Damn Chandlers think they own everything."

"You're welcome," Flynn said, when the other man was out of earshot.

She narrowed her gaze on him, those whiskey-colored eyes shooting daggers. "You expect me to thank you for that little scene?"

"And give me credit for quick thinking," he said. "Because I just saved you from a tedious three minutes on the dance floor during which Walton would try to talk you into a disappointing fifteen minutes in the back of his truck."

"Walton? Is that his name?"

"You didn't bother to get his name before you let him put his hand on your ass?"

"He introduced himself as Cash," she told him. "And his hand was in the same place yours is right now."

"Just playing my role," he said smoothly.

"What exactly is your role?" she challenged. "Are you here on official sheriff's department business, Deputy?"

"I'll pull out my badge if that's what I have to do to stop you from making a big mistake," he promised.

"Oh, is that what I can feel—a badge in your front pocket?"

"Careful, Megan. You don't want to push my buttons tonight."

"You don't have the first clue about what I want," she told him. "Which, right now, is for you to back off, because I came here tonight to forget about you."

His brows lifted at that; her cheeks flushed.

"You want to explain that cryptic remark?" he invited.

"No," she said again.

"You've been thinking about me?"

"No."

He felt his lips curve. "Liar."

"Go away, Flynn."

"So you can go back to flirting with Walton?"

"So I can flirt with whoever I want without worrying that you're going to turn into a Neanderthal and drag me out of here by my hair."

"Women like you should come with warning signs," he muttered.

"Warning signs?" she echoed.

"You know—like kids' toys that are only suitable for ages three and up."

"I'm nobody's toy," she assured him coolly.

"No," he agreed. "But I'm discovering that you've got some sharp edges that need to be handled with care."

"If I do, there's no need for you to worry, because you won't be handling them."

"Sharp edges—" he dipped his head to repeat the words, his breath warm against her ear "—and really tempting curves."

She looked at him then, and his gaze locked with hers.

Out of the corner of her eye, she could see the band setting up, heard the sound system crackle as they made adjustments.

Or maybe it was the air around Meg and Flynn that was crackling with electricity.

A muscle in his jaw flexed. "You shouldn't be here, Megan."

"I'm not breaking any laws, Deputy."

"I wouldn't be so sure. That skirt might qualify as an illegal weapon. Or at least a lethal weapon," he amended. "And one that might be the death of me."

She shrugged, playing it cool so he wouldn't guess how intensely affected she was by his nearness and his words. "There are plenty of women in this bar wearing a lot less than me."

"You're probably right," he acknowledged. "But I don't care about any of them."

"Is that what this is about—the fact that you *care* about me?"

"Turns out I've got a lot of feelings churning inside me right now, Megan."

"And you want to talk about those feelings—here and now?" she challenged.

"No," he said. "What I want is for you to go home."

"Well, that's not happening."

And with that parting shot, she turned and made her way back to the bar.

Of course, he followed.

"Can I get another IPA?" Megan asked the bartender.

Selena pulled a bottle from the fridge and pried off the cap.

"Thanks." She tapped her bank card to the electronic reader to pay for her drink.

Flynn frowned. "*Another*? You don't usually have more than one drink in any evening."

"There are a lot of things I don't usually do."

The bartender's gaze shifted between Meg and Flynn, as if she could sense the tension between them. But apparently seeing no cause for concern, she stepped away to serve another customer.

"So maybe you should slow down," he suggested.

"You don't get to tell me what to do, Flynn Chandler. You're not the boss of me."

"No, I'm not," he agreed, his mild tone a contrast to the heat in his gaze. "But if I was, I'd demand that you turn around right now and march your perfect ass right out of here."

That comment took her by surprise.

"You checked out my ass?"

"Darlin', every guy in this bar checked out your ass."

She ignored the heat thrumming in her veins and arched a brow. "*You* said it was perfect."

"Only stating the obvious," he said.

But she noted that his jaw was clenched, that every muscle

in his body seemed to be tensed. And as she shifted closer, she could feel the tension in him and the heat emanating from his body.

"Did you also happen to notice my bare midriff?" she asked, her tone deliberately casual.

His gaze didn't move from her face, but his hands—as if of their own volition—settled at her waist, his callused thumbs stroking her skin, just beneath her ribs, causing goose bumps to rise on her flesh.

"You're playing with fire, Megan," he warned.

"Then it's probably lucky for me that the guys at that table over there—" she gestured with a nod of her head "—are firefighters."

His gaze shifted for the briefest moment before returning to her again. "You like your men young, do you?"

She almost laughed at the question.

The truth was, she hadn't been with a lot of men—and only one since her messy divorce. An ill-advised encounter that had happened only because she hadn't wanted her ex-husband to be the last man to touch her.

But she didn't share any of that with Flynn now. Instead, she shrugged. "Young guys have a lot of energy."

"And not a clue about how to please a woman," he warned.

"Do you know how to please a woman?" she asked.

Something flickered in his gaze—some indecipherable emotion—and then he deliberately removed his hands from her waist. "There was a time when I did."

"And now?"

His gaze shuttered. "Now I'm a broken man only looking to forget that truth for a little while."

"Everyone's broken," she told him. "It's just that some people are better than others at hiding the cracks."

"You're not going to find anyone here who will treat you with the care you deserve," he cautioned.

"Broken doesn't mean fragile, and I don't need you to look out for me."

"Then I won't bother to tell you that the guy you were dancing with is married."

"I noticed the pale band of skin on the third finger of his left hand."

"And didn't care?"

"It was a dance," she pointed out. "And it wasn't going to lead to anything more—not even a disappointing fifteen minutes in the back of his truck."

"Then I will apologize for my…intrusion."

She nodded. "Apology accepted."

Then she turned and walked away—again—and he watched her go.

Watched her hips sway in that tiny skirt as she slipped into the ladies' room…and wanted.

But she'd made it clear that she only wanted him to back off. That he had no right to be annoyed if she let some guy—a stranger—put his hands on her in a public place. No right to want to punch a guy who was obviously staring down her top as he dipped his head toward her, pretending to listen to whatever she was saying.

She was a smart, strong, independent woman, and if she wanted to hook up with some guy she met at the local dive bar, that was her choice.

Like hell it was.

Without conscious thought or decision, he was suddenly making his way across the floor and waiting for her when she exited the ladies' room.

He grabbed her hand. "Let's go."

She didn't say anything.

Nor did she balk or object as he propelled her toward the exit—except to detour by the bar again to grab the coat she'd left there.

But Flynn knew he was making a mistake.

As soon as he took her hand, he knew it.

Or maybe the mistake had been made the moment he realized the really hot woman in the short skirt was Megan Wheeler.

If he'd been smart, he would have turned around and walked out the door right then.

Obviously he wasn't smart.

At least not when it came to this woman.

Surely, Megan had to know this was a mistake, too.

So why wasn't she digging in her heels?

Or at least yanking her hand out of his grasp?

Instead, she was doing her best to keep up with his long-legged strides. As if she was as eager as he was to get out of there. Even when they exited the bar and he pulled her into his arms in the middle of the parking lot, she didn't resist. She just looked at him, as if waiting and wondering what he would do next.

"I'm not going to apologize again," he said gruffly.

"I don't want an apology," she told him, and lifted her hands to link them behind his head and draw his mouth down to hers.

It wasn't an accidental kiss this time. When she fused her lips to his, the action was both deliberate and determined. And this time, he kissed her back.

Meg might have made the first move, but Flynn took over from there, sliding one hand into her hair to cup the back of her head and change the angle of the kiss. His tongue swept inside her mouth, the sensual glide of his tongue sending a jolt of lust through her system. His other hand came around her back now, drawing her closer to his body. His taut, muscled—and unmistakably aroused—body.

She wasn't just tingling now; she was practically vibrating.

With want.

With need.

Achy, desperate need.

She'd known Flynn for more than a year now. They'd talked to one another about things they couldn't talk about with other people. They'd shared parts of their lives that no one else had seen. As a result, she knew *him.*

And yet, she hadn't known that he held such heat and passion inside.

She'd never guessed that kissing him would be unlike any other kiss she'd ever experienced.

The realization was both arousing and alarming. Because as desperate as she was to scratch that itch, this was *Flynn.*

Her friend.

Emma's friend.

Then his hand slid from her hip to her breast, and her mind emptied of all thoughts. Any concerns she had were annihilated by the flames that licked through her body when his thumb brushed over her nipple. Even through the layers of clothing that she wore, she felt his touch reverberate all the way to her core, making her knees tremble and her panties damp.

It was her soft sigh—a sound of surrender—that penetrated the haze that had clouded his brain.

"This is probably a mistake," he said, muttering the words against her lips.

"Probably," she agreed.

"You need to tell me to stop."

"I don't want you to stop."

"What do you want, Megan?"

"I want you to take me home and—" She whispered the rest of her proposal in his ear, using that forbidden word in such a graphic way that every last drop of blood drained out of his head and into his groin.

Chapter Eighteen

He took her home, and they barely made it through the door before Flynn had Meg pressed against the wall and was kissing her again. Hotly. Hungrily. She kissed him back the same way. Wanting him more than she'd wanted any man in a very long time. Maybe ever.

His hands moved over her body, under her sweater, beneath her skirt. She yanked his shirt out of his pants, desperate to touch him as he was touching her. Eager hands sliding over the taut planes of his chest, the ridged muscles of his abdomen.

God, the man was built.

How had she never noticed that before?

Or perhaps she hadn't let herself notice. Hadn't let herself see him as a man, because she'd needed a friend.

But she was seeing him now.

"I should have walked out of Denim & Diamonds when I saw you there."

She might have taken offense to the words, if not for the fact they were muttered against her lips as his hands continued to explore her body.

Then his mouth moved to her throat, his unshaven jaw rasping against her skin, his lips scorching her with hot, wet kisses. He nibbled on her earlobe.

"Tell me what you like. What you want."

"I want you." She already had his belt unbuckled and his jeans unbuttoned. The zipper required a little more finesse to ease it past the bulge of his erection, but she made quick work of that, too, and reached inside to wrap her fingers around him.

"Megan. Jeez." He sucked in a breath. "Give me a sec. Let me—"

"Now." She pulled a small square packet out of the front pocket of her skirt, tore it open and unrolled the condom over his hard length.

"I didn't realize we were in a hurry." But he slid his hands beneath the hem of her skirt, pushing the denim up to her hips.

"It's been a long time," she told him.

"For me, too." He yanked on her panties, winced when he heard the fabric tear.

"Sorry," he muttered against her mouth.

"Don't be," she told him.

He slid his hand between her thighs, finding her wet and ready. Dipped a couple of fingers into her slick heat and felt her muscles clench—then the flood of her release pour into his hand as she cried out his name.

"Now," she said again.

He gripped her hips in his hands, lifting her against the wall. She wrapped her legs around him, hooking her feet behind his back and fusing her mouth to his as he drove into her, hard and deep.

He swallowed the sound as she cried out a second time, her nails biting into his shoulders even through the layers of cotton and flannel he still wore. She was hot and tight and already coming again, her inner muscles clenching around him, dragging him toward the edge of oblivion.

He fought to hang on, desperate not to explode like a complete novice. He tried to remember some of the focused breathing techniques he'd learned in combat training, but it was hard to think with Meg's tongue in his mouth, mimicking the rhythm of their bodies. Impossible to focus on mind exercises when her soft breasts were crushed against his chest and her naked ass was in his hands. And so, he surrendered to the heat of passion and let the pulsing waves of her climax wash over him and drag him under.

He didn't know how long it took him to become aware of his surroundings again. Minutes? Hours? When he did, he realized that Meg was still in his arms, her back against the wall, her forehead against his shoulder.

"Well, that was unexpected," she said, when she'd managed to catch her breath.

"The condom in your pocket—thank you for that, by the way—suggests otherwise."

"You're right. I should have said that *you* were unexpected."

"You were planning on bringing someone else home with you?"

He somehow managed to ask the question in a mild tone, though the thought of Megan doing what they'd just done with another man, moaning another man's name as she came, evoked feelings on the complete opposite end of the spectrum.

"I didn't have any specific plans," she told him. "And the condom came from the dispenser in the ladies' room at Denim & Diamonds—after you put your hands on my midriff and I realized I wanted to feel them all over me."

"Did you only get one?"

"That's all that would fit in the pocket of this skirt."

"Then it's lucky that I got one, too."

"Did you?" she asked, sounding surprised and pleased. "And do you have plans for yours?"

"I plan to prove to you that young guys aren't the only ones who have energy," he told her. "But next time, I'm going to set the pace. And you're going to be naked."

"As long as you're naked, too."

"But first I need to deal with—" He glanced pointedly at where their bodies were still joined.

"Right." Meg unhooked her legs and let her feet find the floor.

"I'll be right back," he promised.

As he ducked into the bathroom, she made an effort to straighten her skirt. A glimpse of red caught her eye and she bent down to scoop up her ruined panties.

Obviously they were of no use to her anymore, but she thought she might keep them as a memento of the night that Flynn Chandler tore them off her. Because she knew that whatever happened between them tonight couldn't ever happen again.

She heard the toilet flush and quickly stuffed the panties in her back pocket. A few seconds later, he was back.

She yelped, startled, when he scooped her into his arms. "What are you doing?"

"Implementing my plan," he said, already halfway up the stairs.

"Do you think we should talk first?" she asked cautiously.

"I'm not really in the mood for conversation."

"So maybe we could just agree that neither of us will try to turn this into something it's not?"

"As long as what it is—is you and me naked between your sheets." He set her on her feet beside the bed and grasped the hem of her sweater, slowly lifting it up to expose her bare torso, holding her gaze as he did so.

She shivered at the intensity in his eyes.

He didn't ask if she was cold.

He had to know she wasn't.

That she was hot all over and burning inside.

Burning for him.

It didn't matter that they'd already come together—somehow being with Flynn had stoked rather than sated her desire.

The realization caused warning bells to clang in the back of her mind, alerting her to potential dangers ahead.

She ignored them. Simply shut her mind to all the external noise, unwilling to think about all the reasons this was a bad idea—and no doubt there were dozens. Maybe hundreds.

But regrets were for tomorrow.

Tonight, she only wanted to feel again the way he'd already made her feel. She wanted to experience the overwhelming pleasure that shoved everything else aside.

She wanted Flynn. She wanted his weight on top of her, pressing her into the mattress, and the hard length of him deep inside her.

He let the sweater drop to the floor, so that she was standing in front of him now wearing only her cowboy boots, denim skirt and lace bra.

His pupils flared as he cupped her breasts in his hands. He muttered something under his breath—it might have been an oath or a prayer—the words somehow crude and incredibly arousing at the same time. Words that assured her he wanted her as much as she wanted him.

Then he lowered his head and captured one already peaked nipple in his mouth, suckling it through the lace barrier. The gentle tugs of his mouth setting off a chain reaction throughout her body. Desire was a moan in her throat, a quiver in her knees, a pulse between her thighs.

Somehow, while he was tormenting her with his mouth, she managed to remove his flannel shirt. Then he found the clasp between her breasts, released it with a twist, and her focus was lost again. He peeled the cups back to bare her to his avid gaze and hungry mouth. Her fingers slid through his hair, holding his head close, encouraging his attention. He didn't disappoint—nibbling and licking and suckling—first one breast, then the other, until the pleasure was almost too much.

He unfastened the button at the front of her skirt, slowly lowered the zipper. She could barely hear the rasp of the teeth over the sound of her own breathing.

"Apparently I wasn't thinking about taking it off when I put it on," she admitted, as his efforts to gently tug the skirt over her hips proved ineffective.

"You figured you'd just hike it up around your hips and get on with things?"

"I didn't hear you complaining when it was hiked up around my hips and we were getting on with things downstairs."

"And I'm not complaining now," he assured her. "I'm just trying to figure out how to get you naked."

"That's going to take some wiggling," she warned.

His gaze lit with interest and his lips curved in one of those rare half smiles. "I want to see that."

"After you take off your shirt. And your pants."

He lifted a brow.

"To level the playing field," she explained.

He quickly dispensed with the garments—taking a condom out of his pocket and setting it on her bedside table before he kicked his jeans aside—and she found herself once again appreciating how seriously built he was.

Seriously built and hugely aroused.

She wasn't surprised by the scar on his chest, but she wasn't distracted by it, either. She knew he'd been wounded overseas, that his last mission had nearly cost him his life. And she knew that the six-inch surgical cut that had opened his chest to repair his atrial valve had created the most visible and, at the same time, the least of his scars.

"Your turn," he said now.

She hooked her thumbs in the waistband of her skirt and shimmied as she pushed the denim over her hips and down her legs, then she carefully stepped out of the pool of fabric.

"Is that naked enough?" she asked. "Or should I lose the boots, too?"

"You can keep the boots on—for now," he said, sliding his hands down the sides of her torso then around her bottom, cupping her cheeks to lift her up and carry her to the bed, where he dumped her unceremoniously onto the edge of the mattress.

She started to inch her way upward, toward the pillows, but he caught her boots and held her in place.

"Stay right there for a minute," he said.

Before she could form a question or utter a protest, he was on his knees in front of her and draping her legs over his shoulders. Her breath stalled in her lungs as he lowered his head between her thighs and put his mouth on her, boldly going where no man had gone in a very long time, showing her pleasures she hadn't even imagined might exist.

His tongue stroked over her, inside her.

She had little experience with a man focusing on her pleasure ahead of his own—and Flynn was giving her so much pleasure that she had no trouble staying in the moment with him. There wasn't a fraction of a second in which she worried that he might hurt her. There was no fear or apprehension; only joy and wonder.

He continued to lick at her. Slowly at first, as if coaxing a response. Then faster, demanding her surrender.

She gave him what he wanted, helpless to do anything else, as sensations built inside and then exploded out of her like Fourth of July fireworks.

When she'd finished shuddering from the aftereffects of her climax, he tugged her up on the bed and reached for the condom he'd set aside.

She would have expected the first (several) orgasms to have dulled the sharp edge of her desire for him, but as he rose over her, she felt everything inside her trembling with anticipation again. She drew up her knees and dug her heels into the mattress, not just ready for him but eager.

He didn't make her wait but positioned himself at the apex of her thighs and, in one deep stroke, drove into her. She moaned with pleasure as her instincts took over, her hips rising and falling to meet his rhythmic thrusts. It was more than just a mating and merging of their bodies—it was an acknowledgment of long-simmering desire and desperate need.

Every stroke of his body pushed her closer to the edge again. He slid a hand between their bodies, finding the ultrasensitive nub at her center, using his thumb to create more delicious friction. More and more…until it was too much.

Until she cried out with her release and he groaned deeply, yielding to his own.

Meg woke up alone and told herself she should be relieved rather than disappointed.

She stretched, feeling twinges in places she'd forgotten could ache. But they were good aches, private reminders of the intimate workout she'd shared with Flynn.

Yeah, she'd definitely not seen that coming.

Maybe she'd dreamed about him, but she could hardly be held responsible for the fantasies of her unconscious mind. Or was it the subconscious mind? She'd always struggled to differentiate between those two. In any event, she now had to deal with the aftermath of the reality that she'd had sex with Flynn.

And while she had no regrets about anything that had happened between them, she also knew she couldn't let herself think that it was the beginning of something more. She was a woman with a woman's needs that, until last night, had been ignored for a very long time.

Now that those needs had been thoroughly satisfied, it was time to get back to her real life. The one in which she had responsibilities as a mom and a nurse and neither the time nor the inclination to indulge in mind-blowing sex with the hottest cowboy deputy in the state—possibly the country. Untangling herself from the covers of her bed, she grabbed a robe and made her way to the kitchen for a glass of water. She gasped when she turned on the light and revealed a mostly naked man rifling through her cupboards.

Flynn turned, a guilty expression—and Oreo crumbs—on his face.

"I thought you'd gone."

"I just wanted a cookie." He popped the last bite into his mouth. "Did you want me to go?"

She shook her head as she reached into the cupboard above the sink for a glass. "No."

He opened the fridge and retrieved the pitcher of water he knew she kept there and filled her glass.

"Thanks."

"You want to talk now?" he asked her.

She glanced at the glowing numbers on the stove while she swallowed a mouthful of water. "It's 3:36. I feel like I should be texting you."

"Or you could just talk to me," he said.

She finished her drink and set the empty glass in the sink.

"I'm not really in the mood for conversation," she told him, taking his hand to lead him back to her bedroom.

"We're out of condoms," he reminded her.

"I know." She pushed him down on the bed and removed his boxer briefs, then straddled his knees and leaned down to run her tongue along the velvety length of his arousal.

"Meg—"

"It's my turn," she interjected.

"You don't owe me anything."

She licked him a second time, starting at the base again but finishing with a tongue curl around the tip this time, making him groan.

She glanced up, her eyes glinting, her lips curved. "What makes you think this is for you?"

Before he could clear his head enough to respond, her mouth was on him again. Her hot and wet and oh-so-talented mouth—and he couldn't think of any reason to argue with her.

* * *

Flynn was stretched out on the bed, just the hint of a (satisfied) smile curving the corners of his mouth.

Meg nudged him with her elbow.

"Hmm?"

"Are you on call tonight?"

"Nope."

"Well, someone's calling you."

"What?"

"Your phone's vibrating." She gestured to the nightstand.

"Oh." He rose up to a sitting position and reached for the device, frowning at the display. "I've gotta take this."

She nodded, but he was already sliding out of bed, gathering up his scattered clothing.

She might have let herself appreciate the sheer perfection of his naked body if she hadn't been reeling over the name she'd seen boldly displayed on the screen when he turned his phone over.

Caitlyn.

Even before Selena's revelation, Meg had known that he was still in contact with his cousin's girlfriend. Though she didn't know if their communications were frequent or regular, she understood that they were both mourning the absence of a man they'd loved. But Ellis had been gone for a long time now, and she found herself wondering if it was possible that, during that time, Flynn and Caitlyn had grown closer?

She didn't believe for a minute that he would have left Denim & Diamonds with her if he'd been involved with someone else. But the fact that he'd left her bed to take another woman's call in a more private space made her a little…uneasy.

Not jealous.

She had no right to be jealous.

Whatever had happened between them was over and done—a momentary flare of attraction already extinguished.

Chapter Nineteen

Because Flynn ducked away to answer Caitlyn's phone call (and then slipped out of the house without even saying goodbye to Meg), they were able to avoid the awkward "morning after" conversation—or at least postpone it. Unfortunately, not long enough for Meg's liking, as he was the first person she saw when she unbuckled Emma from her car seat at West River Ranch on Saturday afternoon.

"I didn't know you were going to be out here today," Flynn said, falling into step beside them as they made their way to the stables.

"I'm gonna ride Bandit," Emma told him excitedly.

"I'll bet Gramps looks forward to these lessons as much as you do."

"He's a wonderful teacher," Meg said, pleased that her voice sounded normal, without any hint of the irritation that scraped her insides. "And generous with his time."

"He says keeping busy keeps him young."

"He certainly seems to be living proof of that motto."

Raylan was waiting for them in the stables, and after greetings were exchanged all around, he helped Emma change into her borrowed boots, secured her helmet and took her out to the paddock, where Bandit was already saddled and waiting.

"And what are your plans for the day?" Flynn asked Meg when they were alone.

"I'm heading over to see Tess."

"I've got a better idea," he said. "Why don't we saddle up Fred and Wilma and ride over to my cabin?"

"And when we get to your cabin?"

"I'll give you the grand tour," he promised with a wink.

"A grand tour that starts and ends in the bedroom?" she guessed.

"I sure hope so."

"No, thank you."

He was taken aback by her politely dismissive response. "Am I reading things wrong or are you pulling away from me?"

"I'm not pulling away," she denied. "What I'm doing—or trying to do—is get us back to the place where we're friends."

"I can assure you, I'm feeling very friendly toward you right now."

"I'm serious, Flynn."

"So am I. And I'll always be your friend," he vowed. "It doesn't mean we can't be more."

"Friends with benefits?" she said dubiously.

"Why not?"

"Because this is real life, not a rom-com."

"Last night didn't seem like a rom-com to me," he assured her.

"Last night we were two lonely people looking for something to help us forget our loneliness for a while."

"And judging by the nail marks on my back, I'd say we found it."

"And then, before the sun was up, you were gone," she pointed out.

"You're mad that I left?"

"No," she denied. "Only disappointed that you felt it necessary to sneak out without even saying goodbye."

"I didn't sneak out," he denied. "I left because I had to deal with something."

"Something involving Caitlyn."

He frowned. "How'd you know?"

"I saw her name on the display when you picked up your phone."

"You're not jealous of Caitlyn?"

"No," she said again, though not entirely convincingly.

"You know that we keep in touch."

"I know," she confirmed. "But it was still a slap in the face to have you leave my bed to go to another woman."

"I'm sorry if that's how it seemed, but it wasn't like that," he promised. "My leaving didn't have anything to do with you, so I didn't think about how you might feel. I didn't think..."

"About me at all?" she finished for him, when his words trailed off.

He wanted to explain, but he didn't know what to say. Not to mention that the more he opened his mouth, the further he seemed to put his foot in it.

"It was a situation," he said, giving it another shot anyway.

"So you said."

"There wasn't anyone else she could call."

"She has no other friends? No family?"

"Not that she could talk to about this."

"Well, then, it's lucky that you could be there for her," Meg said.

He eyed her warily.

"I mean that sincerely," she told him now. "Everyone should have a friend they can trust will be there when they need them. You've always been that friend for me, too, Flynn, and I hope you'll be that friend again."

"Of course, I will."

"Thank you."

"I'd also still like to take you out riding, if you want. Anywhere you want to go."

"I can't today," she said.

"Maybe next week?"

"Maybe."

* * *

"Raylan said that Emma's coming along really well with her riding lessons," Tess remarked, setting a plate of goodies on the coffee table near where her friend was already seated.

"She certainly seems to be enjoying it," Meg agreed, selecting a pecan tart from the plate.

"And how about you? Are you enjoying your lessons?"

"Sure," she said, biting into the tart.

"So why aren't you out with Flynn today?"

"Because I'm here with you."

Tess nibbled on a brownie. "Something happened between the two of you."

Meg frowned. "Why would you think that?"

"Your gaze dropped away when I mentioned his name."

"I was brushing a crumb off my shirt. Those tarts are delicious but crumby."

"You're calling Gramma Lula's tarts crummy?"

"Crum*b*y with a b," she clarified. "Or maybe crumb*ly*?"

"Forget the tarts," Tess said dismissively. "You slept with Flynn."

"What? No." She shook her head. "I did *not* sleep with Flynn."

Her friend's gaze narrowed. "You had sex with Flynn."

Damn.

"How do you do that?"

"Do what—read you like a book?"

"Yes," Meg admitted.

"I know you," Tess said easily. "And I knew, when you told me about that accidental kiss and the sparks, that it was only a matter of time before you banged him."

"Well, it wasn't on my bingo card," she assured her friend.

"So what happens now?"

"Nothing happens now. It was a one-night stand, and the night is over."

Tess frowned. "You don't do one-night stands. And neither does Flynn."

"There's a first time for everything."

"You're scared," her friend realized. "You've got real feelings for Flynn and you're running scared."

"Not true."

"And now you're not just lying to me, you're lying to yourself."

"Next to you, Flynn is probably my best friend. No way am I going to screw that up by..."

"Screwing him?" Tess suggested in a dry tone.

"Well, I can't undo what's been done. But I can mitigate the potential fallout by recognizing that it was a mistake not to be repeated."

Tess eyed her skeptically.

"No, it wasn't a mistake," Meg contradicted herself. "And I'm not sorry it happened, but that doesn't mean I'm going to let it happen again."

In fact, she was going to make sure it didn't happen again. Because as exciting and satisfying as it had been to make love with Flynn, she knew that letting one night turn into two or three would lead to her developing the kind of real feelings of which her friend had been speaking, and Meg wasn't ready to risk her heart—or Emma's. Far better, she'd decided, to return her relationship with Flynn to the status quo.

Whether or not Flynn agreed with Megan's choices—which, for the record, he did not—he had to respect them. And if she wanted to pretend that the night they'd spent together had never happened, he'd play along for the sake of their friendship. Because it was the only thing she'd asked of him.

He might have been tempted to argue his case, if not for the fact that he knew he'd blown it already. He'd admitted that when he saw Caitlyn's name on his screen, he'd forgotten about everything and everyone else. Yeah, he might as well have strapped a brick of C-4 to said case and ignited the detonator.

So after one mind-blowingly amazing night, they were back to being just friends. Probably he should be grateful that Megan still wanted to be his friend—and he was. But while he valued their friendship more than she knew, now that he'd had the pleasure of making love with her, late-night chats and confidences shared over coffee weren't much of a consolation prize.

But he still had a key to her house and an open invitation to use Tess's former bedroom whenever he had a late or overnight shift, which was where he'd spent the previous night and why he appeared in her kitchen, desperate for a hit of caffeine, Wednesday morning.

Meg, perhaps sensing a presence and likely expecting to see her daughter, glanced toward the entranceway. Finding him there instead obviously gave her a jolt, because she lifted a hand to press it against her chest, no doubt where her heart was racing. "Flynn."

"I'm sorry I startled you," he said.

"It's okay. I just didn't realize you were here."

"I know last night wasn't on the schedule I gave you, but you said I could crash here anytime."

"I meant it," she said, and even managed to sound sincere.

Apparently both of them were tiptoeing around the fact that she'd given him the key weeks before they'd ravished each other.

"I should have given you a heads-up."

"Not necessary," she assured him.

"I would have," he told her now. "But I got called in late and by the time the...situation was resolved, I didn't feel up to driving all the way back to West River."

"Understandable."

"Anyway, it was the smell of coffee that drew me down here."

"You smelled coffee? Or you smelled bacon?" she asked,

taking another mug from the cupboard and dropping a new pod in the brewer.

"If I said bacon, you might think I was trying to wrangle an invitation to breakfast."

"You're welcome to have breakfast with us, if you want."

He suspected she'd only made the offer because she would have done so before they got naked together and was now trying to promote the illusion that nothing had changed between them.

But when his stomach growled audibly, she smiled.

"I'll take that as a *yes*," she said.

"Only if I can help."

"The bacon's already in the oven and scrambling eggs isn't a two-person job… Do you know how to make toast?"

"You don't think the master of teddy bear pancakes can handle toast?" he asked with feigned indignation.

"You're on toast duty then."

He saluted. "Yes, ma'am."

"But coffee first." She handed him the mug.

"Thank you," he said, sincerely grateful.

"So, what time did you get here last night?" she asked, when he was dropping bread into the slots of the toaster.

"It was close to four—or maybe just after—this morning."

"Why are you even out of bed?"

He shrugged. "Habit."

She moved around the kitchen, taking plates from the cupboard and cutlery from the drawer to set the table. "Actually… can I ask you something?"

"Anything."

"I went upstairs the other day—I had to wash my sheets and figured I'd throw yours in at the same time. I would have done the same thing for Tess when she lived here," she hastened to explain. "I didn't think about the fact that I might be invading your privacy."

"I have nothing to hide." The toast popped up, and he occupied himself with the task of buttering. "So, what's your question?"

"Do you even sleep in the bed?"

"I left the blanket and pillow on the floor," he guessed.

She nodded.

"Sometimes I sleep in the bed. Sometimes I start off in the bed and move to the floor." He shrugged. "And sometimes I know the bed isn't going to work and just stretch out on the floor."

"It's not any of my business," she acknowledged. "I was just wondering."

He retrieved another plate from the cupboard for the now-buttered toast. "I wish I knew why there are times that I'm okay on a mattress and other times sinking into it makes me feel trapped, but there doesn't seem to be any rhyme or reason."

"You don't have to explain yourself to me."

"I know."

"I shouldn't have asked."

"I'm glad you did."

"But I'm always here to listen…if you want to talk."

"I know that, too," he said.

Emma wandered into the kitchen then, still in her pj's, her favorite stuffed bunny dangling from one hand.

"Unca Flynn!" Her eyes went wide when she spotted him.

It hadn't been that long since he'd seen her, but she always greeted him with the same enthusiasm. And always, the smile that curved her lips filled all the empty spaces in his heart.

"Are you gonna have breakfast with us, Unca Flynn?"

"I am," he confirmed, helping her into her seat and pouring juice into her cup while Meg served up the bacon and eggs.

Then they sat down and had breakfast together, like they'd done countless times before.

But this time, Flynn found himself looking around and appreciating that Meg and Emma had made a place for him not just at their table but in their lives. And for a minute in time, he'd had the opportunity to cement that place—to be a part of their family.

But that minute had passed, and he told himself that he was relieved and not disappointed. Because Meg was already—understandably—wary of letting anyone get too close.

As soon as I start to rely on anyone else, they let me down.

He wished she didn't believe that was true.

More, he wished he could be someone she could count on.

But the truth was, he couldn't be counted on.

Ellis could attest to that.

Meg had worried that things might be awkward between her and Flynn at the christening, but over the past week, they'd managed to fall back into their usual routines, almost as if nothing had happened between them. Which was exactly what she'd wanted, so why did she find his everything-is-status-quo-and-I'm-completely-unfazed attitude so irritating?

Probably because, despite being the one to push for the return to the status quo, it wasn't really what she wanted. What she wanted was for Flynn to wake up one morning and realize that he didn't want to spend a single minute of a single day without her and Emma. Which only proved that she'd been watching too many Disney movies if she was starting to fantasize about real-life happily-ever-afters.

But she pushed her own conflicted feelings to the back of her mind to focus on the happy occasion of Blake's christening.

The first several rows of the nave were filled with family and friends. Emma was seated the third row back, between Grampa Marshall—husband of Gramma Sunny—and Great-Gramma Lula. The little girl had been happy enough to put on a twirly dress and her fancy shoes to go to church, but her smile turned upside down when she learned that she had to sit with her grandparents because her mom was going to be at the front of the church with Auntie Tess's baby. (No matter how many times she reminded Emma that his name was Blake, her daughter insisted on calling him Auntie Tess's baby, and Meg suspected Emma might still be using that moniker on his fifth birthday—or at least until Tess and Holt had another baby to assume the title.) An injustice no doubt exacerbated by the discovery that her beloved Uncle Flynn was focused on the baby, too.

The ceremony went fairly quickly—a formal welcome, some readings and blessings, then the baptism with water. The guest of honor slept through most of it, only jolting awake—and squawking with distress—when the minister poured the water on his head. After that, nothing would stop him crying, and it was only when two wet spots appeared on the front of Tess's dress that she realized she'd forgotten to put nursing pads inside her bra.

Of course, everyone wanted photos after ceremony, but they had to wait while the new mom excused herself to deal with the baby's crying and her overflowing breasts. And while Blake was soon sated, Tess had to do some strategic positioning of her son so the dark splotches on the front of her dress wouldn't be visible in the pictures.

Through most of the photo session, the godparents flanked the parents, who were holding the baby. Then the photographer suggested some photos of the godparents and baby alone, and Tess handed her son to his godmother and moved aside with Holt so the godfather could step forward to fill the gap.

That was when Meg's traitorous hormones started acting up.

Nothing as obvious as Tess's leaking breasts, thank God—was it okay to use that expression in church?—but enough to make Meg uncomfortable.

"A little closer together," the photographer urged.

Flynn moved closer.

So close that she could feel the heat emanating from his lean hard body. So close that when she breathed, she inhaled his familiar masculine scent.

"You look good," he said, while the photographer was swapping lenses on his camera.

It was a casual enough remark, but there was nothing casual about the way his eyes moved over her, his slow appraisal causing flames of heat to lick through her veins.

Meg had taken extra care with her appearance, because she was Blake's godmother and she knew Tess would want photos, not because she wanted Flynn to look at her. But she couldn't deny feeling some satisfaction in the way that he did.

She tried not to stare back at him. After all, it wasn't the first time she'd seen him dressed in something fancier than a flannel shirt or his deputy's uniform. The first time had been Tess and Holt's impromptu wedding the previous summer. And then, only a few days later, he'd donned a suit again in honor of his grandparents' sixty-fifth anniversary party.

Had she felt a quiver when she saw him on either of those occasions?

If she had, she'd ignored it, unwilling to let herself feel anything other than friendship.

But there was a definite quiver today.

A quiver that somehow managed to shake loose the erotic memories she'd deliberately locked away. Even as she smiled for pictures, those memories played back in her mind, making her heart pound and her body yearn.

No doubt she would go straight to hell for thinking about the things she was thinking about in a church. Maybe she'd even be struck down where she stood—a prospect that encouraged her hasty escape when the photo session was finally over.

Chapter Twenty

Ten months earlier

"You were talking about your last mission—the hostage rescue—when you abruptly ended our previous conversation," Megan reminded him, during another late night call a few days later. "Did you want to pick up where you left off?"

"No," Flynn said, because he didn't.

But maybe he was starting to understand that he needed to talk about some of the events that had happened overseas—and especially those that continued to haunt him.

"Okay," she relented.

He wasn't surprised by her response. She never pushed too hard or in a direction he didn't want to go. Was it a tactic she'd learned in her own therapy sessions? (She'd confided, in an earlier conversation, that both she and her daughter were seeing a therapist to help them deal with the fallout of her ex-husband's abusive behavior.) Or was it a reflection of her own unwillingness to talk about certain topics?

Either way, it had the effect of making him willing to open up and share things with her that he'd never even confided to Dr. Litman.

"My experience with the Rangers taught me to trust my instincts, and when we crossed the border that night, the itch between my shoulder blades warned me that something was about to go wrong.

"Then again, something almost always went wrong. The so-called textbook tactical mission only exists in textbooks. In the real world, snafus happen, and it's up to those of us with boots on the ground to deal with the snafus and get the job done.

"So I ignored the itch, because there were five innocent lives at stake. Five humanitarians who had no stake in the war being fought around them and only wanted to help those in need."

"Proof that no good deed goes unpunished," Megan murmured.

He nodded, though, of course, she couldn't see him.

"Too true," he said, verbalizing his agreement. "They'd been held for thirty-seven days—more than five weeks—while their loved ones begged political leaders to secure their release and their captors made increasingly outrageous demands.

"They'd been dragged from one stronghold to another, their current reported location more than a hundred miles from where they'd been taken, likely beaten for no reason other than that the terrorists wanted to demonstrate their power, and undoubtedly sleep-deprived and malnourished."

"Factors that would hinder their ability to help with their own rescue," she guessed.

He nodded again. "Chatter indicated that there was a lot of action in the area, spreading the guerillas thin and—hopefully—translating to less resistance for us. There were reportedly two guards for the five prisoners and five members of Bravo Group.

"Damn good odds," he told her. "And yet, that itch between my shoulder blades wouldn't go away."

Ghost faded into the night only to return a short while later, as soundlessly as he'd gone, to report that heat signatures confirmed five hostages in the cell.

Their job was to get those hostages out and across the border to safety.

"Good to go," Striker said.

"So when we were told to go, we went. We breached the perimeter, neutralized the guards and made our way to the cell."

The hostages were huddled together, their sunken eyes filled with fear and confusion, but they moved when they were told to move. More than five weeks in captivity had taught them not to question or resist.

"One of the hostages stumbled on his way out the door. Wolf picked him off the ground and tossed him over his shoulder without missing a beat."

Textbook, Flynn had thought at the time, a little uneasily.

"Then I heard Ellis swear—creatively and colorfully—until his words were drowned out by the instantly recognizable sound of an AK-47 coming from a balcony on the other side of the court."

He paused as the familiar *rat-a-tat-tat* echoed in his mind, returning him to the place—the moment—that changed his life. He squeezed his eyes shut, but the image didn't fade; the muzzle flashes didn't stop.

He exhaled slowly, pushing all the air out of his lungs before filling them again, holding his breath for several seconds and then blowing it out. He repeated the exercise several times, concentrating on his breathing, while Megan waited, patiently, for him to resume his narrative.

"Everything that happened next is kind of a blur in my mind," he said, when he was able to continue. "But I remember the bullets striking my body armor… the force of the impact lifting me off my feet…the pain exploding in my chest… and the ground rushing up to meet me."

"That must have been terrifying," she murmured.

"I don't remember being afraid. Or maybe everything just happened so fast that I didn't have a chance to register any kind of emotion," he told her. "But as the world faded to black, I realized that I didn't feel that itch between my shoulder blades anymore. In fact, I didn't feel a single damn thing."

"What's the next thing you do remember?" she prompted gently, when he fell silent again.

"There are some fuzzy memories—or maybe hallucinations—from my time in hospital in Germany and the medevac—but nothing very clear until I woke up in Baltimore, hooked up to various machines that were humming and beeping, with a tube down my throat and a vertical incision on my chest."

"To repair the internal trauma caused by the backface deformation of your body armor," she guessed.

"That's what the doctors told me," he confirmed.

"You *are* lucky to be alive."

The doctors had told him that, too, and though Flynn hadn't been entirely convinced then, the more time he spent with Megan, the more he was starting to believe it might be true.

Chapter Twenty-One

Everyone was invited back to West River Ranch after the christening, and the promise that she would find some of Great-Gramma Lula's brownies on the dessert table had Emma smiling again as they started their journey. Tallulah had tried to beg off the post-ceremony celebration, but Tess wouldn't hear of it, and so she was riding in the passenger seat of Meg's SUV, en route to their destination.

Meg understood her grandmother's reticence. She imagined it would be an uncomfortable situation for everyone—Raylan Chandler's long-ago mistress in the home he shared with his wife of sixty-five years. But since Tess and Holt had married the previous summer, all the players in that long-ago drama were making an effort to get along. And Meg knew for a fact that Eleanor had called Tallulah personally to request that she make the desserts for the occasion—with the exception of the cake, which Miranda had insisted should come from her favorite bakery in town.

The main house had been decorated in accordance with Tess's plans and caterers had taken over the kitchen. Willow hadn't been happy when she learned that Eleanor had hired someone else to take care of the food—as if she wasn't perfectly capable of putting together a spread for thirty-five people—until Eleanor explained that she was expected to attend the party as a guest, and she didn't want any of her guests having to run back and forth to the kitchen to toss a salad or slide another tray of canapés into the oven.

And while thirty-five people was no doubt a modest crowd by Chandler standards, it was still a crowd to Meg, and with her emotions still feeling a little raw as a result of everything that had happened in the past two weeks, she desperately needed a minute alone in which she could let the perpetual smile fade from her face.

Slipping outside for some fresh air, she found her grandmother sitting on the back deck.

"You should have a jacket," Meg admonished gently.

"Probably," Tallulah agreed. "But that would require going back inside to get it, and I'm not ready to go back inside."

"I can't imagine it's easy to be here, but I hope you know how important it was to Tess—and Holt—to include you."

"It's not so hard," Lula said. "Or not as hard as I thought it might be. Eleanor has been much more gracious than I had any right to respect.

"For a lot of years, I blamed Raylan and Eleanor for the fact that I had no relationship with my children," Lula confided to Meg now. "But the fact is, if they hadn't taken in Abby and Sunny along with Wyatt, I would have lost them anyway. Possibly my girls would have been separated and sent to different foster homes. At least they got to stay together here."

"That was a long time ago," Meg said, rising to her feet. "And this is a day for celebrating the future, not lamenting mistakes of the past."

She took her grandmother's hand then, to help her up, too.

"Come on. I promised to introduce you to Willow, who—I should warn you—has already said that she's going to get your pastry recipe, even if she has to arm wrestle you for it."

Amusement twitched at the corners of Lula's mouth. "Do you think she could take me?"

"She's determined," Meg said. "But I'd give you the edge, because you're scrappy."

"Scrappy, huh?"

"As all strong women have to be."

After Meg introduced Lula to Willow and left the two women talking, she checked on Emma, who was hanging out with Gage and Zane, and stole another cuddle with Blake as she made her way through the crowd, trying to exchange a few words with everyone she knew.

A short while later, she saw the twins on the sofa, playing some kind of handheld video game, but her daughter was nowhere in sight.

"Have you seen Emma?" she asked the boys.

They shook their heads.

There were a lot of people milling around, but she couldn't expect that anyone in particular would have been keeping an eye on her daughter. That was her job.

On her way through the dining room, she crossed paths with Eleanor.

"Did you eat?" the hostess asked.

"Too much," Meg said, forcing a smile and pretending the delicious meal she'd enjoyed wasn't now churning in her stomach.

"You should let Emma know the cake will be coming out soon. I know she won't want to miss that."

"Any chance you've seen her recently?" Meg asked.

"Emma?"

"Yeah. One minute she was there and the next…"

"Heading to the stables with Flynn," Eleanor said.

Relief made Meg's knees weak. "Thanks."

She shoved her feet into her shoes and hurried out to the stables. She pulled on the heavy door, sliding it open so she could slip through. As always, she was greeted by the scent of fresh hay with an underlying but not entirely unpleasant hint of animal sweat.

"Emma? Are you here?"

"Here, Mama. We're feeding Bandit apples."

Meg caught her daughter in her arms and hugged her tight.

"You're squeezing too hard, Mama."

She immediately relaxed her hold. "Sorry, baby."

The little girl's brow furrowed. "Are you okay, Mama?"

"I am now," she said. "But I was worried when I couldn't find you inside the house. You know you're not supposed to go anywhere without telling me."

"But I was with Unca Flynn."

"But I didn't know you were with Uncle Flynn."

"It's my fault," he said, sincerely contrite. "I'm sorry."

"There's no more apples, Unca Flynn."

"Which means that Bandit's had enough treats for today," he told her.

"You probably have, too," Meg said to her daughter. "But Mrs. Chandler told me to tell you that they're almost ready to bring out the cake."

Her eyes, predictably, grew wide. "Cake?"

Meg laughed. "Let's get you back to the house."

"Are you comin', Unca Flynn?"

"In a little bit," he said.

So Meg took her daughter back to the house, then returned to the stables to find Flynn exactly where she'd left him.

"If you came back to yell at me, go ahead," he said. "I know I shouldn't have brought Emma out here without telling you."

"No, you shouldn't have," she agreed. "So why did you?"

"I told Tess, but I guess she didn't have a chance to pass on the message."

"Why didn't you tell *me*?"

"You were deep in conversation," he hedged. "I didn't want to interrupt."

"I don't recall any particularly deep conversations with anyone."

But then she remembered that between the time she'd last seen Emma and the time she'd discovered her daughter missing, she'd been chatting with a group that had included her uncle Wyatt and aunt Kristin. Ellis's parents.

No wonder Flynn hadn't wanted to interrupt.

"I'm sorry," he said again.

"It's okay," she told him. "I admittedly had a moment of panic, but as soon as your grandmother said that Emma was with you, I stopped worrying. Because I know you wouldn't ever let anything bad happen to her."

"I would give my life to keep her safe," he confirmed. "But sometimes the willingness to sacrifice yourself isn't enough to stop bad things from happening."

"No one doubts that you did everything you could to save Ellis," she said gently.

He looked at her, a grief in his gaze she'd give the world to fix and that was reflected in his tone when he said, "It wasn't enough."

They'd been keeping a distance from one another—seemingly by mutual if unspoken agreement—since the christening. Flynn suspected that they'd each poked at some of the other's raw spots that day and had subsequently retreated to their respective corners to lick their proverbial wounds.

So when he drove past Holt and Tess's cabin on the way to his own the following Saturday afternoon and saw Meg leaning against the driver's-side door of her SUV with her cell phone against her ear, he had no intention of stopping and making conversation for the sake of it.

But there was something about her posture that triggered his concern, and he impulsively pulled into the drive behind her vehicle.

She'd finished her call by the time he parked. The phone clutched in her hand now hanging at her side, her shoulders slumped and her head tipped forward so that her long hair curtained her face.

He turned off the ignition and climbed out of his truck. Still, she didn't move. Didn't even glance in his direction. As if she hadn't even registered the sound of his vehicle.

And maybe—considering the way she was trembling—she hadn't.

"Jesus, Meg. You're shaking."

She blinked. "I'm sorry?"

"Don't be sorry—tell me what happened."

She shook her head. "It's nothing."

"Bullshit," he said, genuinely alarmed to see her like this and angry that she was obviously holding back.

And apparently that anger was reflected in his tone, because Meg visibly flinched—which only made him angrier.

"And that's bullshit, too," he told her.

"What?"

"You pulling back from me, as if you think I'd ever raise a hand to you."

She had the grace to look guilty. "I know you wouldn't," she acknowledged. "But some learned responses are hard to unlearn."

"I'll give you that," he relented. "And now I need you to give me an explanation for why you're all twisted up inside."

"It's not anything I want to talk about."

"It's me, Meg. You can tell me anything."

She looked at him then, those whiskey-colored eyes filled with anguish. "There are some things about me you don't want to know."

"That isn't true," he promised.

"I'm okay," she said. "Really. I just need a minute."

"I'll give you two," he told her. "Then I'm going to take you to my cabin where we can continue this conversation in private."

"I don't want to continue this conversation."

"It wasn't a suggestion, Megan."

"I need to go get Emma."

"Where is she?"

"At the stables. With your grandfather."

"I'll give him a call," he said easily.

"And tell him what?" she challenged. "That Meg's going to be late picking up her daughter because she's having a meltdown."

He lifted a brow. "Are you having a meltdown?"

"No," she denied. "I'm fine."

"Then I'll simply tell him that I ran into you while you were leaving Tess and Holt's place and waylaid you to talk about Emma's birthday party."

"Fine, we can talk about her party, but I don't want to talk about the phone call."

"Get in the truck, Megan."

She huffed out a breath. "I'm capable of driving myself."

"Are you?" he asked dubiously.

She nodded.

Though he was still skeptical, she admittedly looked less white than she had a few minutes earlier—and a lot more determined. More like the always-confident-and-in-control Megan he knew.

"Okay," he relented, since they weren't going very far. Also, he figured she wouldn't want to leave her SUV parked in Tess and Holt's driveway and then face their questions later.

The old hunting cabin that Flynn had moved into when he was ready for some space from his well-meaning but occasionally intrusive parents was of basic construction and simple design. Originally a single room, perhaps for the efficiency of heating the space through the use of the woodstove in one corner, Flynn had built a wall to separate the bedroom from the main living space. Sometime in the last century, a bathroom had been built off the kitchen—again, likely for the convenience of having all the plumbing close together. When he'd moved in, the windows had been as bare as the floors and though neither had bothered him, his mom had insisted that if he wanted to live out in the foothills—where no one but bears and moose would be looking in his windows—he needed some area rugs and curtains.

Meg had been to his cabin before, but he'd never invited her inside. Not that he worried about her passing judgment—he honestly didn't care what anyone else thought about the place he called home—at least temporarily.

Because when he'd first moved in, he hadn't planned to stay—he'd only wanted to put the pieces back together so he could return to Azerbaijan and bring Ellis home. There had never been any question in his mind that that was what he needed to do. He owed it to his cousin and best friend.

But while time—following surgery and physiotherapy—had healed his body, he was still having some trouble wrapping his mind around the idea of going back. In fact, just the thought made his heart race and his body break out in a cold sweat. But that was a concern for another day—right now, he was focused on Megan.

"I must look bad if you're actually inviting me to cross the threshold," she noted, when he pushed open the door and gestured for her to enter.

He ignored her sarcasm and led the way to the kitchen, which was basically a path straight through the living room.

"Can I get you anything? Coffee? Water?"

"I wouldn't mind a cup of coffee," she said. "Thanks."

He brewed two mugs, then opened the cupboard above the stove and pulled down a bottle of whiskey.

"A little early in the day for the hard stuff, don't you think?" she remarked.

He added a splash to one mug.

"Especially for me," she said, as he handed that mug to her.

"You're still shaking," he pointed out.

She lifted the mug to her lips and cautiously sipped the spiked drink.

"Have a seat," he invited, gesturing.

"There's only one chair," she noted. "Although I guess that's one way to ensure a woman doesn't stay for breakfast."

"Do you need more than one?" he asked, responding to the former part of her remark and ignoring the latter.

"No, but where will you sit?"

"I don't mind standing," he told her.

She frowned at that.

"Or we can both sit in the living room."

Now she nodded, and they returned to the other room. Or rather, the other part of the main room.

Megan perched on the edge of the sofa with her mug cradled between her palms and took a minute to glance around the room. Or probably it was only half a minute, as there wasn't much to see. There was the sofa and a chair—castoffs from the main house during one of his grandmother's redecorating phases—a battered coffee table that was very possibly as old as the cabin itself, a floor lamp from Ikea—because the overhead light fixture sucked for reading—and a cheaply-framed and obviously amateur painting of the Twin Sisters on the wall, created by an ancestor who, perhaps inspired by the mountains, imagined himself an artist.

"I see you're a fan of the minimalist style of decorating," she remarked lightly.

"It's more that I'm not a fan of decorating at all." He settled on the opposite end of the sofa, his back against the arm so that he was facing her.

"Or guests?" she quipped.

"I don't get a lot of company out here," he confirmed.

"There's a surprise."

"But since you're here, you might as well talk."

"It's a good thing you're not a doctor," she remarked lightly, "because your bedside manner sucks."

"Maybe," he acknowledged. "Though you didn't have any complaints about my between-the-sheets manner. Or against-the-wall manner. Or—"

She held up a hand, cutting him off. "Not talking about it," she reminded him.

"If you don't want to talk about that, then tell me about the phone call."

"Okay," she relented. "But it really wasn't a big deal. I just… overreacted."

"That's out of character for you," he noted.

"I was caught off guard."

"By the call? Or the caller?"

"Both," she admitted. "Julia Kendall is a former crime beat reporter who wants to talk to me about a book she's writing."

"What's the subject matter?" he asked, so far not understanding why the request would cause her distress.

"Battered women who take justice into their own hands."

Okay, he could see how that might be a little uncomfortable for her, considering the abuse she'd suffered at the hands of her ex-husband. "Did she think your job at the hospital might have given you some insights? Is that why she sought you out?"

"No." She paused—or perhaps stalled—to sip her coffee again. "She sought me out because I killed my husband."

Chapter Twenty-Two

Flynn didn't show any outward reaction to her revelation.

Of course, he'd always been notoriously difficult to read, rarely giving any hints about what he was thinking or feeling—the sole exception, in Meg's experience, being the night they'd spent together.

Which was definitely not something she should be thinking about now.

Or ever.

"I'm going to need some more details," he finally responded.

She nodded, a wordless acknowledgment of his request. "You know that my ex-husband was abusive."

"I do," he confirmed. "And that you got a restraining order against him when you separated."

"Unfortunately, a piece of paper signed by a judge isn't much of a deterrent to a drunk and angry man who believes he is the boss of his wife and child."

His gaze narrowed at that. "How many times did he violate the restraining order?"

"Three. Well, four, including the night—just about two years ago—he showed up at my door and told me he was going to kill me." She lifted her mug to her lips again and swallowed another mouthful of coffee. "That was the last time—but the first time I really fought back—and he was the one who ended up dead."

"Two years ago, I was still overseas," Flynn noted. "Still, I'm a little surprised that, in all the time I've been back, I've never heard so much as a whisper about something that would have obviously been big news."

"It didn't happen here, but outside Cheyenne," Meg reminded him. "It was only after the divorce—and the restraining order—that I decided to move back to Whispering Canyon with Emma, so we'd have the support of family close by.

"That decision was the trigger that set him off. No way was he going to let *his* wife leave town with *his* daughter—never mind that he hadn't even bothered to exercise the supervised access he'd been granted by the family court judge. But because of that order, I had to apply to the court for permission to move out of town, as doing so would impede his ability to see Emma.

"He showed up in court to object to the application, but because he'd never exercised access, the judge ignored his objections and granted my request. Later that night, he showed up at my door and forced his way inside."

Her hands tightened around the mug, her gaze focused on its contents. She could do this—she'd told the story countless times. She just needed to be dispassionate and objective and not think about the rage on Daymond's face or the terror in her heart.

"Then he started to push me around, berating me for thinking he'd ever let a judge keep him away from his wife and child.

"I promised that I'd be in touch as soon as we were settled to give him our new address and arrange for him to visit with Emma. Not that I had any intention of actually doing so," she confided. "But I was trying to de-escalate the situation."

"I imagine that was like trying to put the pin back in a grenade," Flynn remarked.

"An apt analogy," she agreed. "Daymond called me a lying bitch and knocked me to the floor with a backhand so hard it made my ears ring." She touched a finger to her forehead, subconsciously tracing the small scar that her ex was responsible for putting there. "Then he literally kicked me while I was down. I gritted my teeth, not wanting to cry out and wake up Emma.

"But Daymond liked when I screamed in pain. When I begged him to stop hurting me. Eventually, he got what he wanted. As he always did. And Emma woke up, adding her cries to the mix."

Her expression was blank as she recounted the timeline of events, her eyes seemingly fixed on the wall across from her, though Flynn suspected she was seeing a slow-motion replay of that life-altering night in her mind.

"He announced that he was going to 'shut that damn kid up.' I was whimpering on the floor by then, with three cracked ribs, a dislocated shoulder and a broken wrist, but the pain of my injuries apparently wasn't stronger than my need to protect my child."

Though he was reluctant to interrupt, it seemed to Flynn that Megan wasn't just talking about the night, she was reliving it. And worried that she might be retraumatized, he attempted to ground her back in the present.

"You are a Mama Bear," he said gently.

She blinked then, and managed a small smile for him before she continued. "He started toward her room, and I kicked out—to draw his attention back to me. He wasn't close enough for me to make solid contact, but he instinctively stepped back and lost his balance on the edge of the stairs." She stared into the bottom of the mug that she still held in a white-knuckled grip. "He somersaulted down them…and broke his neck."

Flynn decided the man was lucky he was dead, because listening to Meg talk so matter-of-factly about her ex-husband's threats and abuse, he would have been tempted to hunt down and kill the bastard himself for everything this amazing woman and her precious daughter had endured at the other man's hands. Hands that should have never been raised against his wife and baby.

"I didn't realize he was dead at first," Meg told him now.

"I thought he was just unconscious, and I crawled across the floor to get the cell phone he'd knocked out of my hand. My fingers were shaking so badly, it took me three tries to punch the correct order of numbers for 9-1-1. Then I dragged myself to Emma's room, to soothe her cries."

Her eyes filled with tears, and he gently pried the now-empty mug from her hands to set it on the coffee table so that he could draw her into his arms. She didn't protest, but settled against him as she picked up the thread of her story.

"I was on the floor in her bedroom, with Emma in my lap, when the police came in. I begged them to arrest Daymond for violating the restraining order, but the officer I spoke to said there wasn't any point in reading rights to a dead man.

"I think I started to cry then, not because I was sad or sorry but because I was so relieved that he'd never be able to hurt me again." She brushed an errant tear from her cheek with the back of her hand, and he held her a little tighter. "Never be able to hurt Emma. But the officer's partner wasn't pleased when I admitted that I was glad Daymond was dead, and he suggested that I should be charged with manslaughter. Thankfully, the first guy I spoke with was the senior officer, and a quick survey of the scene and assessment of my injuries led him to determine it was a clear case of self-defense."

"I can't believe his partner came to a different conclusion."

"I found out later that the second cop had dated Daymond's sister, Hanna. She'd told him that I'd made up all kinds of lies to get a restraining order against her brother and deprive him of a relationship with his child."

Flynn touched his lips to the top of her head. "I'm sorry you had to go through any of that."

"Other women have endured much worse," she acknowledged. "I'd seen some of that worse when I worked in the ER, so when Daymond started lashing out at me, I knew the direction things were going and got out as fast as I could."

"But getting out wasn't enough, was it?"

"It often isn't," she confirmed. "But Hanna still blames me for Daymond's death and, every once in a while, she'll reach out to remind me of that fact. At one point, she even had a lawyer send me a letter threatening to sue for custody of Emma. I forwarded the letter to my lawyer, who had a blunt chat with hers about the circumstances of our marriage and divorce. He then followed up with a letter of apology and a promise that he was no longer representing her."

"You think she's responsible for the phone call from the reporter?" he guessed.

"I'd put money on it—if I had any to gamble with."

"Obviously the choice of talking to the reporter or not is your choice to make," he said.

"And my choice is *not*," she told him.

"Okay," he allowed. "But have you considered that telling your story might be therapeutic for you and helpful to other survivors of intimate partner violence?"

"No," she said. "Because I prefer not to even think about that time in my life—and especially that night. And I have no intention of reliving it all again so someone else can twist my experience to fit her story."

"Your choice," he said again. "But does not thinking about it really work for you? Has it healed the scars left by his abuse?"

"Healing is a process," she acknowledged. "As you well know."

He nodded. "I also know that taking control of the narrative might be helpful as you work through that process."

"But would it help Emma, when she's old enough to read what's written?"

"You could put conditions on any agreement to talk to the reporter," Flynn pointed out. "Request your names be changed to protect your privacy."

She pulled out of his arms. "I'm done talking about this."

Flynn rose to his feet. “And there go the walls,” he noted. “Though why that should surprise me, I don't know.”

Meg frowned. “What's that supposed to mean?”

“It means that I'm getting tired of our friendship being a one-way street.”

“It's not.”

“Isn't it?” he challenged. “Because over the past year, I've talked to you about everything, and in all that time, you never even gave me a hint about what happened the night your ex-husband died.”

“Do you want me to apologize?”

“No.” He shook his head. “Because I don't think you're sorry. I think that if I hadn't seen how affected you were by the reporter's call, you never would have told me about that night.”

She didn't, couldn't, deny it.

Instead she said, “I'm sorry.”

“I told you I didn't want an apology.”

“What do you want?”

“Honesty.”

“I've never lied to you.”

“Maybe not,” he allowed. “But I'd hoped we were past the point of having secrets from one another.”

“Says the man who won't tell me why he raced out of my bed when he got a call from his best friend's girlfriend.”

“Okay, let's talk about that night,” he said, aware that the air between them was suddenly humming again. “Let's talk about the fact that I've complied with your directive to go back to being friends even though it's torture to be around you and not be able to touch you.”

“No.” She shook her head. “Let's talk about Caitlyn and your codependent relationship.”

“We're not codependent.”

“Your relationship is the very definition of codependent,” she argued. “You always take her calls. You prioritize her wants and needs over everything else, including what's best for you. And I get it—I do. She was Ellis's girlfriend and you were his best friend, and that created a natural bond between you that you're both clinging to in his absence.

"But every time you see her or talk to her or even get a text message from her, you start to retreat into that dark place inside yourself and shut me out."

He was quiet for a long minute, considering her words.

"You're not wrong about me retreating," he finally acknowledged. "But I don't go to that dark place because talking to Caitlyn makes me think about Ellis—because he's never far from my thoughts. It's because I'm thinking about my failures."

She felt tears sting her eyes. "You didn't fail him, Flynn."

"So why can't I let go of the conviction that I did?"

"Maybe that's something Dr. Litman can help you figure out."

"You're determined to get me to go back to see her, aren't you?"

"You need to talk to someone."

"I'm talking to you right now."

"Are you?"

He paced the width of the cabin. "You want to know why I left that night."

"Only if you want to tell me."

Then back and forth again.

"I left because Caitlyn got a phone call from DHQ." He turned to face her now. "That's the private military contractor we worked for when we left the Rangers."

She could feel the tension in him and felt goose bumps rise on her own flesh. Whatever he was going to tell her, she sensed it was big.

"Since that last mission, the hostage rescue during which Ellis disappeared, there have been reported sightings—infrequent and unsubstantiated. But now DHQ believes they have intel solid enough to go back in." He swallowed. "To bring him home."

Meg was stunned.

Though everyone still talked about Ellis being MIA rather than KIA, she hadn't held out much hope that he'd ever be found, much less found alive.

"That's big news," she acknowledged.

"Or it might be a big nothing."

"But you don't think it's nothing."

"No," he agreed. "For the first time in more than eighteen months, I think it might finally be something."

"Do his parents know?"

"No," he said again, this time adding a shake of his head. "I don't want to get their hopes up. Not yet."

"And how about you?" Meg asked gently. "How are you doing?"

"Trying not to get my hopes up," he admitted.

She went to him then and wrapped her arms around him. He hugged her back, holding her tight. And the way he clung to her, for several long minutes, made her heart ache.

But what started as a simple desire to offer and accept comfort gradually gave way to a deeper awareness. She stroked her hands down his back; he brushed his lips against her temple. She tipped her chin up…he dipped his head toward her.

She pulled out of his arms and took a hasty step back.

"We agreed to go back to being just friends," she reminded him.

Reminded herself.

"And yet, it seems we have…a situation," he remarked.

She blew out a breath. "Apparently so."

The acknowledgment was made with such obvious reluctance, he might have smiled if he wasn't so churned up inside.

"Any thoughts on what we should do about it?" he asked.

"I don't think we should do anything right now. It's been an emotional day—for both of us—and I think we'd both benefit from taking a step back and taking some time to think."

"If that's what you want."

"Plus, I have to get Emma."

"What will you tell my grandfather if he asks about her birthday party?"

"I'll tell him that you convinced me to let her have the pony party she wants to have here at the ranch."

"And how did I manage to do that?" he asked curiously.

"Talking about what happened the night Daymond died reminded me that the first two-and-a-half years of Emma's life were pretty awful, and even if she doesn't have any concrete memories of that time, I want to ensure she has lots of happy memories to balance the scales going forward. And I know that if she has a pony party, she'll be so happy that she'll be talking about her fifth birthday for the next ten years."

"I can't think of any better reason than that," he said. "And if you want to discuss more details—and other things—later tonight, I could pick up a pizza and—"

"I'm sorry," Meg interjected. "But I have a charity event for the hospital tonight."

"The WCMC Annual Black Tie Gala?" he guessed.

"How'd you know?"

"My parents go every year."

"I should have realized."

"Is Emma your plus-one?" he asked, obviously fishing.

"No. She's having a sleepover at my parents' house tonight."

"Do you need a plus-one?" he asked.

"No. But thanks."

She didn't quite meet his gaze as she responded to his question, which made him realize… "You've already got a date."

"I don't know that I'd call it a date," she hedged. "But I am going with one of the surgeons I work with."

"I bet he'd call it a date," Flynn said, not entirely happy to discover that a woman he'd been intimate with not two weeks earlier had already moved on to dating other men.

"He asked me weeks ago. And since I'd planned to attend anyway—my supervisor likes hospital staff to be represented at these events—I figured, why not?"

Why not?

He could think of at least half a dozen reasons—coincidentally the same number of times he'd brought her to climax the night they were together.

But all he said was, "Maybe another time then."

"Sure," she agreed readily. "You know Emma's up for pizza any day of the week. And speaking of…"

He nodded. "You have to go get her."

He walked her out to her SUV, pleased to note that her color was back to normal and she was a lot steadier on her feet than when she'd arrived. Still, he felt compelled to ask, "You're okay now?"

She nodded. "Better than okay, and thank you for that."

"I'm glad." He opened the driver's-side door for her. "Give Emma a hug and a kiss from Uncle Flynn."

"I will."

When she paused before sliding behind the wheel, he impulsively dipped his head and brushed his lips over hers.

"That one was for you—and me," he said. "Something for both of us to think about."

Chapter Twenty-Three

She couldn't stop thinking about it.

All the way to her parents' house, with Emma chattering away in the backseat, she thought about it. The whole time she was getting ready for her not-really-a-date with Nathan Duchesne, she thought about it. Throughout the drive to the Whispering Canyon Country Club, she thought about it.

It hadn't been a passionate kiss. Or even a lingering one. But it had been enough of a kiss to make her remember how it felt to be kissed by Flynn—and yearn to feel that way again.

A situation, indeed.

"Did you say something?" Nathan asked.

She felt her cheeks grow warm. "Just thinking out loud."

His brow furrowed as he studied her face. "Are you alright? You look a little flushed?"

"Now that you mention it, I am feeling a little under the weather. Maybe I should call it a night."

"I'll take you home," he said solicitously.

"I don't want to drag you away just because I'm feeling a little off," Meg protested. "Especially when I know you were hoping to make a pitch for a robotic surgical system to some of the hospital's big donors."

She'd played the right card, because Nathan finally relented in his determination to see her home, though he insisted on ordering and paying for her ride.

He really was a good guy, Meg mused, as he waited outside

with her for the Uber. But he was not the man she wanted to be with tonight.

Not that she had any intention of going to see Flynn.

The kiss had sent her mind spinning, but she needed to be smart. She needed to think about not only what she wanted but what she needed—and especially what Emma needed.

And what they needed was Flynn's presence in their lives. His friendship.

You've got real feelings for Flynn and you're running scared.

She scowled at the echo of her friend's voice in the back of her head.

She'd never denied that she had real feelings for Flynn.

He was one of her best friends—of course she had feelings for him. But real feelings didn't necessarily mean romantic feelings, and considering Meg's romantic history, she'd be a fool to let herself develop romantic feelings for another man—even Flynn.

Or maybe especially Flynn, because he was possibly the only person she knew who was as messed up as she was.

He was also one of the very best men she'd ever known.

So why was she holding back?

Why was she denying what she wanted?

Yeah, they both had baggage, because it was impossible to go through life without going through stuff, and sometimes you had to carry that stuff with you after the fact.

And maybe, if you were lucky, you found someone who cared enough about you to want to help you with that baggage.

Until today, she hadn't told anyone the truth about what happened the night her ex-husband died. The police who'd come to investigate knew the whole story, of course. But they were the only ones. She hadn't even told Tess. Not because she worried her friend would judge her—Tess had been almost as relieved as Meg to learn that Daymond was dead—but because she'd felt that the burden of guilt was hers to carry alone.

But Flynn hadn't blinked when she told him the whole story. And even knowing everything about her now, he still wanted to be with her.

Of course, wanting to be with her in the moment and wanting to plan a life together were two very different things, and he'd given no indication he was thinking about the latter. Possibly because he didn't let himself look too far into the future. And possibly because he didn't think he deserved to plan for the kind of future Ellis might not ever have.

And somehow, while Meg had been trying to sort through all of these thoughts running through her mind, her heart had taken the lead—and taken her back to Flynn's cabin.

He knew the minute she arrived—heard her SUV pull into his driveway and the ignition shut off. But she didn't make a move to get out of the car. He gave her ten minutes to wrestle with whatever questions were keeping her behind the wheel before he made his way outside.

"Do you want to come in?" he asked, his tone deliberately casual.

She nodded and finally opened the door.

"Just in the neighborhood?" he asked, as they crossed the threshold.

That got a half smile out of her. "Not likely."

"So why are you here, Megan?"

"I couldn't sleep?"

He glanced at his watch. "Have you tried to sleep? Because it's not even ten o'clock."

"No, I haven't tried to sleep," she admitted.

He refused to read between the lines. To make it easy. If she wanted him—and the fact that she was here made him think that she did—then she was going to have to say so.

"How was your…event?" he prompted, when she remained silent.

"Successful, I think. It was a nice evening, anyway. We enjoyed a decent meal, spent some time chatting with colleagues and donors, and even shared a couple of dances."

"Feel free to spare me further details," he said.

"There are no further details," she told him. "I took an Uber home with every intention of making it an early night, and the next thing I knew, I was in my car driving here."

"Why?" he asked her again.

"Because being in Nathan's arms didn't make me feel any of the things I feel when I'm with you."

He opened his arms, and she stepped into them.

Then they were kissing and touching and somehow, in the midst of all the kissing and touching, he maneuvered her into his bedroom.

At another time, she might have commented on the obviously new furniture in here—a stark contrast to the rest of the cabin. The neatly made queen-sized bed had head- and footboards that matched a tall dresser and twin bedside tables. Right now, though, she was focused on the man.

And he was focused on her, as he demonstrated when he said, "Let's get rid of this," then lifted the hem of her sweater to tug it over her head and toss it aside.

Meg hadn't bothered with a bra when she'd changed—what was the point when (she hoped) he'd only have to take it off her? And he groaned his approval to find her breasts unencumbered.

"You are…so…unbelievably…sexy."

The way he was looking at her now, Meg felt sexy.

Desirable.

Desired.

Wanted.

She shivered as his callused palms moved over her torso, scraping lightly against her tender skin. Her breath caught in her throat as he captured her breasts, his thumbs brushing back and forth across her nipples, until she was almost whimpering.

Then he lowered his head and took a taut, aching peak in his mouth. He laved and suckled, first one then the other, creating arrows of heat that speared toward her center.

At the same time, she let her hands roam over his torso, marveling at her own power as his muscles tensed and rippled in response to her touch.

The rest of their clothes were quickly discarded, making a pile on the floor. He pulled back the covers on the bed, then tumbled with her onto the mattress, a tangle of limbs and needs.

Meg could feel the press of his erection at the juncture of her thighs as he levered himself over her, and her hips instinctively lifted off the mattress, her pelvis rubbing against his, making him groan.

He pulled back suddenly.

"Condom," she remembered at the same time.

"I bought a box," he told her.

She smiled. "So did I."

He yanked open the drawer on his nightstand to retrieve the box, tearing the cardboard in his haste to get at the contents.

"Maybe I should take over from here," she suggested, removing a single square packet from the box. When it was open, she slowly unrolled the latex over his rigid shaft, a satisfied smile curving her lips as he jerked in response to her touch.

"If you keep that up, I'm going to finish before we get started," he warned, as she stroked him again.

"You have a lot more stamina than you give yourself credit for." She splayed her palm on his chest, her hand covering his scar, and gave him a gentle push. When he was lying on his back, she straddled his hips with her knees.

"This is new," he said.

"You know the saying—save a horse, ride a cowboy?"

"Then I guess I should let you have the reins, so to speak."

She took him inside her, inch by inch, her eyes never breaking contact with his. When he was finally, deeply, buried, she began to move. She started out slow and steady, then increased her pace. A little faster, a little harder. She could feel the tension in his body, knew he was holding himself back, letting her be in control. And she could tell, when his hands clamped on her hips, that he was fighting to hold on, to ensure she found her pleasure before he took his own.

She continued to ride him, every thrust stoking their mutual desire, pushing them both toward the edge of oblivion.

Close…closer…closer…

She cried out as her body convulsed around him, and he groaned deeply as he yielded to his own climax and went over the edge with her.

"I bet I could sleep now," Meg said, her cheek resting against Flynn's chest, where she could hear his heart beating, strong and steady.

His fingertips traced a leisurely path down the length of her spine and back up again. "Does that mean you're going to stay?"

"Do you want me to stay?"

"Well, we do have almost a full box of condoms left," he said lightly.

"Two boxes," she reminded him.

"Where's yours?"

"In the duffel bag in my car, along with my pj's and toothbrush."

"You're not going to need your pj's," he assured her.

"My toothbrush?"

"Give me your keys—I'll go get your bag."

After they made love a second time, Meg fell asleep in his arms. She woke up a short while later, the bed beside her empty.

But she sensed that Flynn hadn't gone far.

Sure enough, when she inched toward the edge of the mattress, she saw he was stretched out on the floor. His hands folded behind his head, his eyes open, staring at the ceiling in the dark.

His gaze shifted. "Did I wake you?"

She shook her head, tugging the comforter with her as she lowered herself to the floor beside him.

He wanted to protest, because he knew the floor wouldn't be comfortable for her. Also, he worried that he might have a nightmare and start thrashing around, and he wouldn't ever want to risk hurting her. But when she snuggled against him, he felt a peace that he'd only previously experienced when riding across the fields on horseback and felt confident that the light of her presence would keep his dark dreams at bay.

"Is this okay?" she asked him.

"Yeah." He wrapped an arm around her. "Better than okay."

"I'm not always good with the relationship stuff," she confided.

"Sometimes the reason we're not good at something is because we haven't had enough practice."

"That might explain it," she acknowledged.

"I haven't had much practice with that stuff, either. The truth is, I was never much interested in that stuff before," he confided. "But with you, I find myself wanting to at least give it a try."

"Trying is dangerous," she cautioned. "Trying implies hope."

"Is hope so bad?"

"Maybe not for consenting adults, who know how to temper their expectations. But Emma wants a dad, and I can't let her hope that a relationship between us might turn into something more."

"I'd never want to hurt Emma," he agreed.

"So maybe we just keep this—I think you called it a *situation*—between us for now?"

"You don't want anyone to know we're…dating?" he finished, for lack of a better term.

"I don't want *Emma* to know we're..." she deliberately paused, as he'd done "...dating."

"Friends with secret benefits?"

"Something like that," she agreed.

"I guess I don't have any objections to keeping our relationship private. Because if my brothers and cousins—or even my grandparents—knew that we were dating, they'd expect a play-by-play and regular status updates. And that's nothing compared to what..."

"Tess," she finished, when his words trailed off.

He nodded. "You're never going to be able to keep this from Tess, are you?"

"She's my best friend. I'd feel guilty if I even tried. And while I might not be able to keep secrets from Tess, she's always kept my secrets."

"You better hope so," he said. "Otherwise, we might as well take out a full-page ad in *The Canyon Whisperer*."

Meg waved a hand dismissively. "Nobody reads the newspaper anymore anyway."

Meg followed the scent of coffee to the kitchen.

"Can't complain about the scenery around here," she said.

"I've been thinking about putting in bigger windows, to take advantage of the view," he said, offering her a mug of coffee.

"I wasn't talking about the mountains," she said. "Although they're pretty spectacular, too."

"You were talking about me?"

"I was talking about you," she confirmed. "There's nothing sexier than a man in the kitchen—except maybe a man pushing a vacuum. Or folding laundry."

"So, basically, a man doing any kind of household chore?"

"Or holding a baby," she said. "There's a reason so many romance novels feature hunky men holding tiny babies."

"Do I need to keep you away from my brother when he's changing Blake's diaper?"

"Hmm…is he wearing a cowboy hat when he's changing the diaper?"

"Does it matter?"

"Oh, yeah," she said. "A cowboy hat increases a man's sexy quotient exponentially."

"Excuse me a minute while I go get my hat."

She laughed and tipped her head back to brush her lips against his. "A badge works, too."

"Good to know." He stroked a hand down her back, over her bottom, in a playful caress. "Now go sit down and watch me scramble eggs."

"The temptation might be more than I can resist," she warned. "But I'll do my best."

"When do you have to pick up Emma today?"

"My mom made plans to take her to a teddy bear picnic at the park, so not until later this afternoon."

"Good. Then we can plan for a picnic, too."

Of course, when Flynn said "picnic" what he really meant was to pack some sandwiches and drinks in a saddlebag and go riding.

"You're determined to turn me into a cowgirl, aren't you?" she asked, as she finished tacking Wilma.

"You do look really sexy in the hat," he said, smiling as he tapped the brim.

She'd gotten used to Flynn's solemn expression, but she was always pleased to see a hint of a smile or his, even more rare, half smile. But this time, it was almost a full smile, and it filled her heart.

It was May now, the sun bright in the blue sky overhead, and as they rode—(trotted!)—across rolling meadows of green, Meg felt some of that elusive peace Flynn had promised. Twenty minutes later, they reached their destination, a babbling brook at the base of a mountain, and he spread a blanket on the grass for their picnic.

Just like her dream, Meg realized.

After they'd had their lunch, they stretched out side by side on the blanket, just relaxing and staring at the sky. As Meg watched fluffy white clouds drift leisurely by, she felt Flynn's baby finger curl around hers, and the simple sweetness of the gesture hooked her heart.

Over the next few weeks, a new status quo was established.

Meg had meant what she'd said about not wanting her daughter to start envisioning Flynn as a daddy figure, so they didn't make any obvious changes to their routines. He didn't eat dinner with them every night or show up for breakfast every morning, and when he was there—which was perhaps a little more frequently than in the past—there were no outward displays of affection. Not until Emma was in bed and confirmed to be asleep.

But Flynn didn't need to touch her to turn her on. All it took was a lingering glance or a slow smile, and Meg was ready to rip his clothes off.

Tess was the only one who knew that Meg and Flynn were "dating"—though she suggested they should come up with a better word to describe the nature of their relationship as they'd never been on a real date. (Leaving a bar together only counted as a hookup, not a date. And going to see a movie with Emma didn't count. Ditto any other event that included a pint-sized chaperone, because Tess apparently had a lot of rules that governed the subject.)

When Meg told Flynn what her friend had said, he decided that they should go out on occasion. Though in the interest of keeping their relationship out of the public eye, their plans usually necessitated going out of town. Since Tess was the only one who knew the truth about their relationship—and Holt, as a consequence of being married to Tess—she became their go-to babysitter. Which meant that, over the next few weeks, Emma spent a lot of time with Auntie Tess, Unca Holt and "Auntie Tess's baby."

Actually, Flynn confessed to Meg one night about three weeks into their new relationship, Hillary knew about the change in their status, too. Not because he'd told her, he hastened to assure Meg, but because the other deputy had (self-proclaimed) finely-honed observational skills. Also, she'd seen them holding hands in Howlett's Pass one night when they'd gone there for dinner.

But for the next few weeks, everything was good. So good, in fact, that Meg let her guard down.

It was a Friday night, after Emma was tucked into bed, and they were arguing good-naturedly over what to watch on TV. Flynn was advocating for one of the Fast & Furious movies—"It doesn't matter which one—they're all great"—while Meg wanted to see a rom-com recently released to streaming that had gotten a lot of favorable buzz. Twenty minutes later, they were snuggled together on the sofa with a bowl of popcorn between them as Brian, Mia and Tego chased down a prison bus to free Dominic.

"I know you're not a pushover," Flynn remarked. "So why is it that we always seem to end up watching what I want to watch?"

"Maybe it's because I feel guilty that you watch more Disney Plus with Emma than I do." She shrugged and reached into the bowl for another handful of popcorn. "Or maybe I just want to make you happy, because I love you."

He pulled his hand out of the bowl and shifted on the sofa, and the kneejerk response made her ache for him.

She'd resisted telling him what was in her heart, because she'd known his instinct would be to reject her feelings, but the words had spilled out, anyway—the feelings too big to remain contained. And maybe it was too much too soon, considering that they'd only been intimate for a few weeks. But she knew Flynn better than she'd known any other man in her life. Certainly, she knew him a lot better than the man she'd married.

She knew what he'd been through and what he struggled with every day. She knew he was still healing—it was something they had in common—but she also knew that beneath the scars, both the visible and invisible ones, was a good man who cared deeply for both her and Emma. And it frustrated her that he was so convinced he couldn't be what they needed that he wouldn't even let himself try.

But maybe the fault was her own. Maybe he'd never wanted anything more from her than friendship and sex and she was the one who'd ruined everything by thinking they could have more.

"If you're waiting for me to say the words back—"

"I'm not," she told him. "I hope maybe, someday, you might come to feel the same way about me that I feel about you. But for now, I just wanted you to know."

"You once told me that hope is dangerous."

"I'm not always good at following my own advice," she confided.

"I don't want to hurt you, Megan."

"Then don't," she said.

"But if I let things continue the way they are, if I let you continue to hope, I will hurt you. And Emma. And that's the last thing I ever want to do."

"Do you think it will hurt us less if you walk out that door right now?"

"In the long run, yes, I do," he said.

"You're actually going to end our relationship because I dared to tell you that I love you?"

"You did dare," he acknowledged. "Because you're strong and brave. Apparently a lot stronger and braver than me, because after everything you've been through, you've somehow managed to put the pieces together.

"And that's something I haven't been able to do. I'm still broken."

"I didn't put the pieces back together by myself," she told him. "I had help from my family and friends. From Dr. Halstead. From you."

But Flynn had already made up his mind.

He set his key on the table and walked out the door.

Chapter Twenty-Four

He'd done the right thing.

Flynn had no doubts about that.

But that certainty didn't stop him from missing both Megan and Emma like crazy.

He'd gone back to his cabin at West River Ranch that night, and when he'd crawled beneath the covers of his bed, Meg's scent had lingered on his pillows from her last visit. A scent that triggered memories of her there, her limbs wrapped around him as he buried himself inside her.

So he'd tossed the pillows aside and dragged his blanket to the floor. But there were memories of her there, too. Memories that proved she understood far more than he'd realized—and accepted him, anyway.

Loved him, anyway.

Or at least believed that she did.

But she'd realize the truth eventually, and when she did, she'd be glad that he'd done the right thing.

For now, he would focus once again on getting through one day at a time. And really, the days weren't so bad, because he had work to keep him busy. It was the nights that were killing him.

And since he obviously wasn't going to get any shut-eye here tonight, he decided to head into the sheriff's office.

Of course, he drove a circuitous route into town.

A route that took him down Walnut Street.

He told himself that he was hoping to find Meg's house in

darkness—and some comfort in the fact that at least she was sleeping. And aside from the almost-imperceptible glow of Emma's night-light, the house was dark.

But Meg wasn't sleeping.

She was sitting on the porch, wrapped in a blanket, in her favorite Adirondack chair.

He knew he shouldn't stop, but his truck slowed, as if of its own volition. Then it was in Park, the ignition turned off and the keys in his hand.

Meg watched him climb the steps, her expression guarded.

"Hello, Megan."

"What do you want, Deputy?"

He leaned a shoulder against the support post, effecting a nonchalance he didn't feel. "I just wanted to make sure that you're okay."

"You don't need to worry about me," she said. "I can take care of myself."

"No one knows that better than me," he told her.

"So why are you here?" she asked.

Was there a slightly hopeful note in her voice? Or was he only imagining—perhaps wishing—it? Was there an answer he could give to her question that would make everything okay? An answer that would allow her to forgive him for not being what she and Emma needed?

"I shouldn't be," he admitted.

"So nothing's changed," she realized.

"Nothing's changed," he confirmed.

"Then you're right—you shouldn't be here."

It was his cue to leave, but his feet refused to move. His eyes studied her face, as if he hadn't already memorized every intricate detail, and he heard himself ask, "Have you missed me at all?"

She shook her head, her expression fierce, almost angry. "You don't get to show up here at three o'clock in the morning and ask me that question."

"You're right. I'm sorry." But he stayed where he was for another long minute, and then he confided, "I've missed you."

"You don't get to say that, either," she told him.

"Not even if it's true?"

She stood up then, the blanket still wrapped around her. "Goodbye, Flynn."

Not good night, but goodbye.

And though she didn't slam the door behind her, he heard the unmistakable click of the dead bolt sliding into place, ensuring that he stayed on the outside—where he belonged.

"If I express an interest in dating anyone ever again, you have my explicit permission to call me out for being an idiot," Meg said as Tess settled on the sofa with her baby at her breast.

They were at her house today, Tess having brought the baby into town for his three-month checkup. And having her friend there, in the house they'd shared together, was making Meg feel a little nostalgic.

"Oh, no," Tess said, sounding genuinely distressed. "What did Flynn do?"

"He decided that continuing our relationship, continuing to let me hope that we might have a future together, would only lead to me and Emma being hurt in the end. So he ended it."

Her friend huffed out a breath. "And hurt you both anyway."

Meg sighed wearily. "Why don't I ever learn?"

"What is it you think you need to learn? To keep your heart under lock and key?"

"That would be a good start," she agreed.

"No. You are an amazing person—warm and caring and capable of so much love—and you shouldn't ever change that."

She sniffled. "I told him I loved him."

"He couldn't have been surprised by that."

"'Panicked' is the word I'd use to describe his reaction."

"I'm sorry, Meg." Tess reached across the nursing baby to squeeze her hand. "Really sorry."

"It's my own fault," she said. "I know better than to think that I can change a person—and I know Flynn, so I should have known that I was imagining a future that wasn't ever going to happen."

"But he *has* changed. He's not the same person now that he was when he first came home."

"How do you know?"

"Well, I didn't know him then," Tess acknowledged. "But I know what Holt told me, which is that he's changed—most noticeably after he met you. And if I had to guess, I'd say that's what scares him. That his feelings for you scare him."

"The man was an Army Ranger who carried out covert missions in hostile territories—I don't think he's afraid of his feelings for me."

"Please," Tess scoffed. "Given the choice, most men would willingly put their lives on the line before their hearts."

Flynn looked around his cabin, hardly recognizing the space after the changes he'd made in the last several weeks. A new table with four chairs in the kitchen, a television mounted on the wall in the living room and satellite dish on his roof, a bin filled with toys and a small shelf packed with age-appropriate books and games for Emma.

Not that Meg and Emma had spent a lot of time there, but he'd wanted to ensure they felt welcome and comfortable when they did visit. But the days of those visits were over—he'd sure as hell guaranteed that.

What was he supposed to do with the stuff now?

Pack it up, he decided. Put it out of sight and out of his mind, because looking at it only reminded him of what he'd had and lost.

He was taping the flaps of a box he'd found in the back of his closet when there was a knock on the door.

"Don't you see enough of me at the sheriff's office?" Flynn said, when he opened the door and found Colby there.

"More than enough," his cousin agreed.

"So what are you doing here?"

"I'm here, as a surrogate for Ellis, to kick your ass."

"Excuse me?"

"My brother would never sit back and watch you screw up your life and I'm not going to, either."

"Am I supposed to know what you're talking about?"

"Your breakup with Meg."

Flynn scowled. "How did you even know we were together?"

Colby snorted. "Did you really think you were fooling anyone?"

"We didn't want anyone to know because we didn't want other people sticking their noses into things that are absolutely none of their business," he said pointedly.

"As much as you might wish otherwise, you're not an island, Flynn. What affects you, affects the people around you. And while no one would describe your usual demeanor as sunshine and roses, you've been downright ornery this past week."

"If I'm really that unpleasant to work with, you could always fire me," Flynn said.

"The thought crossed my mind," Colby admitted. "But it seemed to me the better solution is for you to get your head out of your ass and make up with your girlfriend."

A frustrated curse flew out of Flynn's mouth. "I'm *not* talking to you about this."

"Then talk to her."

"She's not interested in anything I have to say these days."

"Which only proves that you screwed up, not that you can't fix it."

"I did the right thing," Flynn insisted.

"Do you really believe walking away from Meg and Emma was the right thing?"

"I know it was."

"Will you be as certain of that when Meg moves on with someone else?" Colby challenged.

Flynn felt his jaw clench as images flashed through his mind: Meg dancing with Cash at Denim & Diamonds; Meg on a date with the nameless, faceless doctor who took her to the hospital fundraiser; Meg letting any other man touch her, kiss her, make love to her.

Even though most of those images only existed in his mind, they made his chest feel tight, as if it was clamped inside a vise. But that was his discomfort to deal with, and he would. Because he had no right to hold her back from a relationship with someone who could give her and Emma the kind of life they deserved.

For a short while, he'd let himself get caught up in the fantasy of believing he could be the kind of man they needed. The kind of man he wished he could be for both of them. And if he'd continued to labor under that delusion, he would have ended up hurting them both, and they'd already been through more than any woman and child should have to endure.

"I hope she finds someone worthy of her," he responded to his cousin now.

"Because you're not?"

"Not even close."

Colby shook his head. "You need to stop punishing yourself for what happened in the past and let yourself have a future."

"How can you say that when you don't have the first clue about what happened?"

"I can say it because I don't need to know the details to know that you didn't fail my brother in any way."

"He wanted to come home," Flynn said now. "He'd decided the hostage rescue was going to be his last assignment, because he wanted to come home and start a life—and family—with Caitlyn."

Colby was silent for a minute, considering this new information. Maybe reconsidering his determination to offer Flynn absolution.

"And because he didn't get to do so, you don't think you should, either," he concluded.

"When we enlisted, I promised Caitlyn that I'd keep him safe."

"It wasn't your job to look out for Ellis any more than it was his job to look out for you."

"I promised," he said again.

"Now you're using that promise as an excuse not to live your own life," his cousin noted. "How do you think Ellis would feel about that?

"Come on, Flynn," Colby said, when he refused to respond. "You were my brother's best friend. You knew him better than anyone else. Which means that you know, deep inside that heart you pretend is locked behind impenetrable gates, that he'd be seriously pissed at you for throwing away your relationship with Meg and Emma. And you also know that, if he was able, he'd come home from wherever he is and kick your sorry ass.

"So you better get your head out of it fast, because I will step up to do what he can't, and you'll find yourself walking around town with my boot print on your forehead."

Every morning when Emma came down for breakfast, she put a big X over the date on the calendar, counting down the days until the "pony party" for her birthday, the last weekend in May.

Per Eleanor's request, Meg and Emma had gone to the ranch for another planning meeting, and the Chandler matriarch had taken detailed notes of the birthday girl's wishes. Though Meg still had some concerns that spending time at West River Ranch might make it difficult to reconcile her daughter's expectations with the reality of their financial situation, she'd decided that was a worry for another time. Right now, she was basking in the fact that her daughter was finding new joys in each day—and especially the days she spent at the ranch.

As her birthday party grew nearer, the little girl's excitement grew—and so did her mom's trepidation. Not because she had any concerns about the party—with Eleanor Chandler in charge, she knew it wouldn't be anything less than amazing—but because Flynn would be there.

It was funny to think how often their paths had crossed in the past, and how effectively they'd managed to keep their distance from one another since their breakup.

The day of the big event, Meg went early to West River Ranch. She left Emma with Tess and Holt, so the birthday girl wouldn't be underfoot when her mom was trying to set up and decorate, but when she arrived at the stables, Meg found that the hard work had already been done.

"Flynn took care of it," Eleanor told her. "He wanted to make sure everything was exactly as Emma wanted it before he had to go."

"He's not here?"

She wasn't sure if she was relieved or disappointed, though she could guess that her daughter would fall hard on the "disappointed" side.

"Not right now," his grandmother said. "But he'll be back for the party."

Which meant that Meg had nothing to do but greet guests as they arrived and wonder when Flynn would appear.

Once the party got underway, she kept herself busy: offering drinks and snacks, supervising games, handing out prizes, and making sure every child got to take a turn—and later a second turn—around the paddock on a patient and tolerant Bandit, who'd had pink and purple ribbons woven in his mane and tail for the occasion.

It was only when the food had been decimated and Emma was clamoring for cake that Meg realized Flynn still had not made an appearance. Thankfully, there were so many other people and so much going on that her daughter seemed oblivious to his absence.

After cake—which was actually a tower of cupcakes made by Great-Gramma Lula—Emma opened her gifts. There were games and puzzles and My Little Pony figurines and activity kits and, from Raylan and Eleanor, a pair of purple cowboy boots decorated with rhinestones and a matching cowboy hat.

Finally, parents started to round up their kids to take them home, which meant that Meg could start to tidy up. But first she made her way to the stables, where Boone was supervising Gage and Zane's grooming of their pony.

"I wanted to thank you for loaning Bandit to Emma today," she said to them.

"Wasn't my idea," Zane grumbled.

"And nobody said he'd have to wear pink bows," Gage added, carefully unbraiding the horse's tail to remove the offensive ribbon.

"I think what you mean to say is, 'You're welcome,'" Boone told his boys.

"You're welcome," they dutifully intoned.

"And these are a thank-you from Emma," Meg said, offering each a gift card for a local electronics store.

"Oh, wow!"

"So cool!"

"And now you say, 'Thank you,'" Boone instructed.

"Thank you," they echoed, with decidedly more enthusiasm this time.

Meg smiled and moved on to express her gratitude to the senior Chandlers for hosting the party.

"It was our pleasure," Eleanor said.

"I say we do it again next year," Raylan chimed in. "With the addition of a bouncy castle."

"You just want to have a go in one, and I'm not eager to sit around the hospital while you undergo another surgery," his wife admonished sternly.

Meg had to laugh. "And I want at least a week to recover from this party before I even think of another one—even though I didn't have to do any of the hard work."

"It was all worth it, though, wasn't it?" Raylan said. "Just to see your little girl smile."

"It was," Meg agreed.

Eleanor started to respond again, but then her attention was snagged by something in the distance. "Who's that coming down the lane now—kicking up all that dust?"

"Gotta be Flynn," Raylan said. "Three hours late."

As the vehicle came closer and Meg was able to confirm that it *was* Flynn's truck, her heart jolted inside her chest.

It was only when he pulled up alongside the paddock that she noticed the horse trailer hitched to the back.

He hopped out of the driver's seat and, after giving the adults a wave of acknowledgment, turned his attention to Emma.

"There's the birthday girl," he said, offering her his trademark half smile.

Instead of running to him, as she usually did, she stood with her feet apart and her fists propped on her hips and said, in an accusatory tone, "You din't come to my birthday party."

"Isn't this your birthday party?" he asked, gesturing to the streamers and balloons that Meg hadn't yet gotten around to taking down.

"It was," she confirmed. "But everyone's gone now—and so are the cupcakes."

His brows lifted at that. "You didn't even save me one cupcake?"

She looked to her mom then, as if not entirely certain of the answer.

"There are a few left," Meg said.

"I'm sorry I'm late," Flynn said, his focus on Emma again.

"But I ran into a little trouble trying to get your birthday present here."

"What kinda trouble?" she asked, her tone softened by his apology.

"Blew a tire on my trailer," he said.

Her brow furrowed. "How do you blow a tire?"

"I mean it went flat," he explained.

"Did you hafta call a tow truck?"

"No, but it took some time to change it, and that's why I'm late."

"It's okay," she decided.

"So…are you ready for your present?"

She nodded.

Knots of apprehension formed in Meg's belly as Flynn made his way to the back of the trailer.

Surely, he wouldn't have—

But of course he would.

And he had.

He'd bought her a pony.

And as he guided the animal out of the trailer, Emma's jaw dropped open.

"It's for me to ride?"

Flynn nodded. "For you to ride and groom and feed and take care of."

She moved forward and lifted a hand to touch the animal's flank. Gently. Reverently. "What's her name?"

"She's your pony, so you get to decide."

"Thank you, Unca Flynn." Now she did throw her arms around him to hug him tight, happy tears squeezing out of her eyes as she did so. "Thank you. So. Much."

"A little over the top, don't you think?" Meg said, when her daughter had brushed away the tears and turned her attention back to the pony.

"Tess assured me that 'over the top' was a requirement of a grand gesture."

"Tess knew you were planning to buy Emma a pony?"

"And the fact that you didn't know proves she can keep a secret," he remarked. "But the pony is only the first part of the plan."

"Come on, Emma," Eleanor said, offering her hand to the birthday girl. "Let's take your pony to see her new home."

Raylan took the reins from his grandson then and they made their way to the stables, leaving Flynn and Meg alone.

"Are you mad?" he asked.

She took a minute to consider the question and sort through the various emotions warring inside her. "I'm not mad," she decided. "I'm just trying to figure out what you thought buying a pony for Emma would accomplish."

"It's not that complicated," he told her. "I simply wanted to give you both a reason to come out to the ranch."

"You could have tried issuing an invitation," she said dryly.

"And if I'd asked, what would you have said?"

She sighed then. "I don't know."

"I've missed you, Megan."

She closed her eyes, so that he couldn't see how much those simple words made her heart yearn. "I can't do this again, Flynn."

"I'm not asking to go back to the way things were. That's not what I want."

She looked at him again—at the man she'd gotten used to seeing almost every day and missed unbearably every day that he'd been gone. "What do you want?"

"A chance to show you how sorry I am for letting go of the two best things that ever happened to me," he said.

"So why did you do it?" She felt her throat tighten with emotion and had to work to swallow around it. "Why did you push me—push us—away?"

"I was scared," he confided now. "Afraid to admit how much you and Emma meant to me. Afraid to tell you I loved you, even though I did. And afraid to let you depend on me, in case I let you down."

"You did let me down," she said. "When you walked out on our relationship, as if it wasn't worth fighting for."

"I didn't walk out because our relationship wasn't worth fighting for, but because I didn't feel that I deserved everything you were offering—all the things I never knew I wanted until you and Emma came into my life.

"Ellis was the one with the traditional dreams of a home with a white-picket fence and a wife and a family. But he doesn't have any of those things now, because I failed to bring him home. And, as a result, I didn't think I had any right to them, either."

She looked at him carefully. "So what's changed?"

"I have. At least, I'm trying to," he said. "I've got twice-weekly appointments to see Dr. Litman, to work on moving beyond the past so I can move on with the future. Hopefully with you and Emma."

His gaze held hers, his expression serious and intent and somehow hopeful. And while she didn't have any doubt that he believed what he was saying, she was afraid to believe it, too. Afraid that she'd be the one who ended up hurt again. Or—even worse—that Emma would.

"And you expect me to believe that you suddenly changed your mind about what you want—and trust that you won't change it again two weeks from now?" she challenged, even though she wanted to do exactly that.

"I don't expect anything." He reached for her hands then and drew her closer. "But I'm hoping you'll give me a chance to prove that what I'm telling you now is true. Because living without you and Emma these last few weeks hasn't felt like living at all, and I don't want to spend another minute of another day without you."

And with that simple but obviously sincere declaration, the last of Meg's resistance melted along with her heart.

She looked at him through eyes blurred with tears. "For a man usually of few words, how is it that you somehow managed to find just the right ones?" she wondered aloud.

"Maybe I'm finally listening to my heart?" he suggested. "Because I do love you, Megan."

"Exactly the right ones," she murmured.

"Now might be an appropriate time for you to tell me that you love me, too," he told her.

"You know I do," she said, tears trembling on the edges of her lashes.

He lifted a hand to gently brush away the single droplet that slid down her cheek. "Still?"

"Always," she promised.

He lowered his head to kiss her then, long and slow and deep.

"I did miss you," she confessed, whispering the words against his lips.

"I missed you more."

After several more minutes and kisses, they eased apart to catch their breaths.

"I know it's Emma's birthday, but I have something for you, too," he said, holding up a diamond solitaire in a platinum band.

And Meg, who always had something to say, could only stare at the ring, speechless.

"This is the second part of my plan," he told her. "I understand that you might need some time to trust that I'm going to stick. And I realize that you might have reservations about walking down the aisle again, so I'm not asking you to marry me right now, I'm only asking if you might be willing to consider marrying me in the future. Or at least consider spending the rest of your life with me, even if you don't want to do the vows thing."

"For a man usually of few words, you also somehow managed to tangle up what should have been a simple question with a lot of them," she said, her lips curved in an indulgent smile. "So I'm going to give you a simple answer—*yes*."

Epilogue

"This was. The. Best. Birthday. Ever," Emma said, after Flynn and Meg had tracked down the little girl and the senior Chandlers in the stables to share their happy news. "I got cowboy boots *and* a pony *and* a daddy."

"It has been a really good day," Meg agreed, leaning her head back against Flynn's shoulder.

"We're so happy for both of you—all of you," Raylan said, hastily amending his statement to include Emma.

"Absolutely thrilled," Eleanor confirmed. "And I realize this is probably premature, but did you have any thoughts on a wedding date?"

"Very premature," the future bride said.

"Well, don't wait too long," Raylan cautioned. "We'd like to be able to dance at your wedding and we're not getting any younger."

"We'll keep that in mind," Flynn promised.

The birthday girl paused her grooming of the pony then to ask, "After the wedding, can you put a baby in Mama's tummy, Unca Flynn?"

Meg felt her cheeks grow hot. "That's a topic of conversation best left for another time."

"But I really want a sister," her daughter said.

Flynn looked at Meg. "What do you think? You want to have a baby?"

And her heart, already full of so much love, overflowed with joy. "I think I do."

"Yay! I'm gonna have a sister," Emma announced, as if it was a done deal.

"You might get a brother instead," Raylan warned. "It's been a long time since there's been a girl born in the Chandler family."

"Five generations," Eleanor confirmed.

"I guess a brother would be okay," the little girl said. "But I'd really rather have a sister to play My Little Ponies with me."

"Let's start with the wedding first," Flynn suggested.

"Good idea," Meg concurred.

Raylan and Eleanor headed back to the main house then, and Meg texted Tess to share the happy news while Flynn helped Emma finish grooming the as-yet-unnamed pony. Following the exchange of about a dozen messages with her friend, Meg tucked her phone away. Almost immediately after she'd done so, Flynn's phone rang.

"I bet that's Holt," she said, because she knew her BFF would have already recounted every detail to her husband.

But when Flynn turned his phone over, it was Caitlyn's name on the display.

"Answer it," Meg urged.

He swiped to connect the call.

Flynn's single-word questions and answers didn't reveal much about the subject of their conversation, but when it was over, tears shimmered in *his* eyes. He reached one arm out to Meg and the other to Emma then, drawing them both close and holding them tight.

"Ellis?" The name was a tentative whisper from Meg's lips.

Flynn nodded, his body vibrating and his voice raw when he said, "He's coming home."

Meg's eyes filled again. "Just in time to be your best man."

"Like he promised," her future husband agreed.

"Why are you crying, Mama?" Emma wanted to know.

"They're happy tears," Meg assured her.

"But why?" the little girl pressed.

She smiled. "Because this really was the best day ever."

"So far," Flynn clarified, hugging her a little tighter. "But we're going to have every day of the rest of our lives together to try to top it."

"And I can't wait to get started," Meg said, tipping her head back to touch her lips to his.

* * * * *

Look for Ellis's story,
the next installment in
The Cowboys of Whispering Canyon
award-winning author Brenda Harlen's
new miniseries for
Harlequin Special Edition.

Coming soon!

And don't miss Tess and Holt's story
The Rancher's Temptation

Available now, wherever Harlequin books
and ebooks are sold.